O9-AID-264

At seventeen, she'd never seen a more perfect example of manliness,

Madelyn thought, thinking back to when she first met Luke. One look and she'd wanted him to be the first to make love to her. Now, watching him sleep, a shimmer of female appreciation still ran through her.

She wasn't sure about anything when it came to Luke. She just knew he was important to her—and not just as her doctor.

His lashes fluttered as he opened his eyes, and he frowned.

"Maddy?" His voice was rusty and threaded with disbelief.

"Go to sleep, Luke," she soothed.

"Baby?" he muttered.

"He's fine."

His mouth moved. "Sorry he's not mine."

"So am I," she said on a suddenly shaky breath.

He smiled then. "Keep you safe, sweetheart," he murmured. "Even from me."

It was at that moment that she realized she still loved him.

Dear Reader,

This is a very special month here at Intimate Moments. We're celebrating the publication of our 1000th novel, and what a book it is! *Angel Meets the Badman* is the latest from award-winning and bestselling Maggie Shayne, and it's part of her ongoing miniseries, THE TEXAS BRAND. It's a page-turner par excellence, so take it home, sit back and prepare to be enthralled.

Ruth Langan's back, and Intimate Moments has got her. This month this historical romance star continues to win contemporary readers' hearts with *The Wildes of Wyoming—Hazard,* the latest in her wonderful contemporary miniseries about the three Wilde brothers. Paula Detmer Riggs returns to MATERNITY ROW, the site of so many births—and so many happy endings—with *Daddy by Choice.* And look for the connected MATERNITY ROW short story, "Family by Fate," in our new Mother's Day collection, *A Bouquet of Babies.* Merline Lovelace brings readers another of the MEN OF THE BAR H in *The Harder They Fall*—and you're definitely going to fall for hero Evan Henderson. *Cinderella and the Spy* is the latest from Sally Tyler Hayes, an author with a real knack for mixing romance and suspense in just the right proportions. And finally, there's *Safe in His Arms,* a wonderful amnesia story from Christine Scott.

Enjoy them all, and we'll see you again next month, when you can once again find some of the best and most exciting romance reading around, right here in Silhouette Intimate Moments.

Yours,

Leslie J. Wainger
Executive Senior Editor

Please address questions and book requests to:
Silhouette Reader Service
U.S.: 3010 Walden Ave., P.O. Box 1325, Buffalo, NY 14269
Canadian: P.O. Box 609, Fort Erie, Ont. L2A 5X3

PAULA DETMER RIGGS

DADDY BY CHOICE

Silhouette® INTIMATE™ MOMENTS®

Published by Silhouette Books

America's Publisher of Contemporary Romance

If you purchased this book without a cover you should be aware
that this book is stolen property. It was reported as "unsold and
destroyed" to the publisher, and neither the author nor the
publisher has received any payment for this "stripped book."

For Annette Broadrick
A great Texas lady and a treasured friend.

 SILHOUETTE BOOKS

ISBN 0-373-27068-2

DADDY BY CHOICE

Copyright © 2000 by Paula Detmer Riggs

All rights reserved. Except for use in any review, the reproduction
or utilization of this work in whole or in part in any form by any
electronic, mechanical or other means, now known or hereafter
invented, including xerography, photocopying and recording, or in
any information storage or retrieval system, is forbidden without
the written permission of the editorial office, Silhouette Books,
300 East 42nd Street, New York, NY 10017 U.S.A.

All characters in this book have no existence outside the imagination of
the author and have no relation whatsoever to anyone bearing the same
name or names. They are not even distantly inspired by any individual
known or unknown to the author, and all incidents are pure invention.

This edition published by arrangement with Harlequin Books S.A.

® and TM are trademarks of Harlequin Books S.A., used under license.
Trademarks indicated with ® are registered in the United States Patent
and Trademark Office, the Canadian Trade Marks Office and in other
countries.

Visit Silhouette at www.eHarlequin.com

Printed in U.S.A.

Books by Paula Detmer Riggs

Silhouette Intimate Moments

Beautiful Dreamer #183
Fantasy Man #226
Suspicious Minds #250
Desperate Measures #283
Full Circle #303
Tender Offer #314
A Lasting Promise #344
Forgotten Dream #364
Silent Impact #398
Paroled! #440
Firebrand #481
Once Upon A Wedding #524
No Easy Way Out #548
The Bachelor Party #656
Her Secret, His Child #667
*Mommy by Surprise #794
*Baby by Design #806
A Perfect Hero #889
Once More a Family #933
*Daddy by Choice #998

*Maternity Row

Silhouette Desire

Rough Passage #633
A Man of Honor #744
Murdock's Family #898
*Daddy by Accident #1073

Silhouette Books

Silhouette Summer Sizzlers 1992
"Night of the Dark Moon"

36 Hours
The Parent Plan

A Bouquet of Babies
*"Family By Fate"

PAULA DETMER RIGGS

discovers material for her writing in her varied life experiences. During her first five years of marriage to a naval officer, she lived in nineteen different locations on the West Coast, gaining familiarity with places as diverse as San Diego and Seattle. While working at an historical site in San Diego she wrote, directed and narrated fashion shows and became fascinated with the early history of California.

She writes romances because "I think we all need an escape from the high-tech pressures that face us every day, and I believe in happy endings. Isn't that why we keep trying, in spite of all the roadblocks and disappointments along the way?"

IT'S OUR 20th ANNIVERSARY!
We'll be celebrating all year,
Continuing with these fabulous titles,
On sale in April 2000.

Romance

#1438 Carried Away
Kasey Michaels/Joan Hohl

#1439 An Eligible Stranger
Tracy Sinclair

#1440 A Royal Marriage
Cara Colter

#1441 His Wild Young Bride
Donna Clayton

#1442 At the Billionaire's Bidding
Myrna Mackenzie

#1443 The Marriage Badge
Sharon De Vita

Desire

#1285 Last Dance
Cait London

#1286 Night Music
BJ James

#1287 Seduction, Cowboy Style
Anne Marie Winston

#1288 The Barons of Texas: Jill
Fayrene Preston

#1289 Her Baby's Father
Katherine Garbera

SECRETS! **#1290 Callan's Proposition**
Barbara McCauley

Intimate Moments

#997 The Wildes of Wyoming—Hazard
Ruth Langan

#998 Daddy by Choice
Paula Detmer Riggs

#999 The Harder They Fall
Merline Lovelace

#1000 Angel Meets the Badman
Maggie Shayne

#1001 Cinderella and the Spy
Sally Tyler Hayes

#1002 Safe in His Arms
Christine Scott

Special Edition

#1315 Beginning with Baby
Christie Ridgway

#1316 The Sheik's Kidnapped Bride
Susan Mallery

#1317 Make Way for Babies!
Laurie Paige

#1318 Surprise Partners
Gina Wilkins

#1319 Her Wildest Wedding Dreams
Celeste Hamilton

#1320 Soul Mates
Carol Finch

Prologue

It was hotter than hell the day Luke Jarrod returned to West Texas. Overhead the merciless sun beat down on the cab of his truck, while inside the air conditioner blasted ice from the vents.

Slouched behind the wheel, his eyes gritty from too little sleep and his shoulders stiff from too many hours driving without a break, Luke was sweating like a bridegroom with a .12-gauge shotgun at his backbone. Which was real appropriate, considerin' he was about to become a daddy at eighteen.

It scared him some to think of his Maddy girl having a baby, her being so tiny and all. And only seventeen. Too damn young to know better, so *he* should have.

It had been opening day of the Whiskey Bend Stampede at the county fairgrounds when he'd first laid eyes on her. A bunch of ROTC kids from Whiskey Bend High School had been bringing in the flag, just like every other rodeo in every other town he'd seen that season. Strung tight and desperate for prize money to keep himself in tacos and his cutting horse, Cochise, in oats, he'd been standing with the more seasoned competitors in the dusty ring with his hand over his heart, watching the chicks twirling batons when his buddy Buck Mehan had dug an elbow into his ribs.

"Son," he said, "were I ten years younger I'd be all over that little yeller-haired darlin' in the third row, the one swishing all that glorious hair like there was no tomorrow. Man could die happy did he belong to her."

Luke had never wanted to belong to anyone. Belonging meant obligations and responsibilities, two things he'd avoided for as long as he could remember. But one look at those slinky tanned legs and tight little butt sashaying past him, her itty-bitty skirt swishing this way and that, and he'd fallen about as hard as a man can fall without cracking wide open.

Her name was Madelyn Sue Smith, and she'd been flat-out adorable, her crazy little cat's face lit with excitement and her eyes full of spirit. It had been high noon, and the sun had coated her honey-colored hair with shimmering gold. He'd never seen hair like hers, bunches of tousled curls all the way to her shoulders. It had been prettier than a palomino's coat, which was just about the prettiest thing he'd ever seen. When they'd been together, he'd spent hours running his hands through all that glorious stuff.

Lord help him, he hadn't intended to let things get out of hand. But she'd been so sweet, and her smile had taken the edge off the sadness that had plagued him from the moment his mother had abandoned him when he was only nine, taking the baby sister he adored and leaving him to cope with his father's bitter rages.

His body stirred at the memory of the stolen hours they'd spent together in a cheap motel room near the fairgrounds. That last night he'd bought her flowers— white carnations with petals almost as silky as her skin—and made sure the sheets had been clean. She'd been a virgin, and he'd tried to be gentle.

A thousand times he'd played back that scene, the teasing flick of her tongue against his, the purr of need in her throat. The adoration and trust in her eyes when she'd told him she loved him. A thousand times these past eight months he'd taken out that memory, hoarding each flash of those river green eyes, each dimpled smile, the soft little huff of wonder when she'd explored his body for the first time. When she'd finally worked up the courage to touch him, he'd damn near come right up off the bed.

For the first time since quittin' school at sixteen to join the junior circuit, he'd been reluctant to move on. Especially when she'd cried and clung to him like there was no tomorrow.

I'll write every day, she'd promised between frantic kisses. And she had at first, four letters for every one of his, telling him over and over how much she missed him—and how she couldn't wait for him to come back when the season was over with the engagement ring he'd promised.

The more she wrote about them getting married, the tenser he'd become. Hell, he'd just gotten old enough to drink legal in a few enlightened states. The last thing he wanted was a noose around his neck. Thing was, though, he'd promised, and like his old man always said, a Jarrod never broke a promise.

Bent a few, though. And it wasn't like he'd been real specific about *when* the season ended.

What with one thing and another, he'd started looking for reasons to put off goin' back. Things like not havin' enough money to support a wife. Or even the prospect of a steady job. Hell, he had no education to speak of. Nothing but a talent for stayin' glued to the back of a raging tornado in horseflesh for the eight seconds it took to put money in his jeans.

Since his father had remarried and started another family, he didn't even have a home to offer her—not a real one, anyway. So he kept puttin' off that long drive back to Texas. As the months rolled by, there'd been other dusty towns and inevitably, other girls. Soon he'd been impatiently scrawling a few lines on a post-card. And finally he'd stopped writing altogether.

So had she—eventually—which was why he'd been so surprised to see the letter waiting for him at his daddy's ranch outside Wickenburg. Damn thing had followed him halfway around the country—Canada, too—forwarded so many times the envelope had been raggedy and smudged.

All the way from Arizona he'd been picturing her with a big belly. The more he'd thought about it, the more awestruck he'd become. That sweet girl was havin' his baby. *His.* It humbled him as much as it scared him.

Sweat beaded under the band of his dress Stetson hat as he made the left turn that would take him to her place. What was done was done, he told himself as he pulled into the driveway of the ugly brown house. He'd had his fun. Now it was time to pay the piper.

But as he climbed down from the truck and straightened his shoulders, he realized he was glad she was pregnant. Maybe it wasn't the best way to start out a lifetime with his lady, but he'd make it work. If it took him a lifetime, he was determined to show her just how much he loved her. His Maddy girl.

Chapter 1

Twenty-two years later

''I don't mean to frighten you unnecessarily, Maddy Sue, but I wouldn't be doing my duty as your doctor if I didn't lay out the worst-case scenario.''

Sixty-seven-year-old Dr. Horace Austin Morrow had been Madelyn Smith Foster's doctor from the moment she was born. Or, more precisely, from the moment of her conception, as he liked to tease with a twinkle in those still-bright blue eyes whenever she was being mulish.

Madelyn trusted him implicitly. She also loved him like the father she should have had. She liked to think he cared deeply for her, as well. Certainly he had stood by her when almost everyone else in her life had turned against her.

After Luke had broken her heart, she'd cried on

Doc's broad shoulder so many times she'd come to associate the smell of his starched lab coat with fathomless sorrow. When Doc had haltingly told her that the odds of her ever becoming pregnant were too minuscule to measure, she'd collapsed in those strong arms, sobbing until she was empty inside.

Five months ago, when he'd given her the astounding news that she'd beaten those odds and had actually conceived, she'd also cried in his arms. From joy this time. But now...

"You said I just had a small cyst, that it was nothing to be concerned about." Her voice was a thread, pushed past the sudden constriction in her throat.

"Actually it's more like a benign tumor. Folks generally call these things fibroids, but the correct medical term is *myoma*."

Instinctively her hand went to her tummy where the fragile little soul she already adored was curled into a warm ball under her heart. "You mean I...I could lose this baby?"

"It's possible, honey. These here myomas are like West Texas weather—real unpredictable. Sometimes the weatherman forecasts a big old tornado, and all we get is a piddling little blow. On the other hand it only makes sense to duck on down to the cellar when you see the warning signs."

Madelyn bit her lip, her gaze fixed on the fuzzy black-and-white image of her child in the ultrasound photo. Along the curve of her uterus was a black smudge, more like a thickening than her idea of a tumor. Certainly it didn't look menacing, at least not to her untrained eye. However, the dark shadow was bigger in this photo than the one taken a month earlier, which Doc claimed was a big old red flag.

"Would you mind going over the possible…
complications again, please?" she asked when he remained silent, his homely face set in somber lines.

"I wouldn't mind at all, honey." The springs of
Doc's chair protested as he shifted his bulk a little
closer to where she was perched rigidly on the edge of
her chair. "These are only maybes, you understand,"
he said, lifting his shaggy salt-and-pepper brows.

"Yes, I understand." And if she didn't, she soon
would—even if she had to steal Wiley Roy's precious
laptop computer and search every database on the Net.

Doc held up the same gnarled hand that had held
hers while she'd screamed in agony during her first
delivery. One by one he ticked off potential problems.
Each one was worse than the one before. Each one had
the potential to precipitate early labor or worse. By the
time he finished, she felt light-headed and her throat
was dust dry.

"What do you suggest I do?" she managed to
squeak out after swallowing several times.

"Get yourself to a specialist who handles these kinds
of cases on a regular basis, one of those new high-risk
docs that are all the rage these days. I've been doin'
some callin' around just in case, and I've come up with
five names." He reached for a folder and flipped it
open. "Two are at Baylor, one at UC San Diego, one
at Mount Sinai and one up in Oregon at Portland General."

Madelyn cast a wary glance at the collection of faxes
and printouts he was shuffling through, refreshing his
memory. "Is there one that's better than the others?"
she asked when he glanced up.

"They're all excellent. Some I've heard tell of here
and there, some I haven't. I met Candace Marston once

at an internists' conference in Austin three or four years ago. She's a few years younger than you, but sharp as a tack. The others are all men.''

''I don't care about gender. I care about my baby, and I want the best, whoever he or she is.''

Doc studied her in thoughtful silence through his half glasses for a long tense moment before nodding. ''In that case, this is the man you should see. The best of the best.'' He lifted a sheet of paper with a brief bio typed at the top of a long list of published articles and honors.

Her breath dammed up in her chest when she read the name printed in bold letters at the top: LUCAS OLIVER JARROD, M.D.

''It can't be,'' she said, her voice flat.

''According to everyone I asked, Jarrod's considered the premier expert on myomas, among other things. Way I heard it, he's got women flying in from all over the world, just so's he can watch over 'em.''

''I don't care.'' Her heart seemed as if it would pound clear through her chest, and her blood felt hot in her veins. Not once, in all the years since the social worker had taken her child away forever, had she stopped loving her daughter or wondering about her. Nor in all that time had she ever stopped hating Luke Jarrod or blaming him for her loss.

Yet, paradoxically, the man she'd married had the same lean build and pantherlike way of walking that had first attracted her to Luke.

''It took me years to stop hating him. I…it can't be good for the baby to stir all that up again.''

''Then don't let it be stirred.'' Stern, suddenly, and intense, Doc's eyes bored into her. ''If you want to give that little one a chance, get yourself on the next plane to Oregon. Charm the man if that's what it takes. Play the guilt card if he balks. Remind him of all he cost you if you have to, but convince him to take you on.''

Madelyn bit down on the urge to refuse point-blank. This baby meant everything to her. *Everything.* Yet, how could she bear to rake up the misery of the past all over again?

''Maddy, you're a strong woman,'' Doc said gently but with audible conviction. ''You've handled much worse than this and survived. You've made yourself into a real role model for the young folks in this sorry old town. You even married a man who didn't value you near enough because your folks liked him.''

At the mention of the baby's father, her gaze dropped. The eldest of eight children, Wiley Roy Foster had been adamant in his desire never to be a father. Since four specialists had told Maddy she would almost surely never conceive again, theirs seemed an ideal match. And they *had* been happy in the beginning. Gradually, however, the hopeful early years settled into a mundane routine. Wiley Roy wasn't so much a bad husband as a complacent one. Nothing she tried could shake him from his rut, while little by little, she found herself feeling lonelier and lonelier.

When she'd told him she was pregnant, Wiley Roy had stunned her by issuing an ultimatum. Perhaps he'd provided the sperm, he'd said but he was in no way a father. She had to choose between him and the child. He'd moved out of their split-level Spanish colonial home on the day she refused to terminate this pregnancy. His rejection had hurt, but the pain was already fading. The hurt Luke had caused never had.

Sensing the tangle of emotions, Doc reached over to

take the hand she'd clamped like a talon around the arm of the chair. "Madelyn, I've checked this man out thoroughly. He has some of the most impressive credentials I've ever seen and an impeccable reputation, both professionally and personally. Everything I've learned tells me he's no longer that callous hell-bent-for-leather rascal who sloped out on you when you needed him most."

"What if you're wrong?" she asked, studying the familiar face carefully.

"Read his curriculum vitae, and then if you're not convinced, we'll move on down to the next name on the list."

Still she hesitated, dropping her gaze to hide her eyes from Doc's too-perceptive gaze, her stomach in knots and her heart beating so fast she had trouble catching her breath.

"Maddy, I know I didn't take as good care of you as I should have the first time, but believe me, I wouldn't recommend this if I didn't think it was exactly what you needed right now." Very gently Doc's hand squeezed hers, drawing her gaze back to those kindly eyes. "Think of the precious little one who's counting on you to protect him or her, Maddy. Think of your baby."

It hurt to talk. Hell, it hurt to breathe. Since Luke was pretty much forced to do both, he set his jaw and pushed himself past the pain. It was a skill he'd developed a lot of years back and had saved his sorry ass more than once.

"You gonna give me your opinion or are you just gonna stand there, wasting time neither of us can spare?" he grumbled at the big blond man leaning with arms crossed against the sink in one of the emergency-room cubicles, watching him through narrowed eyes.

Boyd MacAuley was one of the best neurosurgeons in the country. He was also a good friend. Luke's *best* friend, if he had to choose. Although it was only a little past nine in the morning, Boyd had the look of a man in need of eight solid hours of deep sleep. It was a feeling Luke knew all too well. In the past thirty-six hours he'd only managed a couple of catnaps between deliveries.

"You know my opinion, hoss." Boyd's voice was edged with an impatience to match Luke's own. "I've given it to you at least once a month for the past two years. You need to have those disks repaired. As it is, I'm amazed you're still on your feet."

"I don't have time for more surgery."

"Make time."

Luke sucked in his breath and sat up. He was used to the sharp stab of pain in his lower back every time he moved. It had been the sudden weakness in his right leg that had nearly sent him crashing to the floor in the operating room. Fortunately he'd already performed the emergency C-section on Phyllis Greaves and was fixing to apply the staples to the incision when his left leg had buckled on him.

As luck would have it, the first-year resident assisting him had once been a linebacker for Oregon State, which meant that he'd been strong enough to catch Luke's one hundred and ninety pounds without keeling over himself. Otherwise Luke was pretty sure he'd be nursing a few major bruises, as well as a battered ego.

Now, an hour later, the numbness was gone, replaced by a throbbing that felt exactly like a red-hot poker had been jabbed through his calf muscle. He knew the cause of course—scar tissue surrounding the fourth and fifth lumbar vertebrae impinging on the sciatic nerve. Mostly he could ignore it, but when he was tired, like now, he tended to limp badly. Today was the first time his leg had actually gone numb, however.

"If I do let you cut, how long before I can go back to work?" he asked when it was safe to breathe again.

"Two, three weeks, then six, eight more of restricted activity. In a brace of course."

"Bull. I've done my research. I figure three months before I can handle even routine deliveries. Longer for the high-risk moms."

Boyd let out an exasperated sigh. "So you scale back for a while. I know a half-dozen third-year ob/gyn residents who would kill to work under the great Luke Jarrod."

"Shove a sock in it, MacAuley."

Luke swung his legs over the edge of the table, then waited out the renewed surge of pain. An accident his last year on the circuit had blown out his back. High-risk surgery had gotten him back on his feet. The brace he hated had kept him going through his last two years in med school. Years of back-strengthening exercises and therapy had gradually allowed him to shuck the brace.

After the accident his mentor at Stanford, Dr. Danton Stone, had done his best to tout him off obstetrics, telling him repeatedly about the toll a specialty like that would exact on his ruined spine. Dan was right, Luke thought with a pang of resignation. So, unfortunately, was Boyd. Much as he hated to admit it, he couldn't keep up his present pace much longer without surgery.

"All right," he conceded with a sigh. "Give me a few months to scale back my patient load."

Boyd shook his head. "A week, two tops."

"Not a chance. I have a dozen ladies ready to go any minute now, almost all of them having potential for major complications."

"*You* have a potential for major complications—like permanent paralysis if those wonky disks cut into your spinal cord."

"Unlikely."

Boyd snorted. "Lord save me from stubborn jackasses."

"Stubborn, hell. I agreed to let you cut into me, didn't I?"

"Fine. Let's nail down a date."

Ninety minutes and counting after Madelyn had walked into the ugly redbrick medical building, she was perched on the padded paper-covered table with the dreaded stirrups, waiting for Luke.

She had a lot of experience at that, she realized, fighting the sudden urge to laugh hysterically. Agonizing months of waking up every morning expecting her shy lanky bronc buster with the amazing blue eyes and irresistible smile to walk up the crumbling front steps of the shabby old house on Alamo Street, a wedding ring in the pocket of his Wrangler's. Just like a movie she'd seen once—except that *her* hero hadn't come in time.

Half out of her mind with grief, she'd sent him away, then regretted it with every atom in her body. If he loves you, he'll be back, her pastor had told her over and over. But he hadn't come back, and her life had gone on. Obviously his had, too. Very nicely, it seemed, she decided, glancing around for the umpteenth time.

Though the examination room was small, the signed lithograph of a lone rider silhouetted against a dying sun was by a famous Southwestern artist. The diplomas and certificates that marched next to the print were even more impressive. A bachelor's in biology from Arizona State, a medical degree from Stanford. A chief residency at Portland General. A clutch of fellowships and honors. Not bad for a high-school dropout with lousy grammar who'd sworn up one side and down the other he'd never set foot in a classroom again.

A knock on the door had her pulse skittering. But it was Esther, the rotund nurse with smiling eyes, who entered. "Doctor just phoned from the hospital and he's on his way," she offered as she wrapped the familiar black blood pressure cuff around Madelyn's arm. "Shouldn't be long now."

The sky was a solid gunmetal gray and the air smelled like rain as Luke limped across the grassy median separating Port Gen from the medical building.

In spite of the three cups of coffee he'd gulped down with the breakfast he'd grabbed in the cafeteria, he was still a little queasy from the meds he'd reluctantly taken to soothe the inflamed tissues in his spine. Though he'd showered and shaved, he still felt grimy and battered, pretty much how he'd felt after a day on the rodeo circuit.

Dorie Presley, his iconoclastic frizzy-haired receptionist, looked up as he slipped through the back door to his ground-floor office suite, her Celtic blue eyes sharply assessing. A transplanted Californian who had grown up in a San Francisco mansion, she was married to a surgical resident who adored her enough to overlook her haphazard housekeeping and lousy cooking.

Luke couldn't care less about her lack of domestic skills. All that mattered was her ability to keep him organized and halfway on schedule, a skill he'd never mastered. She also made the best coffee he'd ever tasted, which meant a lot to a man who lived on caffeine.

"You look terrible, L.J."

"Thanks, I needed that," he muttered as he shrugged into the starched white coat he'd learned to wear because some patients had trouble trusting a doc who wore frayed jeans, scuffed cowboy boots and plain old cotton work shirts.

"This should help," she said, handing a mug of the extra-strong boiling-hot French roast she'd started brewing the instant he'd called to say he was on his way.

"Darlin,' you're a pearl beyond price."

He took a greedy sip, far too aware that he really should cut back. The chronic burning in his gut wasn't exactly an ulcer, but it had the potential.

"How's Mrs. Greaves?" Dorie asked, looping his stethoscope around his neck.

"Awake and thrilled with her twin daughters."

"Congratulations, boss!" she said, grinning. "You beat the odds again."

Luke allowed himself a private moment of deep satisfaction. Phyllis Greaves had lost four babies before coming to him. The Greaveses were nice people who would make wonderful parents. "Thanks, but most of the credit goes to Phyllis." The determined lady had spent the last two months of her pregnancy in bed and never once complained. He admired her grit.

"Your messages are on your desk in order of priority. Nothing urgent, but Dr. Horvath at Rogue River definitely needs a return call before five.''

''Remind me, okay?''

Dorie's grin flashed. ''I live to serve, oh exalted healer.''

Luke snorted. ''Do we have a full house or did some of my ladies get tired of waiting?'' he asked over the muted ringing of the phone.

''Definitely stacked full, so don't dawdle,'' she said before snagging the phone.

While she dealt with the call, he slugged down the rest of his coffee, then patted his pockets, looking for his reading glasses before he remembered he'd left them in his locker at the hospital.

While dealing with a question for the patient on the other end, Dorie fished his spare pair from her bottom drawer and handed them over. He grunted his thanks before tucking them safely into his breast pocket, along with a pen he filched from the jar on her desk, and heading down the hall toward the examining rooms.

All four doors were closed, with patient charts lined up neatly in the Plexiglas slots on the wall. He stopped at number one. The folder was yellow and tagged in blue and red. A new patient, high risk, the only kind he had time to treat these days.

Moving his shoulders to relieve the tension that had started the instant he'd walked through the back door, he plucked the chart from its plastic slot and flipped it open.

The name was printed on the tab in Dorie's neat boarding-school script. *Madelyn Smith Foster.*

His breath dammed up in his throat. My God, Maddy? Here? The last time he'd seen her he'd been standing on her porch with his hat in his hand, begging her to forgive him.

While he'd been having a high old time in Canada, flirting with more pretty girls than there were fleas on a dog, she'd been twisting and turning through two days of torturous labor, only to hemorrhage and nearly die before the frantic GP had taken the baby by cesarean. Her parents had waited less than twenty-four hours before offering her an ultimatum—give the tiny but perfectly formed baby girl up for adoption or take the kid and leave.

It hadn't been much of a choice for a seventeen-year-old schoolgirl with no job skills and no money, so she'd signed the papers that had taken her baby away forever. It hadn't been easy for her, however. Anything but. Her eyes had still been puffy and glazed with grief two weeks later when she'd opened the screen door to his nervous knock.

Forcing himself to breathe again, he scanned the patient-info sheet. Thirty-nine years old. Employed as a guidance counselor at Whiskey Bend High School. Divorced. His mind stuttered over that fact before moving on to the medical history—the usual childhood illnesses, an appendectomy at the age of seven. On the night they'd made love she'd been embarrassed to let him see the scar—

"Luke, are you all right?"

His head shot up and for an instant he felt disoriented. "What?"

"Don't take this wrong," Dorie murmured, looking both concerned and amused. "But you look exactly like a man who's taken one where it hurts the most."

He managed an off hand grin. "It's my office. I can look anyway I want, sugar."

Unimpressed gray eyes, sharp as lasers, zoomed in on his face. Heat crept up his neck as he dropped his gaze to the chart. "This…this patient, what do you know about her?" he asked, careful to keep his voice low.

"Just that she's a referral from a GP I never heard of, has excellent insurance through a group policy for Texas-state employees, arrived early for her appointment, seems a bit aloof, but pleasant—and definitely anxious, though she hides it well. On a scale of one to ten, style-wise, I give her a twelve."

"What the hell is 'style-wise'?" Luke muttered. He was always edgy when he was caught off-guard.

"You know. Style. Presence." She lifted an eyebrow and he frowned. "The way a woman dresses and wears her hair and carries herself."

"Mrs. Foster is a twelve?"

"Absolutely." Dorie grinned, clearing enjoying herself. "If I had to guess, I'd say she bought the suit she's wearing from Neiman Marcus, probably not on sale. Same with her shoes. Lizard pumps, probably Italian. And hair to die for. Thick, sun-streaked and blond, which has to be natural or the best dye job I've ever seen."

Luke felt a little dizzy. The Maddy he'd known had worn jeans or short cotton skirts and flirty shirts that showed off her ripe breasts to perfection. Her hair had definitely been glorious, however. Long and silky and the exact color of honey shot through with sunlight.

"You're sure she's here as a patient?" he pressed, more confused than ever.

Dorie offered him a curious look. "Since she filled out the new-patient forms, I think that would be a safe assumption, yes."

"Damn." He raked his hand through hair still damp from his shower. The rare nervous gesture from a man who prided himself on his control had Dorie narrowing her gaze.

"Luke, is there a problem?"

"Hell if I know."

Dorie regarded him strangely for a beat, then broke into a knowing grin. "Aha, an old girlfriend. And from the panicked look on your face, I'd say the flame is still flickering inside that lean mean bod of yours."

Luke bit off a crude reply. "Don't you have insurance forms to fill out?"

"Yes, sir." Dorie snapped him a mock salute before disappearing into the reception area.

Luke braced one hand against the wall and dropped his head. His heart hammered his chest as he fought to regulate the breathing that threatened to tear through his throat like a feral howl.

He'd struggled for years to drive his darlin' Maddy Sue out of his head. Years and years of going weak in the knees whenever he heard bubbling laughter or caught a glimpse of thick blond hair shining in the sunshine. Of feeling his gut knot and twist whenever he saw a woman holding a baby.

He should have figured God wouldn't let him slide forever, he thought as he pushed himself away from the wall, squared his shoulders. He'd sell his soul for a drink right now, he thought as he took another ragged breath, then opened the door.

Chapter 2

The white coat with his name embroidered in red above the pocket said he was an MD. The calendar said he was six weeks away from his forty-first birthday. Two steps into the room and he was an eighteen-year-old rodeo bum, with a crushing pressure in his chest and shock waves in his gut from a hard-knuckled punch in the solar plexus.

It was exactly the same as it'd been that blistering-hot day in Texas, he realized with a kind of stunned dismay. One minute his life had been under his control, the next he was reeling.

Maddy had been as pretty as a picture at seventeen. Now she was stunningly beautiful. A sophisticated lady exuding poise and a quiet confidence, even perched on the end of his examining room table with her spine as straight as a die and her chin pridefully high.

The big hair that had mesmerized him was gone, but the glorious color was that same shade of honey shot with sunshine. Once it had spilled to her shoulders in glossy waves, swishing like molten silk with every sassy toss of her head. Now, however, it had been tucked back out of the reach of man's hands into a chic twist right out of one of Dorie's glossy magazines. He wanted to ask why she felt she had to keep all that wonderful sunshine hidden away, but he'd lost the right to ask her that kind of question.

"Hello, Maddy," he said after closing the door behind him. He hadn't felt this wired since the last time he'd dropped from the top rail of the chute onto the back of a nightmare.

"Doctor." She inclined her head, queen to subject. Damn, but she was something, he thought, fascinated in spite of the wariness skimming his nerves.

Ordinarily he offered his hand to a new patient, the first fragile thread of trust. Only the certain knowledge that it would cost him more to touch her than he wanted to risk had him trying a smile, instead.

"You look terrific." His voice came out rusty as hell, but he had a feeling it was the words themselves that had her eyes narrowing between those long fluttery lashes.

He let his gaze drift lower, skimming the curves that filled out the pale yellow jacket in all the right ways to mess with a man's head. She was also pregnant, he realized with a jolt that twisted all the way through him, leaving him a little breathless. About six months along was his best guess.

He still remembered the jagged despair in her voice when she'd told him that the surgical field had gotten contaminated during her C-section, and the resulting infection had scarred her fallopian tubes, rendering her sterile. The guilt he'd carried had been a bloody hole in his gut ever since.

"So you really are a patient," he added when she remained silent. "I wondered."

"I didn't lie to you when I told you I was sterile," she said, her drawl softer than he remembered, though flavored now with a hint of tension. "According to Doc Morrow, the odds of my ever conceiving again were too small to even measure."

"Doc Morrow?"

"My family doctor in Whiskey Bend. He delivered me when I was born and he delivered my...*our* baby." She took a quick breath, the only sign of distress he could detect. "He was also the one who arranged for the adoption."

Pain was a vicious hand wringing him dry. "I'm sorry, Maddy. Deeply sorry."

A hint of some fierce emotion darkened her eyes. "Sorry enough to make sure I keep this baby?"

He had a long list of questions, all of which filtered down to one. "Why me?" he asked quietly.

"I have a fibroid that's growing." She hesitated, then added with the barest suggestion of a tremor in her voice, "Doc's only treated one similar case, and that patient went into premature labor at six months." She took a breath, her eyes suddenly sad. "She lost the baby."

Luke cursed silently, one pithy vehement expletive. It could be worse, but not much, he thought as he leaned his butt against the edge of the sink and shifted most of his weight to the leg that didn't throb.

For years he'd tortured himself with thoughts of how it would be if he saw Maddy again. It was a game he played with himself when he had trouble sleeping.

Mostly his fantasies had been shaded toward raunchy—
in a respectful sort of way, of course, since Maddy was
a good girl. But this... His chest tightened, the way it
used to right before a ride. Like a fist grinding against
his sternum.

"There are a lot of good baby docs in Texas," he
hedged. "Marston and Wong at Baylor, to name two."

She dismissed that with a brief frown. "I contacted
them both. Each said you were the leading doctor in
this area. As did the two other experts in high-risk
pregnancy I consulted. I've also read the article you
wrote about treatment of fibroids during pregnancy."

"Which one?"

"The one in the *Journal of the American Medical
Association.*"

He nodded. "*JAMA* published three. Which one did
you read?"

That brought her up short, but she recovered quickly.
"The one that explained why the kind of fibroid I have
can't be surgically removed without risking a miscarriage." Her hand crept to her belly. "The more I read
the more I realized how easy it would be to lose this
child."

He crossed his arms over his chest and marveled at
the woman she'd become. Bright, confident and way
way out of his league. "I'm sure your research told
you that myomas are unpredictable. They can cause
some really mean complications one month and go dor-
mant the next." They were also decidedly dangerous
when they took a notion to grow, a fact she obviously
knew as well as he did.

"Since this...this baby means everything to me, I'll
do whatever it takes to carry it to term."

"Even tolerate my presence in your life again?"

"Obviously." Her chin came up. "Since you're considered the best, you were my first choice."

It was an answer that should have pleased him. Instead, it terrified him.

When he'd been facing a tough ride, he'd survived by paring his mind to the basics. Things he knew how to do, like shoving his butt hard against the rigging and keeping his head tucked tight so his neck didn't snap. Skills he'd practiced until they'd become second nature. It was a knack he'd come to value during life-and-death emergencies he'd learned to expect every time he walked into a birthing suite. It was a knack he fell back on now.

"You realize you'll have to move to Portland until you deliver?"

"I'm prepared to do that, yes."

"What about your job? Your...family?"

"My mother has agreed to look after my house and garden, and I've already arranged to take a leave of absence from my job for the next school year. The principal has four children of her own, and she's been wonderfully understanding. A godsend, really."

He nodded. Cleared his throat. "It says on your info sheet that you're divorced."

"Yes, for almost four months now."

"I assume Mr. Foster is the baby's father?"

"Yes, although I think that if he could, he would erase every scrap of his DNA from the baby's cells."

"I take it he's not gonna be interested in participating in the baby's delivery?"

"No, he's relinquishing paternity." She hesitated, then added, "Wiley Roy never wanted children, and since I thought I was sterile, he didn't bother to get a vasectomy when we married. When I found out I was pregnant, he…he gave me an ultimatum—the baby or him. I couldn't have both.'' She glanced down at her hands. At the thin white line on her finger where he deduced her wedding band had been. Her mouth firmed as she folded her hands, then lifted her gaze to his. ''I chose the baby. The next day he went to Juarez and divorced me.''

''Man's a fool.''

She shrugged. ''He's a decent man and a wonderful teacher. He prides himself on being an example for his students, and in his own way, he was a good husband. He simply doesn't want to be a daddy.''

And neither did you, her expression said loud and clear. She was wrong. Once he'd gotten over the shock, he'd wanted that very much, but he doubted she would believe him. He straightened, sucking in a breath against the hot jolt of pain in his spine. ''Is that your medical record?'' he asked, indicating the bulging brown folder next to her on the table.

''Yes, everything from the moment I was born until my last visit with Doc right before I left Texas.''

''Which was when, exactly?''

''Two days ago, I took the 6:00 a.m. flight from El Paso yesterday morning.''

''May I?''

''That *is* why I brought it,'' she said as she handed it over. ''The information dealing with this pregnancy is on the top. Doc included his phone number, and I've already signed a release form authorizing him to answer any questions you might have.''

''Very efficient.''

She dismissed the compliment with an impatient frown. ''I can't afford to waste time. I doubt you can, either, Doctor.''

''True enough.''

After fishing his reading glasses from the pocket of his white coat, he leaned back against the sink again, flipped open the folder and started to read.

Madelyn kept her gaze trained on Luke's face, scarcely daring to breathe. Beneath the tailored lines of the loose-fitting linen jacket, her heart was racing wildly, just as it had been that hot September day at the fairground when her gaze had met his across the dusty ring.

He'd changed of course. Grown older and...harder somehow. Inside and out, she decided after a good long look at the set of his jaw. Certainly he was more physically powerful, which surprised her, though perhaps it shouldn't have. Luke had always been very strong. Growing up on horseback had given him incredible power in his legs, especially his thighs and buttocks. Twenty-two years had added breadth to his shoulders and packed hard muscle onto his chest and arms.

The glossy black hair that had always smelled of wind and baby shampoo was now liberally threaded with silver. For such thick hair it had been surprisingly silky. Though shorter now, it still fell into a rebellious off-center part where a cowlick defied taming.

The too-handsome face she'd never quite managed to purge from her mind for all her years of trying was now all hard lines and stark angles. The mouth that had thrilled her every time he'd slanted her a lopsided shy-at-the-edges grin was controlled now and bracketed by deeply gouged creases. His eyes, Paul Newman blue and once full of the devil, were somber now, even guarded, with the war-weary look of a man who'd left innocence behind long ago.

Unfortunately, however, the aura of raw masculinity that had both exhilarated and frightened her was as potent as ever. More so, she realized with a hard thud in the vicinity of her still-queasy stomach. Buried somewhere in this quiet-spoken professional with a calm manner and a way of looking directly into her eyes was the first man she'd ever loved.

As a high-school guidance counselor, she'd seen parts of herself in every girl who'd sat across from her, bewildered and scared and hurt because she'd trusted her heart to the wrong boy. Ancient history, she reminded herself as he turned back another page with a large heavily veined hand and continued reading. Being here wasn't personal, nor was it really a choice.

Instinctively she pressed her hand against her stomach, a gesture she'd repeated many times since Doc had given her the astonishing news. The reminiscent smile that started to bloom died as those amazing blue eyes shifted to capture hers, sending what felt like a white-hot shiver all the way to her womb. Only years of rigid self-control kept her from flinching.

"According to this, you were already nine weeks along when you consulted Morrow." Though soft-spoken, his voice had a gritty quality that had her tensing all the way to the bone.

"Yes, that's right." She kept her voice calm and even, the exact tone she used when soothing angry parents or troubled adolescents. "My periods have always been erratic, and they got worse after that C-section. Doc had told me not to worry, so I didn't, but when I started having other symptoms, I decided to have a thorough checkup."

"Other symptoms?"

"A thickening in my waistline and tenderness in my

breasts.'' To her dismay she actually blushed. He glanced down quickly, his gaze running over the page again before he closed the folder.

''Why did you wait so long to consult me?''

''Doc wasn't concerned until he sent me for this latest ultrasound.''

Luke's mouth compressed, giving his face an even tougher texture. Behind the thin dark rims of his glasses, his blue eyes had taken on flecks of steel. ''You're an intelligent woman, Madelyn. It's obvious you want this child. My question is, why did you trust yourself to the same doctor who in your last pregnancy misdiagnosed preeclampsia as indigestion?''

''It's easy to diagnose after the fact,'' she replied, her voice sharper than was fitting for a well-bred Southern lady. ''But in those days Doc was the only doctor in the county, and he'd been run ragged by an outbreak of chicken pox.'' She took a breath, hating the painful memories her words had stirred. ''I was lucky to have him, especially since my daddy had no money and no insurance. Without Doc's compassion and generosity I would have had to drive 150 miles to the charity hospital in El Paso for my checkups. And God only knows what would have happened when I hemorrhaged.''

His jaw went white. ''Maddy—''

''No, let's get this all out, Luke.'' She sat straighter and kept her gaze on his. ''You're the last person I want to need in my life. I couldn't sleep for two nights before I made the decision to ask for your help. Just being in the same room with you brings up memories I've worked hard to erase. But I want this baby more than I've ever wanted anything in my life. I'll do whatever it takes to give him or her the best possible chance.''

He studied her thoughtfully, then frowned. ''Maddy—Madelyn—I can't treat you without touching you.''

''I realize that.'' She drew a breath. That had been the worst of it, coming to terms with the enforced intimacy that childbirth imposed on doctor and patient. ''I also realize that in all aspects but one we're strangers to each other, so it shouldn't be that difficult to maintain a strictly professional relationship.''

''You're the mother of my only child, Madelyn. I would have married you if you'd said yes. I can never think of you as a stranger.''

Something barbed twisted around her heart. ''We don't have a child, Luke. She belongs to someone else, thanks to you. To survive I had to accept that. Just as I had to accept responsibility for mistaking sexual attraction for love. I know the difference now.''

His jaw tightened for the briefest of moments before he lifted a hand to rub the back of his neck. His sigh was heavy as he lowered his hand. ''Tell you what, you get yourself out of that fetching suit that's got my staff green with envy and into that paper gown yonder while I go see if I can scare up some professional detachment.'' He left before she had a chance to reply.

After asking Esther to prepare Maddy for a thorough exam, Luke went into his office and shut the door. Though he had other patients waiting, he needed a minute for himself.

He felt as though he was strangling, and his back was threatening to seize up again. Beneath his shirt and starched coat, his skin was slick with sweat, and his knees were as wobbly as a newborn colt's.

Heckfire, he was a freaking basket case here, he thought as he eased his aching body into the chair behind his cluttered desk, tossed his glasses on top of the latest *Physician's Drug Reference* and slumped back against the cool leather upholstery.

God only knew how much he wanted to help her, he thought, letting his head fall back. Anything he had that she needed, it was hers. If she wanted money, he'd beggar himself. If she needed a place to stay, he'd buy her a frigging mansion. Transportation? No sweat. A call to his friendly BMW dealer and the keys to a new Beemer would be in her hands within the hour.

With a long-drawn-out groan that sounded depressingly like a whimper, he raked both hands through his hair, then balled them into fists on the arms of his chair. Damn, but this was pure misery. As rough as it was on him, however, it had to be about a million times worse for her.

He'd known right off she had a healthy amount of grit. It had been there in the rigid angle of her head when she'd looked at him, and in the straight line of her back as she'd perched there on the edge of the table, a lady from the top of her shiny head to the toes of those city-lady shoes.

Asking for help from a man she'd sworn to hate had cost her. A woman with her spirit and class, ready to humble herself.

Because she loved the child she carried. Loved it as she'd loved their daughter.

Damn, but he admired her. Flat out respected the hell out of her. It was clear as glass she wanted this baby about as much as he figured he wanted her to have it.

Letting his shoulders slump, he dropped his hands and willed himself past the pain. Concentrate on what you know, he reminded himself. Diagnostic tests and procedures first, then a carefully considered, strictly monitored regimen of care. His mind clicked through the familiar routine, weighed pros and cons of radical new theories, considered options, then roughed out a plan.

Preliminary decisions made, the hard angry knot beneath his breastbone loosened. When he figured he had enough control to keep his voice steady, he picked up the phone and punched out Boyd's private number.

"MacAuley, here, and you have two seconds to state your business before I'm outta here."

Luke grinned. Poor guy sounded so harried he almost hated to add to his stress level. "Jarrod here, and I can state it in one. Cancel the surgery."

"The hell you say!" The bellow in his ear had him flinching.

"You heard me."

"Give me one decent reason."

He could give the guy a dozen. About how he still woke up in the middle of the night with his heart pounding and Maddy's small white face shimmering in his head. About how he hated the selfish ass he'd been at eighteen. About how he'd sworn to become a better man. But all those decent reasons came down to one.

"I promised a lady a miracle, and I intend to do my damnedest to give it to her," he said quietly before hanging up.

Chapter 3

"Is this your first?" Esther asked as she set out instruments.

Madelyn pressed her hand to the gaping front of the paper gown and wondered how a woman was supposed to maintain her poise with her bare feet dangling two feet above the floor. "No, my second. But there are complications, and it's possible I'll deliver too early."

"Don't worry, Mrs. Foster. Dr. Jarrod will take good care of you." The nurse covered the instruments before adding with a grin, "He might look like he just ambled out of a Louis L'Amour novel, and sometimes he can be a little abrupt when he's worn-out, but he's the best doctor I've ever known—and I've known plenty."

Madelyn returned Esther's smile with one of her own. In her heightened state of nervous tension, her lips felt numb—and just a little shaky. "Thanks, I—"

A sharp rap on the door had her jerking her head toward the sound. A split second later the door opened and Luke walked in. It was still there, that indefinable something that always made her think of wind racing across a barren mesa. Her lungs seemed suddenly starved for oxygen. Jet lag, she told herself firmly. Combined with stress.

"Ready for me, ladies?" he asked, his gaze sliding past her to his nurse.

"Ready, Doctor," Esther replied as she snapped on the lamp attached to a long gooseneck.

Suddenly nervous, Madelyn shivered, drawing another quick gaze from those intense blue eyes.

"Cold?"

"More like apprehensive." She licked dry lips and tried to ignore the ugly stirrups that Esther had just clicked into an upright position.

His expression was surprisingly sympathetic. "Took me a bad fall once and spent a little time hooked up in traction. Darn near made me crazy dangling there with my legs halfway to the ceiling."

He slipped his hand into the glove Esther held for him. "You ever been in the Pacific Northwest before?" he asked.

"No." Madelyn's reply came out thin, and she cleared her throat. "It's very...uh, lush. It seems like we flew over acres and acres of trees. And then, of course, there are all those rivers. Well, two here in the city, according to the guidebook I read on the plane. The Willamette and the Columbia. It was pretty hazy, so I didn't really get a good look, though." She realized she was babbling and clamped her mouth shut.

"Darn cold, too, for someone born and reared in desert country." He plunged his other hand into the matching glove, then flexed his long fingers. "Took me a couple of years before I stopped feeling like a

Popsicle six months out of every year. Esther still knits me sweaters for Christmas. Soft as a baby's bottom they are. And as pretty as they are soft. Had me three offers to buy the last one right off my back last year.''

Esther did her best not to preen. ''You keep on gorging yourself on that junk food and I'm gonna have to buy another skein for this year,'' she muttered as she uncovered the instruments.

Tensing, Madelyn fought the urge to scramble down from the table and hightail it all the way back to her hotel. A bubble of laughter caught in her throat as she pictured the unflappable always ladylike Mrs. Madelyn Smith Foster racing through an Oregon drizzle in her paper dress.

''Lie back, please,'' Luke said, his tone as impersonal as Doc's when he was performing a similar exam.

Paper rustled as she swung her legs to the table. His arm supported her as she lay down, his strength as intimidating as it was reassuring. ''Comfortable?'' he asked, sliding his arm free.

Her skin tingled from the brief pressure of his hard muscles. She put it down to heightened nerves. ''Fine, thank you.''

Her tummy made a nice little mound, and she concentrated on studying that sweet bulge. Beneath the gown, she was naked. As naked as the first time they'd made love.

''I can't do this,'' she said, her voice catching. ''I thought I could but—''

''Maddy, it's all right,'' he said, his voice soothing. ''We can reschedule, give you some time.''

Esther was right, Madelyn thought. Even garbed in the starched white coat, with a stethoscope casually looped around his neck and his diplomas hanging on

the wall behind him, he was every inch a man of the
Old West. Like a working cowboy, he had skin permanently darkened from years of working cattle and
mending fences under the hot sun, his temples scored
by squint lines and an implacable strength etched into
the weathered lines of his face.

When he'd competed, he'd worn a white straw Stetson, pulled low and tight against the whiplash snap of
his head when the bronc twisted and whirled and
bucked. One of the good guys, she'd thought then. A
hero.

"Do you still ride?" she asked before she realized
how silly that must sound. But she didn't care, not
when panic was licking at her again.

"Not much anymore, although I still stable a couple
of horses on a little place near Hillsboro. Two pretty
ladies, both palominos." He hooked one foot around a
stool on wheels and pulled it closer. "A couple of in-
terns from the hospital exercise them for me a couple
times a week," he said as he lowered himself with a
surprising stiffness onto the padded black seat. She
smelled him then, wind, sky, sun and a hint of soap.

"Molly—she's the mom—is part Arab and real
high-strung. Last time I paid her a visit, she got it into
her head I didn't love her anymore and took a chunk
outta my shoulder." He shook his head, his gaze flicking to the nurse, who looked surprisingly relaxed.
"How many stitches did I have?"

"Fourteen, and you hollered bloody murder the
whole time."

"Well, heckfire, woman. You were using a railroad
spike, instead of a needle. And jammin' it in real good,
too."

Esther rolled her eyes before meshing her gaze with

Madelyn's. Humor gleamed in the dark depths, and her expression dripped feminine disdain. "Pathetic the way a grown man turns to jelly the instant he feels the slightest prick of pain, isn't it?"

Madelyn felt a surge of gratitude toward the empathetic nurse. And Luke, too, she realized. Never in a million years would she have credited him with the kind of sensitivity he'd just displayed. For the first time since she'd locked her rental car and walked through the door of Luke's office she felt herself relaxing.

"It's genetically linked," she replied, falling in with what was obviously a familiar routine. "Like the utter inability to ask directions or find anything remotely smaller than a '57 Chevy in a bureau drawer."

Luke snorted, but his eyes held a lazy amusement, and the fine web of lines fanning the corners deepened. "Hey, I'm the boss around here, remember? Which means I get to make the rules. And rule number one is no male bashing allowed."

"It's not bashing if it's the truth," Esther said, sharing a smug look with Madelyn. "Right, Mrs. Foster?"

Madelyn nodded solemnly. "Absolutely."

Luke emitted a drawn-out sigh. "I can tell when I'm outnumbered." He offered Madelyn a crooked smile. "So, you want to get this exam thing over with, or should I have Dorie reschedule you for tomorrow?"

Madelyn blinked. "Do you have office hours on Saturday?"

"Not usually, but we've been known to make an exception in special cases." He glanced Esther's way. "What time is Walter Junior's game tomorrow?"

"It's been changed to Sunday at two."

He frowned. "Should I have known that?"

"Dorie put it on your calendar," Esther said with a

smile. "Tomorrow I can come in any time before noon."

Madelyn was enormously touched. Maybe big cities weren't as impersonal as folks back home claimed. "You'd do that for me?"

Luke's expression was suddenly dead serious. "Especially for you, Maddy."

"Because you think you owe me?"

"Because I know I owe you," he corrected, his voice thick.

Then it was there in her head, the excruciating pain that went on and on, the race to the hospital, screaming his name as the contractions ripped through her. She swallowed hard, turned her face away.

"Esther, can you give us a minute?" he asked quietly.

"Of course." The nurse offered Madelyn another reassuring smile before she left, closing the door behind her with a soft click that seemed unnaturally loud to Madelyn's ears.

"This was a mistake," she said through a constricted throat when they were alone. "It seemed perfectly logical when Doc and I were discussing it, but now..." She drew in a breath before sitting up. "Obviously there are a few unresolved issues from that particular period of my life that escaped my attention."

He ran his thumb over the thin scar riding the edge of his jaw. A tussle with a barbed-wire fence when he'd been five, he'd told her once when she'd traced it with her fingertip. "Guess I've been called a lot of things in my time, most of them deserved, but I can't ever remember being called an 'unresolved issue' before."

His dry tone charmed her into a shaky laugh. "Sorry, that's the guidance counselor in me talking."

He nodded. "Professional jargon. Makes it easier to handle the scary stuff."

His insightfulness surprised her. "Exactly."

"If it would help to take a swing at me, go ahead."

"I don't want to hit you, Luke," she said with a large measure of surprise. "Although I admit there was a time when I wanted to empty my daddy's shotgun in…well, places best not discussed in polite company."

That hard mouth softened into a rueful grin. "I can understand that, and I surely do appreciate your restraint." Grin fading, he scooted the stool closer. "I'll do everything I can to make this easier for you, Madelyn, but you have to give me some guidance here. Which, considerin' that's your profession and all, should be a dead-bang cinch."

"That's just the trouble," she said, her voice strident. "I don't know how to handle this. Ever since I found out about the baby, I've been an emotional basket case."

He nodded, serious as a judge. "Those baby-nurturing hormones can be a real pain sometimes."

She gurgled a laugh, then bit her lip, fighting an overwhelming urge to cry. "It's so…frustrating," she muttered as a tear drizzled down her cheek. "See what I mean?" she added, dashing it away.

Smiling, he captured her hand in his. "I want to help you. I think I can, but first I have to know exactly what kind of problems we have ahead of us."

"There is no us, Luke. There never was."

"I was speaking medically, not personally." He hesitated, then said gently, "I'm not asking you to forgive me. Or even to like me, though that would make things easier. But I am asking you to trust me professionally."

She felt a wave of relief. A professional relationship was exactly what she wanted. All she wanted.

"I hope you warm up that…that thing," she said, her gaze going to the shining speculum on the tray. "Otherwise, I swear I *will* shoot you."

His eyes crinkled. "I'll remember that," he said before releasing her hand and scooting to the door to call Esther in again.

Forty minutes later Madelyn was dressed and waiting in Luke's oak-paneled office while he finished with another patient.

Seated stiffly in one of two chairs by the desk, her hands folded in what was left of her lap and her mouth dry, she glanced around, distracting herself by absorbing the sights and smells of Luke's private domain.

Like the rest of the office, it was furnished in Southwestern pastels. The chairs for visitors were well padded and covered in soothing shades of green and beige. His own chair was upholstered in brown leather that looked butter soft and showed definite signs of wear.

A Navajo blanket of excellent quality covered part of one wall, and a signed lithograph of the desert at dawn hung behind the desk. As far as she could see the only visible sign of his rodeoing days was a small bronze statue of a wild-eyed stallion trying to unseat its rider, used as a paperweight on the desk.

Both her charts were there, as well, sitting squarely in the middle of the blotter. Though she knew it was inappropriate, she was sorely tempted to take a quick peek at the notes Luke had jotted down in his left-handed scrawl. Only the knowledge that she would feel horrendously embarrassed if he caught her kept her hands in her lap.

Though by necessity intimate, the examination itself had been virtually painless. As he'd worked, he and Esther had ragged each other about a dispute over a called third strike during her son's last Little League game.

By the time they'd finished insulting each other, the exam had been finished and Luke was helping Madelyn to sit up. Before she could launch into the anxious questions tumbling in her mind, he'd stripped off his gloves and been on his way out.

"We'll talk in my office," he'd told her with a non-committal smile before disappearing.

So here she was, fully dressed again in her new maternity power suit, so uptight she was surprised she didn't creak when she moved. Certainly she couldn't sit still, she realized as she got up from the chair and went over to inspect the snapshots and children's artwork pinned to a large bulletin board opposite the desk. Most of the drawings were addressed to "Uncle Luke," the letters printed laboriously in crayon or pencil. Several, however, had obviously been done by an older child and showed a definite flair.

One in particular caught her eye. It was of a cowboy astride a yellow horse, his gloved hands crossed over the pommel, his hat pushed to the back of his head, the way Luke used to wear his when he was feeling playful. At eighteen, he'd been breathtakingly earthy, the epitome of untamed masculinity to a naive girl raised on cowboy lore.

"That was a Christmas present from my goddaughter."

Startled, she whirled around. "She's very talented."

"I think so." After closing the door, he crossed the room to stand next to her. She'd forgotten how tall he seemed when they stood side by side, how he filled up the room with restless energy even when he was standing still. She felt that same energy seeping into her now.

"That's her there," he said, indicating a glossy photo of a young girl perched in front of Luke on the saddle of a breathtakingly gorgeous palomino. About five or six, she had dark braids, big brown eyes and looked impossibly dainty snuggled against his broad chest.

"Her name's Tory MacAuley," he said, his voice a little gruff. "Her mom's a kindergarten teacher and her dad's a neurosurgeon at Port Gen."

Madelyn forced herself to smile. "How old is she?"

"Five and three-quarters. A real proper lady already. Reminds me a little of you, actually." His grin transformed his face, erasing years and strain. "She informed me a few weeks ago that all the boys in morning kindergarten were pigs."

Madelyn laughed softly. "She'll change her mind soon enough."

"That's a fact, though I wouldn't care to be in her daddy's shoes when it happens." A look she couldn't decipher crossed his face for an instant before he glanced toward the desk. "How about we have that talk I promised you?"

"Yes, fine." Madelyn hurried to the chair she'd just left. Outside an ambulance wailed as it sped along the hospital access road, and rain pelted the twin windows. Luke snapped on the brass lamp, then waited until she'd seated herself before settling with surprising stiffness into his own chair.

"The baby's a good size for twenty-three weeks with a good strong heartbeat. The two ultrasound photos Dr. Morrow included show a definite increase in the size of the fibroid, which is a concern. But your blood pressure is fine and from what I've seen, you're in excellent health. Just to be on the safe side, though, I'd like to have Esther draw some blood and we'll set up an appointment to do another ultrasound. After that, I'll have a better idea—''

The door flew open, startling them both. "Sorry to interrupt, Doctor," the redheaded receptionist exclaimed as she rushed in. "We just got a call from the ER. Marlene Gregory was hit by a car as she was crossing Powell Street, and the baby's in trouble. The trauma surgeon said he'd meet you in the OR stat."

Luke was already on his feet by the time the receptionist ran out of air. "I'm sorry, Maddy, I have to go."

"Of course," she said, rising. "I'll wait."

He hesitated, then came around the desk. "Look, I don't know how long I'll be. Where are you staying? I'll call you when I'm done, and we can set a time to meet."

"I'm at the Mallory Hotel downtown. But I don't mind waiting. Really."

"Go back there, order yourself a blood-rare steak with all the trimmings for lunch and then take a nice long nap."

"But—"

"Doctor's orders, Mrs. Foster." He gave her a quick—and impersonal—smile before hurrying out.

Chapter 4

Built in the early twenties on a hill overlooking Portland's central district, the Mallory Hotel retained all the elegance of an earlier more gracious era. In the lobby glittering crystal dripped from a magnificent chandelier while classical music soothed tempers and set the mood.

Madelyn's room was on the fourth floor. Discreet signs directed Luke to the right and down a long dog-leg. Thick green carpet splashed with pink and purple roses muffled the sounds of his boots as he checked the shiny brass numbers affixed to the old-fashioned doors. Her room was the second from the end and looked out toward the business district wedged between two mighty rivers.

The Willamette and the Columbia.

He chuckled to himself as he recalled her nervous travelogue in his office. That first night in Texas she'd chattered a mile a minute all the way to the motel, her breath coming out in cute little bursts. And when she hadn't been chattering like a magpie, she'd been gnawing on that curvy little bottom lip. A classic response to anxiety. Him, he tended to dive a little deeper into that private place inside no one had ever seen. He knew the stony silence made him seem grumpy and maybe a bit remote, but anything was safer than having his insecurities hanging out naked for the whole damn world to kick.

His gut tightened as he lifted a hand and knocked. While he waited, he worked at blocking out the screaming ache in his spine. Just as he lifted his hand to knock again, the door swung open. It took him a moment to connect the rumpled sleepy-eyed angel in the purple robe with the sophisticated woman he'd left almost six hours ago in his office.

"Luke! I thought you were going to call." Her voice had the throaty quality of someone who'd been asleep only seconds before.

"I thought about it," he admitted, trying his damnedest not to notice the tendrils of pale hair that had slipped free of the classy twist to frame her face, but even a man with promises to keep could only stretch professional detachment so far. "But then I, uh, thought about how long it'd been since breakfast and I figured we could talk over dinner."

She blinked, then frowned. Damned if she wasn't adorable, standing there with bare feet and her mouth pursed in the closest thing to a kissin' invitation he'd ever hoped to see on a pretty woman. Hell had to be a lot like this, he decided. Condemned to want the one thing you can never have, no matter how many years of penance you've paid.

"What time is it?" she asked, peering up at him distractedly.

"Goin' on six."

Her eyes flew wide. "Gracious, I slept four hours."

"As your doctor, I have to say I'm mighty pleased to hear it. But as a man who's got an empty space the size of Crater Lake in his belly, I'm wondering how long it'll take you to decide on dinner."

Those sexy green eyes darted a quick look at his midsection. He nearly sucked in his gut, before he caught himself. He was in some fairly major trouble here, he realized. Wantin' to show off for the lady like the conceited fool he'd been at eighteen. Block it out, Jarrod, he told himself firmly. The lady was his patient. Only his patient.

"Oh, right, dinner, then conversation," she said, stepping back. "Please come in while I get myself together." She turned away, leaving him to close the door.

"How's Mrs. Gregory?" she asked, glancing over her shoulder. No longer sleepy, her eyes were dark with what looked like genuine concern. He liked that about her, he decided, the fact that she could step outside her own anxiety to care about a woman she'd never met. He liked it a lot.

"She's holding her own," he told her with a smile. "The next twenty-four hours are crucial."

"But she has a chance?"

"She has a chance."

Relief bled into her eyes, but there were still shadows. Bad memories, he thought, the kind he'd never been able to shuck for all his trying. "And...and the baby?"

"A little boy, four pounds, six ounces. He has a

chance, too.'' He hoped she didn't ask him how good a chance.

''Was the daddy...where was the little boy's daddy?''

''Last word I got he was on his way home from a business trip to L.A.'' He lifted a hand to scrub some of the tiredness from his face. The past two days were starting to catch up with him. ''Turns out the elderly man who hit her had a heart attack. His chances ran out on Powell Street.''

A fleeting expression of sorrow crossed her face. ''I'm sorry.''

''Yeah.'' He shifted his weight to his good leg. The numbness hadn't returned, but the ache left behind refused to ease. ''I, uh, figured we could eat in the dining room downstairs, if that's all right.''

''Fine.''

She started to turn away, then swung around with a taunting swish of silk to look at him with a mixture of curiosity and suspicion. ''I don't remember giving you my room number.''

''You didn't. I got it from the desk clerk.''

''They do that in Oregon? Just give out a room number to anyone who asks?''

''Not in the Mallory they don't, so don't be worrying yourself.''

''But you just said they gave it to you.''

''I told the desk clerk I was checking on a patient.''

Skepticism filled her eyes. ''And she believed you? Just like that?''

''Actually I delivered a baby here once. On the third floor. A tourist from Japan who'd been too polite to call for help until it was almost too late. I was just leaving the restaurant when the desk clerk got the call and started yelling. Same one's on duty tonight and she remembered me.''

Her expression cleared. "Let's hope history doesn't repeat itself in my case."

"Just remember not to worry about calling for help, even if you're not sure you need it. Us doctor types would rather handle things in a well-equipped hospital than a hotel room. Makes us real nervous when it's a room-service waiter passing the instruments.''

She choked a laugh. "I'll make a note."

Since she hadn't invited him to sit down, he checked around for something sturdy enough to lean against while he waited.

"How long has it been since you slept?" she asked, studying his face.

He shrugged. "Baby docs learn to sleep in snatches.''

"In that case why don't you grab a quick nap while I shower?''

Luke glanced at the bed, still made but a little rumpled from her nap. The idea of shutting down for a few minutes was nearly irresistible. "Better not. I've been known to crash hard when I'm this tired, and I still have rounds to make tonight."

"At least sit down and rest. I won't be long," she said before disappearing into the bathroom with another maddening swirl of silk against sleek calves. An instant later he heard the rush of water through the pipes in the connecting wall.

Feeling as though he was strangling, Luke managed to lower his aching bones to the mattress, found the remote and turned on the TV. After surfing until he found a Mariners game, he eased to his side, bunched the pillow she used under his head and set his mental alarm for fifteen minutes. Between one breath and another his mind simply shut down.

Through the closed door Madelyn heard the indistinct sounds of a baseball game on TV as she unzipped the small brocade bag containing her jewelry. She had one pearl drop affixed to her lobe and was searching for its companion when she heard the muffled ringing of the phone by the bed.

Muttering a curse, she hurried from the bathroom in her stocking feet. Luke was asleep, sprawled on his belly with his scarred boots hanging over the edge of the bed and his head turned toward the TV. His long arms were wrapped around the pillow, his cheek half-buried in the soft foam. His corners of his mouth were still tense, however. And his black brows were drawn together in a frown, as though something in the fathomless void of sleep was troubling him.

She managed to snatch up the phone on the third ring. He didn't move. Turning away, she whispered an impatient hello into the receiver.

"Madelyn? Is that you?" Her ex-husband's voice carried the strident edge of irritation that had become far too familiar.

"Wiley, how'd you get this number?"

"From your mama. She also told me you were consulting a specialist, but then, you always did overreact."

She glanced over her shoulder, her stomach knotting. Only Doc and her best friend Emily Weldon knew the name of the man she'd come to see. The last thing she needed right now was another scandal. "What do you want, Wiley?"

"Simply to complete the dissolution of a marriage that's become intolerable for both of us."

Madelyn closed her eyes and used her free hand to rub at the pinprick of pain in her right temple that invariably exploded into a full-blown headache whenever Wiley started in on her. "Intolerable," she repeated in a low tone. "Yes, I suppose it is now."

It hadn't been so intolerable when he'd come to her every Saturday night for an hour of regimented sex that had left her feeling more and more lonely and unsatisfied, however. Or when she'd nursed him through a battle with lung cancer, holding the basin as he retched after surgery and emptying bedpans because he was too modest to ask the nurse. No, good old Wiley hadn't found her intolerable then. Shaking with hurt and a healthy dollop of disgust at the loyalty she'd shown a man who so clearly had none for her, she stiffened her spine and took a bracing breath.

"All right, Wiley. I'll get an attorney. We'll work out a settlement."

"No need. Judge Berdette and I have already worked out the details."

"I'll just bet you have."

"The judge was my father's best friend before Daddy passed on to his heavenly reward, as you well know, and as such has always looked out for the best interests of the Foster family."

When had the stability she'd valued so much in Wiley Roy turned to a really ugly stuffiness? she wondered.

"Perhaps you'd better explain the details of this settlement."

"I suppose I must." His voice was perilously close to a whine. "I'll deed my share of the house over to you as well as your car and a third of our joint stock portfolio in return for your absolving me of any and all paternal obligations, now or in the future. In addition, you agree not to give the child the surname of Foster. My preference would be that you revert to your maiden name, as well, but that's your own choice. I would, of course, want those points spelled out in writing, duly witnessed and notarized. In addition, I never want to see the child or have him think of me as his father. You will not put my name on his birth certificate or on the form when you enroll him in school.''

Madelyn's knees were turning to jelly, and the pulsing in her head took on jagged edges. If she'd been alone, she would have sunk to the mattress and conducted the rest of this slimy discussion from a fetal position. As it was, she hated the thought that Luke might surface at any moment. A quick look over her shoulder reassured her that he was blessedly oblivious.

Turning back and ducking her head, she curved her hand around the mouthpiece. ''Wiley, think about that a minute,'' she whispered urgently. ''I can understand if you're angry, even though we both know I never lied to you. Take it out on me if you have to, but for God's sake don't punish your own flesh and blood.''

''I told you I never wanted a child, Madelyn.''

''But he's going to grow up in the same town. He'll hear gossip. Kids can be so terribly cruel, and even if they aren't, sooner or later he'll realize you don't want him.''

''You should have thought of that before refusing to terminate this pregnancy.''

Madelyn realized it was futile to argue. Besides, the pain in her head was truly vicious now. Icy fingers

gouging chunks from her skull. It was an effort to form
coherent sentences.

''Your terms are acceptable,'' she managed to enun-
ciate before removing the phone from her ear. Jagged
zigzags of phosphorescent light shot across her field of
vision as she attempted to return the phone to the cradle, causing her to miscalculate. The phone fell from
her fumbling fingers, hitting the table with a noisy clat-
ter.

''Oh God, oh God, oh God,'' she whispered, bracing
a shaking hand on the slick tabletop. Her knees were
water. Nausea roiled in her belly, and her throat
burned. She swallowed against the urgent need to physically purge herself of the ugly feelings inside her.
Gagging, she clasped her hand over her mouth.

''Easy, darlin', I've got you.''

Before she'd even known he was awake, Luke had
scooped her into his arms, carrying her with long swift
strides into the bathroom where she was noisily mis-
erably sick.

Luke pressed two fingers against the carotid artery
in Maddy's neck as she lay on the bed, his gaze on the
second hand of his watch. Her pulse had settled nicely
since she'd dozed off, and the flow of blood was re-
assuringly strong. Slowly he withdrew his hand, his
gaze focused intently on her face. Though her skin was
still pale, her breathing had evened into a normal
rhythm.

Silently he brushed the back of his hand against the
satiny curve of her cheek, his brow still knitted.
Though still too cool, her skin was no longer clammy.

''Luke?'' she murmured, nuzzling his hand. Curly
golden eyelashes fluttered as she struggled to focus.

"I'm here, Maddy." He removed the folded wash-cloth from her forehead, replacing it with one he'd just dipped in ice water and wrung nearly dry.

Even as she sighed in relief, eyes the color of a Mexican sea and glazed with pain blinked up at him. The helpless vulnerability shimmering in the depths squeezed his heart. "My baby?"

"Sleepin' most likely. Those little critters are real tough."

Her brow puckered as she stared at him, her eyes huge with fear and pain and her pale mouth trembling. "I'm…so scared of losing him."

"Go back to sleep and let me take care of both of you." He smoothed back her hair with a hand that wasn't at all steady. "Things will look brighter when you wake up."

"I hate this…needing you."

"I know."

"Part of me still hates you."

"I know that, too."

"They wouldn't even let me nurse her, our baby. They said they didn't want her to bond with someone who wasn't going to be her mama. I begged and begged…" She blinked. "You would have made them give her to me, wouldn't you, Luke?"

A hole opened in his gut. "Yes, I would have made them."

"I still hear her crying sometimes. Crying for her mama." She sighed, her eyelashes drifting closed. "Did I ever tell you?" she mumbled in a voice barely above a sigh.

"Tell me what, Maddy?" he asked gently.

For a moment he thought she hadn't heard him. And

then her pale lips curved into a soft smile. "Our baby, she looked just like you."

Luke sat on the edge of the mattress for a long time, silently stroking her hair while his heart seeped blood, his mind filled with an image of Maddy cradling a tiny black-haired baby in her arms. He'd thought nothing could make him hurt worse than that day on her porch when she'd told him he would never see the child he'd fathered so carelessly.

He'd been dead wrong.

Chapter 5

Maddy stirred restlessly, then surfaced from a twilight sleep with a nagging sense of anxiety. The room had grown darker, she realized as she opened her eyes. The TV was on in the room next to hers—she could hear it faintly—and on the street below, a horn blared, the sound muffled by both distance and the old hotel's thick brick walls. She had no concept of time, just that the worst was over and she'd survived.

Lifting her hand, she touched the cloth on her head. To her surprise it was still cold. Slowly she turned her head, expecting to see Luke sprawled in the chair, his feet propped on the edge of the bed, his eyes heavy lidded and lazy as he watched over her.

She was already rehearsing the words that would send him down to dinner without her when her breath dammed up in her throat. There was a woman sitting where Luke had been, a tiny woman with bright copper curls and an even brighter orange sleeveless shirt who was watching her with big brown eyes. Madelyn guessed her age to be late thirties, early forties. Her contemporary certainly.

Seeing that Madelyn was awake, she smiled and held up a hand. Madelyn noticed that she wore a wedding ring. She'd removed her own on the day Wiley had rejected their child. "Don't panic, I'm a nurse. Luke had to leave to make rounds, and he asked me to hang out here until he got back."

Madelyn cleared the sleep from her throat. "I'm Madelyn Foster," she said before finding a smile of her own.

"Yes, I know. I'm Prudy Randolph. I work with Luke at Portland General. He's also a good friend." She unfolded her legs in order to lean forward. "How's the head?"

"Better, thanks. Sleep almost always does the trick. The hard part is *getting* to sleep."

Ms. Randolph offered a look of sympathy. "Think you can manage some water?"

Madelyn was so thirsty she decided to risk unsettling her stomach. "Yes, please."

"I just got some ice from the machine for the compress," the woman said as she sprang to her feet and headed for the bathroom.

While the water ran and the pipes rattled, Madelyn carefully moved the compress from her head to the nightstand. After a few testing breaths she sat up. She felt woozy, but much better.

"Luke tells me you're from Texas," Ms. Randolph said when she returned, a glass of water in one hand and a bucket filled with what sounded like ice and water.

"Yes, ma'am," Madelyn replied, taking the glass

between both her hands as she added a polite thank-you.

"Please, call me Prudy. I have this overpowering urge to run to the mirror to check for crow's feet and sagging eyelids whenever anyone calls me ma'am."

"I know the feeling." Madelyn took another sip of the cold water, then held the glass against her forehead for a long soothing moment before glancing Prudy's way again. The instinct honed over the years told her this was a woman who could be trusted.

"Feeling any discomfort in your belly? Cramping? Unusual pressure?" she asked when Madelyn's gaze met hers.

"No, thank goodness."

"More?" Prudy asked when Madelyn set the empty glass next to the phone.

"No, thank you. I think I've tested my stomach enough for the moment."

"With my second I had morning sickness for five endless fun-filled months. Luke put me in the hospital twice on force fluids before I could become seriously dehydrated."

"How many children do you have?"

"Two redheaded daughters, or as my husband, Case, calls them, the two terrible terrors of Maternity Row."

Madelyn blinked. "Maternity Row?"

Laughing, Prudy pulled up her tanned legs, encircled them with her arms and leaned her chin on her knees. She was barefoot, Maddy noticed, and her toes were painted a fluorescent orange to match her shirt. Her shorts were fuchsia splashed with green triangles. It was a combination that should have looked garish. On Prudy, however, it seemed utterly right somehow.

"Maternity Row is our pet name for this little section of the old city overlooking the Columbia. Its real name is Mill Works Ridge, but Case took to calling it Maternity Row because almost everyone who moves in is either pregnant or about to be.'' She paused. ''Well, except for Harriet Finkle, who's going on seventy now, but since she retired from her job at Northwest Financial, she's almost always off on one of her 'life adventures,' so she doesn't really count.''

Madelyn laughed. ''Sounds like a very special place.''

''Oh, it is that. Very…healing somehow.'' Prudy's eyes twinkled. ''If I weren't such a practical soul, I'd call it magical.'' She twisted in the chair, draping her legs over the padded arms. Energy crackled from her small frame. The word *dynamo* popped into Madelyn's mind and stayed.

''One night a month the guys get together to play poker and the moms take the kids to a kiddy movie or rent videos and pig out on junk food. Last month we took the little ones to a petting zoo at the mall, which actually turned out not to be a good idea, because one of the Paxton twins got nipped in the bum by a baby goat who'd taken exception to having his ears tied in a knot.'' Her grin flashed again. ''Raine Paxton swears her boys can run rings around my girls in the terror department any day of the week. We've decided to blame L.J. since he's delivered most of the Maternity Row babies. But we forgive him because he's everyone's favorite uncle.''

Glancing down, Madelyn smoothed the coverlet with fingers that were still a little icy. ''I saw the artwork in his office addressed to Uncle Luke,'' she said softly.

''He calls that his gallery wall and is always pointing out new additions whenever I go in for a checkup.''

"Is he married?" The question was out before she realized it had been on her mind.

"No. Never has been, either." Prudy sighed. "If ever there was a man in need of a family of his own, it's L.J."

It had been there for him, Madelyn wanted to shout. A wife who would have adored him, a darling baby daughter with shiny black hair like his. "Perhaps he has other priorities," she said a little too stiffly.

A speculative gleam popped into Prudy's eyes, making Madelyn wonder if her voice had betrayed her thoughts. She prepared herself for the barrage of prying questions so common among women in Whiskey Bend, but to her surprise—and relief—Prudy's expression grew rueful.

"The other ladies of the Mommy Brigade and I have tried for years to fix him up with a nice lady, but he's one slippery dude. Oh, he's perfectly charming in that 'yep' and 'nope' way he has, but as far as any of us know, he never takes a woman out more than three times. He—" She was interrupted by a sharp knock at the door. "That must be the cowboy now."

Beneath the flowered coverlet Madelyn's stomach was jumping again. Little jittery pulses that had nothing to do with the lingering remnants of her migraine and everything to do with the way this man had always affected her.

"How's my patient?" he asked in a tired voice as Prudy stepped back to allow him to enter.

"Better than she was when you turned her over to me of course."

"Modest as always," he drawled as he stepped inside. In one hand he carried a plastic sack from a nearby drugstore, in the other a physician's black bag. He seemed to limp slightly as he walked.

"See for yourself if you don't believe me," Prudy said blithely as she closed the door behind him.

Madelyn summoned a polite smile as his gaze shifted her way. He looked rugged and worn and as tough as an old saddle. His hair was windblown and curling over his collar in a provocative mix of raven and silver, and his face was seamed with weariness. He was still dressed in the pale blue shirt and jeans one washing away from raggedy. His boots were only slightly less worn.

"You're not curled in a tight little ball and your color's better, so I reckon you're over the hump," he drawled after studying her for a long moment.

"Thanks to you and Prudy."

"Trust me, I enjoyed the peace and quiet," Prudy said before shoving her feet into green flip-flops.

Luke set his bag and sack on the table before giving Prudy a quick hug. "I owe you one, toots."

"Nothing I like better than having a gorgeous hunk a' burning love beholding to me," she said, giving Madelyn a sisterly grin. "I hope we meet again, Madelyn, but if not, the best of luck with that little one you're growing."

Madelyn returned her smile gratefully. "Thanks so very much. I appreciate your being here. It helped."

"My pleasure."

Luke looped an arm around Prudy's shoulders and ambled her to the door. Madelyn had an acutely vivid sensual memory of that steely arm draped across her own shoulders and felt an odd slippery feeling inside.

With a final wave for Madelyn, Prudy departed.

Madelyn cleared her throat. "I'm sorry about this, Luke."

"No need to be sorry for somethin' that's not your fault." Jaw tight, he returned to the bed and lowered himself into the chair.

"Have you eaten?" she asked, alarmed at the pallor beneath the tan.

"Yeah, I figured you wouldn't be in the mood for dinner anytime soon, so I grabbed a bite at the hospital."

Something about the tone of his voice had her narrowing her eyes. "In the cafeteria?"

"Not exactly."

"How, exactly?"

He leaned back and stretched out his legs. "I hit the vending machine in the staff lounge."

"Luke, you need more than junk food!"

He blinked at her through eyes that were dull with fatigue. "Are you playin' doctor, Miz Foster?"

She flushed, appalled that she'd been fussing at him like a wife. "Even a high-school guidance counselor can see you're staggering from exhaustion," she said. "And you're changing the subject."

"Yeah, but I appreciate your concern." He surprised her by easing forward to take her hand in his. His fingers were warm and strong, the pads slightly roughened by a wrangler's calluses.

"I owe you a talk," he said, his voice husky. "If you feel up to it, we can do it now."

Her heart leaped and her free hand crept to her belly. "Just tell me if you can help me keep this baby." Her voice had gone thin with anxiety. "I'm not sure I can concentrate on anything more complicated than that right now."

He glanced down, turned their hands until hers was resting atop his. She felt his weariness and, paradoxically, a steely strength. His expression was somber as he lifted his head and steadied his gaze on hers. "I can't promise you a perfect baby, because that's out of my control, but what I can control, I will. You'll need constant monitoring, and you'll need to do exactly what I tell you. But between the two of us I think we can give this little one a fighting chance." He took a breath, then curled his fingers around hers tightly, as though she was his lifeline, instead of the other way around. "Do you believe me?" he asked, his gaze watchful and just a little wary.

"Yes, I..." She had to take a breath. She had to believe him. She had no choice. Otherwise, she would fret herself into a blind panic—or worse. "I believe you."

A look she couldn't decipher crossed his face. And then to her utter shock, he lifted her hand to his lips and kissed it before returning it gently to the bed. "Now that that's settled how about I order you up some soup from room service?"

Her mind had to struggle to ignore the traitorous warmth that had spread through her the instant his mouth had brushed her skin, so it took a moment for her to catch up. Something about soup—and room service.

"Only if you order a real dinner for yourself," she replied quickly, pouncing on the distraction.

"Back to that food thing?"

She thought of the orders he'd given her in his office earlier and smiled. "Steak with all the trimmings. And a big spinach salad. You need iron and potassium."

His mouth slanted. "Yes, ma'am," he said as he

reached for the phone. While Madelyn leaned back and closed her eyes, he ordered enough food to feed a small army for a week.

"I hate warm milk," she murmured, rousing herself to interrupt.

"Make that hot cocoa," he told room service before hanging up.

"Are you going to be this autocratic throughout my entire pregnancy?" she asked as he climbed slowly to his feet.

"Nah, this is piddling little stuff. I'm saving the major bossiness until later." He braced his hands on his lean hips and rolled his head, obviously trying to loosen taut muscles in his neck and shoulder. "Lady said twenty to thirty minutes. Time enough to grab a quick shower."

"I've already had a bath," she reminded him.

"Not you. Me."

Just like that, those jittery little pulses were back. "What do you mean?"

He stifled another yawn before giving her a crooked bone-melting grin. "I don't remember much about my mama 'cause she took off when I was nine, but I do remember the unholy fuss she used to make when my daddy came to the dinner table smellin' a little ripe."

Madelyn clutched the edge of the coverlet with fingers that had suddenly gone numb. "I'm sure you can wait until you get home," she hastened to assure him.

"Suppose it could, if I was goin' home. But since I'm not and I have rounds first thing tomorrow morning, I'd best sluice off the grime while I have the chance."

Madelyn's brain was still a little fuzzy, so it took a moment before his words sank in. "You don't...surely

you don't intend to sleep here?" Terribly conscious
that she was clad in nothing more than a slip and her
underwear beneath the coverlet, she glanced uneasily
at the empty expanse of bed to her left.

His sigh seemed to come all the way from his rundown boot heels. "Guess we need a little clarification
here."

"We certainly do," she declared stiffly.

"Shove over, then, and let's get to it."

Her slip made a whispery sound against the blanket
as she scooted over to make room for him to sit on the
edge of the bed. A hazy memory surfaced suddenly of
Luke unbuttoning her blouse and easing off her skirt
before folding one-half of the quilted bedspread over
her like an afghan.

"I won't sleep with you, Luke," she said. "I don't
care how good a doctor you are or how much I need
you."

A silence hung between them, hot and dangerous. It
was just beginning to dawn on her that she'd made a
bad mistake when his eyes narrowed.

"I left my house almost forty-eight hours ago for a
delivery. I've been at the hospital or the office or here
since then. I'm tired and I'm grumpy and my patience
is stretched as thin as cellophane. So yeah, I intend to
sleep here, on top of the covers if that makes you feel
easier. As for sex, even if you were willing, I'm not.
You're my patient, and I do not sleep with my patients."

Shame was spreading heat over skin his gaze had
iced. "Luke, I—"

"I've already told Dorie to schedule an appointment
for you on Monday, at which time we'll do another
ultrasound. I'll probably ask you embarrassing ques-

tions about bodily functions, so be prepared. I don't mind if you blush, but I expect you to answer truthfully and in as much detail as I require.'' He paused, speared her with an impatient look. ''Clear so far?''

''Perfectly clear, although I'd just as soon not dwell overly long on the bodily functions part.''

Surprise burst in his eyes, erasing the angry impatience. ''Yeah, well, neither would I, but it comes with the job.'' His voice was still cool, but a hint of his drawl had crept back. ''Anything else we need to get straight between us before I head for the shower?''

Her heart was still racing, but not from fear. The young bareback rider she'd known had been cocky and easygoing and heedless of his own mortality. What he hadn't been was kind when he'd taken her virginity. The man he'd become had shown her incredible kindness, but he'd also shown her temper and a hint of an implacable will. Even though she'd grown up around strong quick-tempered males, the tough lean cowboy doctor with the tired face and steely eyes was possibly the most formidable man she'd ever met.

''Actually there is something I think you should know before this goes any further,'' she said, folding her hands primly over the coverlet.

His eyes narrowed. ''What's that?''

She drew a breath, then sighed. ''I snore.''

The soup was vegetable beef, served hot, with crusty French bread. She ate it all, then worked at finishing her hot chocolate while he methodically worked his way through a huge steak dinner.

The shower had removed some of the fatigue from his face. He'd washed his hair and slicked it back, giving his aggressively masculine features a naked vulnerable look. His eyes, however, were guarded, his thoughts hidden. Though he appeared relaxed, she knew he wasn't. But then, neither was she, though she was putting up a decent facade.

"How long have you suffered from migraines?" His question came between bites of the peach pie he'd ordered for dessert.

"I had the first one the day I signed the paper giving up my baby."

His fork froze halfway to his mouth, and his eyes took on a tortured sheen before he slowly lowered the fork to the plate, then pushed it away. "Have you ever consulted a specialist?" he asked, reaching for his coffee cup.

"Several." She toyed with the knife she hadn't used. "None could help me."

His cup clicked against the saucer as he set it down. "It's possible the headaches will get worse during your pregnancy."

"Yes, I know."

Easing back, Luke studied her face. Her skin had regained color, especially along the rise of those classy-as-hell cheekbones. Though still shadowed, her river-green eyes reflected a lively intelligence and something he couldn't quite tag, which always made him edgy. Those soft pale lips, though, they made him want to beg.

"Acupuncture helps some, so does Midol, though I'm not sure why," he said because it was true. And because he needed to remind himself that he was here as her doctor, and a doctor's sole concern should be for his patient's well-being. How she looked and smelled and riled his blood had no place in the doctor-patient relationship.

"I like your friend, Prudy. If you wouldn't mind giving me her address, I'd like to send her some flowers as a thank-you."

Because he was so tired, it took Luke a moment to realize she'd asked him a question. Somehow he summoned enough energy for a polite smile. His lower back was one angry pulsating knot, and his own head had begun to ache.

"She'd like that," he managed.

"Have you known her long?" He heard the note of polite tea-party conversation in her voice and felt empty inside.

"About twelve years, I guess. She's the head nurse of the trauma unit." He drained his cup, grimacing a little at the bitter aftertaste. He'd ordered espresso, double strength. About halfway through the meal, however, he'd begun to fade and now not even the added jolt of caffeine could counteract the sleep deprivation that was fixing to take him down for the count.

"Working in the ER must be very demanding."

He managed a nod. "Worst rotation I ever had as an intern."

"Was it difficult, going back to school?"

"Yes, and you're not really interested in hearing about my life." Ignoring the flash of hurt in her eyes, he pushed back his chair and managed to get to his feet without flinching. "If you don't mind, I'm going to sack out now." He grabbed the toothbrush he'd bought at the drugstore near the hospital, and somehow he made it to the bathroom without staggering. But it took him a good five minutes leaning against the closed door before he could move again.

Chapter 6

Madelyn came awake to the sound of water gushing through pipes. Someone on the floor above was taking a shower. Frowning and still groggy from the deep sleep that always followed a migraine, she struggled to bring the red numerals of the bedside clock into focus. To her surprise, it was barely five. The last time she'd looked at the clock before sleep claimed her, it had been past midnight. Luke had been asleep for a good hour by then.

When he'd come out of the bathroom, he'd ordered her to jab him hard in the ribs if her headache returned, then shucked his shirt, eased himself onto the mattress as though every movement was agony and closed his eyes. Then, between one breath and another, he'd simply shut down.

He was still lying in the same position, his broad chest rising and falling in a slow even rhythm. His jaw was dark with morning beard, his brow slightly furrowed, his mouth relaxed. One hand was splayed over his flat belly, the other tucked under the pillow. His chest was bare, his shoulders wide, his skin permanently burned to bronze. He had huge arms, the bulging biceps roped with prominent veins that meandered in twisting lines along his wide forearms and muscular wrists to large very clean hands ridged with the permanent calluses of his years working the family ranch.

Fanned over his chest was a pelt of soft dark hair liberally salted with silver. Below his rib cage a downy line bisected his belly before disappearing beneath the unbuttoned waistband of his jeans. Her body gave a silent yelp when her gaze skimmed his distended fly.

"Sorry, it's not personal. Purely vascular."

Her gaze snapped to his face. He was watching her through thick inky lashes, his expression guarded, his vivid blue eyes still faintly shadowed by weariness. He'd missed sleep and it was her fault, she realized, fighting off a strong urge to apologize. She'd blackmail the devil himself if that's what it took to keep this baby safe.

"I was just seeing if you were awake," she said truthfully if a bit curtly.

"You fixin' to throw me out?"

"Yes."

He chuckled, then yawned hard enough to crack even that hard jaw, before drawing up his leg, tactfully hiding his distended groin from her view.

"Give me a minute to shake off the cobwebs and I'll give you back your privacy."

The baby kicked, and she shifted her attention to her belly. "Good morning to you, too," she murmured, rubbing what felt like a little foot.

His quick grin was more than professional, less than intimate. "Gave you a kick, did she?"

"He's a morning person."

"Think it's a he?"

"The tech who did the last ultrasound tried and tried to find out if this is a boy or a girl, but the baby was being stubborn. She decided it just had to be a boy because he was being so contrary."

"Guess I can't argue with that."

He lifted his hand from his chest to rake back his hair, then returned it to his chest, curled into a relaxed fist. She couldn't help noticing that he wore no rings and that his broad square nails were closely clipped. One knuckle was scarred, another badly misshapen. Probably broken in a bar fight.

Reminding herself that she wasn't interested in the life he'd led over the years, she turned her head and regarded the fuzzy outline of the skyline beyond the gauzy window sheers.

She was here because of the baby growing inside her now, not the one she'd had to give away. Fate had brought them together as temporary allies. As such, Luke deserved her respect and—she admitted with a mental gritting of her teeth—her courtesy.

"I'm being ungracious, and I don't mean to be," she said. "You've been extremely kind, and I do appreciate it."

"Not ungracious, Mama, just a little out of sorts. Nesting jitters, we call it in my business." His lazy grin was a white slash against his outlaw stubble. "Don't worry, I won't hold it against you."

"Big of you," she muttered on a sudden flare of anger that was utterly out of character for her.

"Yeah, ain't it?" he said before his grin dissolved

into another face-stretching yawn. "How're you feeling this morning?"

"A little achy, but nothing major." As she scrambled out of bed and reached for her robe, he stretched his long arms over his head like a big cat still drowsy from a long nap, then turned to look at the clock.

"You havin' any trouble with morning sickness these days?"

"I had a little queasiness for a week or two, but I thought it was indigestion. Last night was the first time since I've been pregnant that I've, well, you know…" She glanced away as a vivid memory of the humiliating scene in the bathroom flashed into her mind.

"Hey, I've hugged a few porcelain bowls in my time, too. At least you tossed your cookies in a good cause. Me, I was just stinkin' drunk."

A fleeting smile crossed her lips. "I think last night had more to do with the migraine than the baby."

"Diagnosin' again, Miz Foster?"

She felt a swift pang of alarm. "Are you saying it might have been something more serious?"

"Relax, Maddy…Madelyn. I was just trying to fill up all that tense silence I could just feel comin' on between us."

"Tense, maybe, but silence, never. In the long illustrious history of the Lone Star State, no self-respecting Texas lady has ever allowed a pause in the conversation to last longer than ten seconds. And that was only because it took her that long to wrestle herself out from under the hand her husband had clamped over her mouth."

His grin flashed, crinkling his eyes and arousing a slow melting feeling inside her. She turned away to take clean underwear from her suitcase.

"You have any plans for this afternoon?" he asked a moment later.

"Yes, I'm going to buy a newspaper, then spend the day checking out apartments for rent. Something small, preferably furnished and in a good neighborhood that I can rent month to month," she admitted as she slipped her blouse and skirt from the hangers. "At a ridiculously low rent of course."

"Sounds doable." He closed his eyes. She could have sworn he was asleep by the time she closed the bathroom door behind her.

Luke was sitting on her side of the bed, talking on the phone in a low tone when she returned. He glanced up as she entered, lines fanning deeper into his temples as he spoke into the receiver. "Yeah, I love you, too," he said with a laugh as Madelyn turned away to grant him what little privacy the room afforded.

So Prudy was wrong, she thought with an odd little tug inside. Luke did have someone special in his life. And really, why shouldn't he? Certainly it was no concern of hers.

The sleek light-rail trolley swooshing past on the street below drew her attention to the window. The sun was up now, splashing the dark-green carpet with a band of gold. Spirits rising, she followed a sunbeam to the window. Warmth bathed her face as she drew back the curtains to look out over the city.

One of the oldest cities to spring up in the Oregon Territory, Portland had the look of a bustling dynamic riverfront community. Two bridges were visible from her vantage point, spanning a river that glistened like a pale blue ribbon in the sunshine. In the compact central district, a number of smaller more traditional buildings constructed of weathered stone blocks sat like sturdy supplicants at the feet of ultramodern structures of glass and steel. She liked the blend, she realized. The old and the new. A perfect metaphor for her life at this moment.

"Nice day for apartment huntin'."

She turned to find Luke off the phone and watching her. Madelyn felt a skitter of nerves along her spine. Old tapes, she told herself as she curved her lips into a polite smile. "It's a *glorious* day for apartment hunting," she corrected. "I have a feeling I'm going to find the perfect place."

"Were I a bettin' man, I'd say it was a sure thing," Luke drawled as he got to his feet and ambled loose-hipped and lazy into the bathroom.

He returned a few minutes later to find Madelyn sitting at the small table near the window, writing in a bulging leather-bound notebook. Seeing her with sunshine in her hair made him ache.

Spending the night had been pure misery. When his back hadn't been giving him fits, he'd been staring at the ceiling, trying not to remember how her body had looked in that frothy excuse for a slip he'd found under the demure schoolteacher's skirt and blouse. His hands had itched to dive under the silk and lace to stroke the even silkier skin beneath.

Reminding himself that he was her doctor, for thirteen more weeks, anyway, Luke strapped his watch to his wrist and slipped his beeper over his belt, then stuffed his keys and wallet into his pockets before sitting down on the edge of the bed to tug on his boots. "What's with the Yellow Pages?" he asked as he got to his feet, his attention on the buttons of his shirt.

"Rental agents. I'm making a list to consult in case I don't find anything in the paper."

"Waste of time." A quick glance at his watch told him his was running short. At this rate he'd be lucky to snag a cup of lousy staff coffee before he had to conduct teaching rounds. His mood dipping and his thoughts already turning to the patients he had waiting, he unzipped his jeans, shoved the shirttails out of sight, adjusted his briefs, then did himself up again. He was rolling up his sleeves when he realized she was scowling at him. He lifted his eyebrows. "Something wrong?"

Her gaze narrowed. "Are you always this…casual around your patients?"

"Casual?"

"Undressing publicly," she amplified with prim irritation.

Swallowing the laughter that wanted to spill out, he made a big show of glancing down at his favorite shirt, well-seasoned jeans and worn-in boots. He waited a beat, then let his gaze find hers again. "How much more dressed you want me to be, exactly?"

She blinked, then fought a smile. "I sound like a real prude, don't I?"

"Uh-uh," he drawled, lifting both hands. "No way am I gonna answer that question. No, ma'am."

Her smile burst free, giving him a real good look at that little dimple just above the right corner of her mouth. His mind stuttered.

"I'm sorry, Luke. I know this is difficult."

"Once you get used to me, things will even out."

Her smile faded and her eyes grew cautious. "I knew this was going to be stressful on some level, but—" She stopped abruptly, then dipped her head and rubbed her fingers over her forehead before glancing up again. "I was prepared to use whatever means necessary to force you to help me. I didn't expect to resent you because you're making it so easy."

"Then don't." He checked his watch again, then grabbed his bag and walked to the door. After releasing the dead bolt, he turned. "I'm scheduled to conduct teaching rounds this morning, but I should be able to shake loose about nine, nine-thirty. Prue's workin' seven to three today, but she's gonna leave the key with a neighbor."

The nervous little frown he hadn't quite forgotten formed between her eyebrows. "What key?"

"The key to the house on Mill Works Ridge I arranged for you to rent from one of Prue's neighbors who's lookin' for a house-sitter for the next four or five months," he said as he pulled open the door.

"What?" She shot to her feet so fast her tummy bumped the table. "Luke, wait!"

"Make sure you drink your orange juice, Mama," he ordered before shutting the door behind him.

Madelyn drank her juice. But *not* because he'd told her to. And not until she'd satisfied her craving for caffeine.

The first day of the rest of her life was going to be a beauty—and a perfect day for apartment hunting. Which she fully intended to do after she'd taken a polite look at the place Luke mentioned.

To her surprise and delight, the room-service waiter had delivered a copy of the *Oregonian* with her breakfast, and she'd seized the opportunity to quiz the congenial young man on the most likely areas of the city to begin her search. The university district seemed the most promising place to find furnished units. It was also conveniently located—and safe for a woman alone, the waiter had assured her. She'd already circled several possibilities in the classifieds, but since it was still only seven-thirty, she decided to wait another hour or so before she began calling.

Nibbling toast, she leaned back and enjoyed the first easy breath she'd taken since picking up the phone in her old-fashioned country kitchen to make the appointment she knew would dredge up old hurts. So far this reunion of sorts with Luke had been far less painful than she'd anticipated, and she was honest enough to admit a large measure of the credit belonged to him.

He wasn't at all the man she'd imagined him to be on those rare occasions when she couldn't quite shove thoughts of him out of her mind. It was both unsettling and…what? Amazing?

It was almost as though she'd imagined those four days with an uneducated brash hell-raising bronc buster. A frown creased her forehead when she realized she was rubbing the cesarean scar, which was the only tangible reminder she had of the child she'd given up.

To survive the pain she'd compartmentalized her thoughts about that baby into tiny boxes, like perfect gems in a nest of cotton.

Did the people who'd taken her child cherish her the way she would? Did they tell her every day how precious and wonderful she was? How utterly loved she was and always would be, no matter how many times she stumbled? Did her daddy teach her things and praise her beauty?

Except Luke wouldn't have been around long enough to teach their daughter anything.

No, she'd made the right decision, she told herself

yet one more time. The couple who'd adopted Jenny were good people, Doc had promised. College-educated, financially welloff, stable and responsible. A loving couple. Everything she and Luke hadn't been.

After putting her breakfast dishes outside the door, she retrieved her address book from the table and carried it with her back to the bed. Settling back, she flipped to the *W*'s, then she picked up the phone.

"Weldon residence. Jason speaking."

Madelyn's lips curved at the six-year-old's careful diction. "Hi, Jasey, it's Aunt Madelyn. How're you doing today?"

"Hi, Aunt Mad'lyn. We have a new puppy!"

"You do?"

"Yep. She has floppy ears and big feet."

"What's her name?"

"Mama calls her Peaches, but Daddy says her name should be Misery."

Madelyn laughed, but the pressure around her heart increased. This might have been *her* life if only... Sucking in a breath, she pulled herself up short. Recalling old angers and resentments would only serve to complicate an already complicated situation. "Is your mama available, honey?"

"Uh-huh. Mama, Aunt Maddy's on the phone!" Jason yelled. Wincing, Madelyn held the phone away from her ear.

"She's comin'," she heard Jason say in normal voice again.

"Thanks, sweetheart. You enjoy your puppy now, you hear?"

"Yes, ma'am."

They said goodbye and the phone clunked down. In the background Madelyn heard a baby wailing, followed by the sound of what Emily Weldon called her "mommy" voice, which was in sharp contrast to the authoritarian brusque tones of the harried high-school administrator she was during the week.

If anyone deserved to have it all, it was Emily, Madelyn thought, rubbing at the residual ache in her temple. A doting husband, a passel of beautiful healthy kids, a useful satisfying job she loved. She was also an incredibly nice person.

Tall, plump and brilliant, with a Ph.D. in elementary education and administration from UCLA, she'd taken over as principal of Whiskey Bend High the same year Wiley Roy had been hired to teach mathematics.

Madelyn had been in college then and hadn't met Emily until the day she'd interviewed for the position. They'd become friends, as well as colleagues.

A woman who'd made some bad mistakes herself, Emily had made it clear to the town busybodies that she wasn't interested in listening to gossip—about Madelyn or any other member of her staff. She always said it was one of her biggest regrets that she hadn't found an excuse to fire Wiley before he'd turned his attention in Madelyn's direction.

Emily had been one of the first people to learn of her pregnancy. Madelyn would always cherish the memory of the unflappable administrator's uninhibited squeal of delight as she'd raced around her desk to give Madelyn a hug.

Emily had been furious when she'd learned of Wiley's decision to divorce the mother of his child. Since she was also Wiley's boss, she'd been in a tough spot, but she'd handled it professionally. Privately, however, she'd come up with some highly imaginative ideas for the punishment she thought he deserved.

"Madelyn, honey, I'm so glad you called." Emily's voice was slightly breathless, her normal state on a Saturday morning, Madelyn suspected. "How did it go?"

"Surprisingly well. Dr. Jarrod—Luke—has agreed to take me as a patient."

"Oh, honey, I'm so pleased. What did he say about the baby?"

Madelyn gave her a brief rundown of the visit, ending with the emergency call that had cut it short. "I have an appointment to see him again Monday."

She heard the sound of chair legs scraping against the floor and pictured Emily perched on a stool at the breakfast bar. "Pardon me for being indelicate, but was it awful, his doing the examination, I mean?"

"Not at all." She found herself smiling. "In fact, it was, well, fun."

"Excuse me, but we are talking about an internal exam, are we not?"

Madelyn laughed. "You'd be amazed."

"I already am." Emily cleared her throat. "Seriously, how was it, seeing *him* again, I mean?"

"Stressful, but I got through it."

"Any lingering…attraction?"

Madelyn twisted the phone cord around her finger and told herself not to think about the half-naked body that had lain within touching distance last night. "Not enough to worry about."

"I don't suppose he's gotten fat and bald?"

An image of that massive chest and hard belly shimmered into her mind. In another lifetime she would have snuggled next to all that latent power, lulled to sleep by the steady beating of his heart. And in the morning, when he'd awakened aroused and vulnerable, she would take him inside her body and make long lingering love to him the way she'd done so many times in her dreams.

Her breathing faltered, then picked up. "He's still a very attractive man," she said primly. "Not that it matters."

"Is he married?"

Madelyn set her jaw against the sudden acceleration of her pulse. "No, not that it matters one way or another. He's my doctor, nothing more."

The pause was nearly imperceptible. "Works for me, honey," Emily assured her, loyal as always. "I just wanted to know which way to direct my good thoughts, that's all. You know, toward a fairy-tale ending where the two of you ride off into the sunset on his majestic white horse or the distinctly less satisfying *The Way We Were* scenario."

Madelyn laughed. "I can't sing a lick, but go ahead and picture me as Barbra Streisand."

"So much for romance," Emily said with an exaggerated sigh.

"As I've told you countless times before, dear heart, we can't all have a happily-ever-after."

"And as I've told you, there's almost always another chapter if you have the courage to turn the page, which— Oh, *hell.*" Emily's exclamation was followed by a furious high-pitched yapping. "Honey, I have to go. Sissy just dumped a pitcher of maple syrup on the pup's head."

Madelyn laughed. "I'll call again when I have a permanent phone number and address."

"You'd better, girl! Oh, and Maddy, when you go

back for that appointment on Monday, take a good look around. I have a feeling you just might see a white horse tethered to a parking meter out front.'' She hung up before Madelyn could reply.

Chapter 7

It had stopped raining during the night. By nine-thirty when Luke pulled away from the Mallory with Madelyn sitting primly in the passenger seat of his Cherokee, the clouds were gone, and Portland sparkled like a new penny in the clean air. Figuring she'd enjoy the sunshine, he took her on a scenic tour of the downtown district before heading east toward Mill Works Ridge.

"First thing Monday I'm going to get a library card and hit the history stacks," she said, folding her hands primly over her baby Buddha tummy. "Baby and I will have a lot of time to read over the next few months, and I intend to enjoy every luxurious minute."

"You sound like Raine." He glanced over in time to see her inquiring look. "Raine Paxton. She owns While Away Books in the university district. Mostly used, but some new, too. And darned if she doesn't know every single book on the shelf without having to look it up."

"Sounds intimidating."

"Nah, she just has one of those photographic memories I would have given a large chunk of my future income to borrow when I was in med school."

"Since I doubt Stanford is in the business of handing out diplomas on a whim, you must have managed somehow."

His heart jerked at the grudging compliment. If he thought it would redeem him even a little in her eyes, he'd trot out the whole damn list of honors he'd accumulated. Because he suspected it would only make him look like a braggart, or worse, a sinner looking to buy his way out of hell, he settled for a shrug. "I got through it okay."

He braked for a red light, then shifted to ease the tightness in his shoulders. She adjusted her skirt, then turned a curious gaze his way. "Did you ever win that silver belt buckle you were always talking about?"

"Yeah, the year I turned twenty."

She glanced at his belly. "How come you're not wearing it?"

He hesitated, wondering how much of himself to reveal to her. "After the presentation I threw it in the nearest river, which happened to be the Colorado. Figure it's still there." The light changed, and he concentrated on navigating past a utilities crew digging up the street.

"Were you drunk?" she asked. "When you threw it in the river, I mean?"

His mouth quirked in a smile that had nothing to do with amusement. "Not then, no."

"Then why would you throw away something that meant so much to you?"

"Hell if I know." But he did. Going after his place

in the sun had cost him his shot at real happiness, the kind that didn't tarnish. It had cost him Maddy and his child, and he would regret that for the rest of his life.

Now, as he turned onto the street bordering the Columbia, he let himself imagine what his life would have been like if he'd stayed in Texas. But every time his mind started down that road, he smacked up against the brutal truth. If he'd wanted to stay, he would have stayed. Instead, he'd wanted good times and applause, not responsibility and restrictions.

"The hospital is only ten minutes away," he said as he braked for the light at the intersection of Columbia Heights and Waverly Lane. "Five, if you hit the lights right."

She gave him a considering look. "Is that why your friends from the hospital live there?"

"Part of the reason, yeah."

"How come you don't live there, too?"

"It's strictly a single-family type of place. Big yards full of jungle gyms and kids." Kids he'd tried hard not to love too deeply because it only made it more difficult when he went home to silent rooms.

"That's the Columbia down beyond that little park yonder," Luke said as he braked for the sharp left. "And this is Mill Works Ridge. Only two blocks long, but I think it's the prettiest street in town."

Still enthralled with the shimmering ribbon of the famous river visible through the screen of pretty bushes, Madelyn took a moment to turn her attention to the houses on the other side of the narrow street. When she did, she couldn't prevent a low exclamation of delight.

The neighborhood was enchanting. Six sparkling white-frame cottages, lined up three to a block like graceful Victorian debutantes in fussy lace-trimmed party dresses. Each was different and yet equally charming. Bright bunches of flowers bordered neatly trimmed lawns bisected by rust-red brick walks.

Luke flicked her a look before parking in front of a two-story gem at the western corner of the first block. The shutters and front door were a soft slate blue. Lace curtains swept back from the front windows in twin swags, reminding Madelyn of shimmering cobwebs. Lush lavender roses the size of cabbages framed the porch steps, and pink and white petunias spilled from boxes beneath a large front window.

"Is this it?" she said, her voice coming out in an embarrassingly eager rush. "The house I'm…considering?"

"Nope. This one belongs to the Paxtons." He opened the door and climbed out. Disappointment crashed over her as she fumbled with her seat belt. She had simply assumed that because the key was here, the house must be in this neighborhood. Never assume, she reminded herself. Yet another in an increasingly long list of painful lessons, she told herself with a sigh.

Reminding herself that brooding was bad for the baby, she grabbed her purse and reached for the door handle, only to find Luke had beaten her to it. Bracketing her thickened waist with those big hands, he helped her down from the Cherokee's high seat, then touched her shoulder.

"That one over there is yours," he said, indicating the house on the opposite corner. The smallest of the six, it had sparkling curlicue trim along the eaves and bright emerald shutters on the windows. "You said you wanted small."

He shoved his hands into his pockets, then pulled

them out again. It was the first time she'd seen Luke look unsure of himself. "Prue said to warn you it's not real modern inside."

But there were white and pink peony bushes blooming along the walk and a birdbath on the lawn.

Luke saw the direction of her gaze and frowned. "I, uh, forgot to ask if Miz Finkle pays for a gardener."

"Hmm."

"Look, it was just an idea. I know I kinda ran over your objections, so—"

"Is that a cherry tree in the side yard?"

He turned to look, his eyes crinkling against the sun's glare. "Looks like it, yeah."

She sighed, already picturing herself walking barefoot in the lush green lawn. "I don't suppose it comes with a puppy?" she mused half to herself.

He lifted a hand and rubbed a jaw that had lost the teeth-gritted hardness of a moment ago. "Would you settle for a cat?" he asked cautiously.

"It comes with a cat?"

"Yeah. Miz Finkle travels a lot, so she hacks off a chunk of rent in exchange for pet care."

"How big a chunk?"

"A hundred a month."

She blinked. "That much?"

His cheeks creased in a wry smile. "Apparently Miz Finkle is right fond of that cat."

She glanced toward the house again. "Did I ever tell you how much I've always wanted a cat?"

His grin flashed, pushing a crescent dimple into one austere—and now clean shaven—cheek. "Then let's go get you one, Mama."

More polite now than she remembered, he slipped his hand under her elbow to help her up the two shal-

low steps to the front walkway. It was subtle, the way
he shortened his long stride to match hers, something
Wiley who was almost as tall had never done. What
wasn't so subtle was the way her heart raced whenever
he looked at her. The chemistry between them was
more powerful than any rational argument she'd been
able to muster so far. Well, she would simply ignore
it. After all, she was a mature professional woman with
a couple of fairly impressive diplomas of her own
hanging on her office wall.

"That's the MacAuleys' house yonder. Boyd's a
neurosurgeon at Port Gen, and Stacy usually works
part-time as a kindergarten teacher, but she's on maternity leave until September. She just had a baby."

Tightening his hold, he guided her up porch steps
still slippery with morning dew. When he released her
to ring the bell, she eased back a few inches. Away
from the heat of his big body and the provocative scent
of his skin.

"How old's the baby?" she asked when he turned
his head to give her a faintly mocking look.

"Three months. Boyd James MacAuley III. They
call him B.J."

He lifted a hand to smooth back his wind-tossed hair.
The generous salting of silver added depth to the glossy
softness and gave character to his face. In addition to
shaving, he'd exchanged his sadly wrinkled cotton shirt
for one of western design the exact blue of his eyes.
In deference to the warmth of the day, he'd rolled the
sleeves above the elbow, displaying arms that looked
too brawny to belong to a skilled healer.

She wondered what it would have been like to sleep
in those arms night after night. To cuddle close to that
long hard body, safe in the knowledge he loved her as

she loved him. If he'd come back and married her, they would have struggled, yes, but they would have been struggling together. They would have raised their daughter with love and acceptance.

Her emotions scrambling, she leaned over the porch railing to stroke one of the spectacular blooms. The door opened then, and she whipped around so fast she staggered. Luke's arm was around her waist, steadying her before she could topple.

The dark-haired, pretty woman in shorts and T-shirt who greeted them had a toilet plunger in one hand, a miniature high-top sneaker in the other. Luke held up a big hand. "Easy, darlin', we come in peace."

"If this is a bad time, we can come back later," Madelyn hastened to assure her after Luke introduced them.

"Oh, no, actually this is fairly calm. My husband usually takes weekend duty, but—"

She stopped short when a towheaded little boy wearing only a disposable diaper and a devilish expression shot past her.

"Hold up, partner," Luke ordered, scooping the toddler into his arms.

"Unca Luke!" The boy's face lit up and he gave Luke a smacking kiss.

"Hey, Matthew. What's goin' on?"

"We's pumming."

"Uh-huh." Luke looked at Raine for clarification.

"My sons and I are playing plumber this morning," Raine translated, sharing a smile with Madelyn. "Alex swears Matt stuffed both his new Nikes into the john, but so far we've only gotten one out." As though to prove her point, water dripped on the toe of her scuffed loafer. "I don't suppose either of you know anything about unstuffing a john?"

"Probably not much more than you do, I'm afraid," Madelyn admitted, her fingers itching to smooth the soft flaxen curls tumbling over the little boy's round face.

Raine shifted her attention to Luke, who shook his head. "I sweated through four miserable years in med school just so's I wouldn't have to do manual labor." His grin flashed. "I'll pass you the tools if that helps."

Raine rolled her eyes before giving Madelyn a "gotta love 'em" look. "I think it's time I admit defeat and call a plumber," she said, stepping back to let them enter.

The entryway was small but bright. Ahead was an ornate staircase fashioned of some dark gleaming wood and a colorful cotton runner protecting the hardwood floor. To the left was an antique umbrella stand festooned with a collection of hats, one of which bore the logo of the much respected TV news magazine produced and hosted by—

"Morgan Paxton lives here?" The shock in her voice had both Raine and Luke grinning at her.

"Most of the time, yes," Raine said with a laugh. "Surprising, isn't it?"

Madelyn felt herself flushing. She'd seen the charismatic journalist countless times on the nightly news, reporting from some international hot spot or other, sometimes with starbursts of high-tech weaponry filling the night sky behind him, his tawny hair ruffling in the breeze and his eyes intense as he personalized the impersonal.

"I have to admit to being a fan," she said. "And

forgive me if I sounded rude, Mrs. Paxton. Your house is lovely.''

"Not to worry. We're used to people who don't know us well wondering why we don't live in a huge mansion in Lake Oswego. Or Westchester County for that matter.'' She smiled warmly. "And, please, call me Raine.''

"Where is Pax, anyway? Hiding out in the den?'' Luke asked, shifting the toddler to his other arm.

Raine laughed. "No, but I suspect he would be if he were here. At this precise moment my darling husband's in Mexico filming a story. He's due back Tuesday morning, thank goodness.''

Madelyn smiled at the stir it would cause in Whiskey Bend when her mama spread the word that the girl they'd scorned before she'd clawed her way back to respectability was living next door to a world-famous journalist. *If* she took the house, Madelyn cautioned herself firmly. Nothing was settled.

"Prue dropped off Harriet's key on her way to work this morning,'' Raine explained, leading them to the left through a living room filled with flourishing plants, little-boy toys and comfortable-looking furniture. A fascinating collection of artwork and artifacts from all over the world were displayed on the walls. A huge bouquet of those marvelous lavender blooms sat on a carved chest under the window, dew still glistening on the velvet petals.

"What a magnificent dollhouse,'' she marveled, her gaze lovingly tracing the outlines of a miniature replica of this house sitting on its own stand in one corner. Obviously made with meticulous attention to detail by loving hands, it was as much a work of art as a child's delight.

"Morgan made that for our daughter Morgana," Raine explained with visible pride. "She's Lebanese by birth and was nearly three when we adopted her last year.

"She's visiting with my father at his cabin down near Diamond Lake for the next two weeks. He's teaching her how to fish."

"Is Stace around?" asked Luke. "She sent word with Boyd that Tory had another drawing for my wall."

Raine shook her head. "Case had to go in to work this morning, so Stacy took Chloe and Lily and her girls to Story Hour at my shop," Raine explained as she led the way to the kitchen. "With any luck they'll be back before you leave."

"Unca Luke!" Another little boy came barreling into the kitchen from a door opposite the one they'd used, his chubby arms already reaching upward. He, too, was barefoot and wearing only a diaper. His hair wasn't quite as curly as his brother's, Madelyn realized. And he was slightly larger. Otherwise they were identical.

Luke hesitated, then reached down and scooped him up with his free arm. Madelyn thought he winced as he straightened. But his eyes were crinkling with affection as he accepted the toddler's exuberant kiss.

"Hey, Alex, big guy, I hear you're in trouble."

"Uh-uh. It's Matt's fault."

"Is not!" The twins glared at each other, identical chins jutting and little fists waving.

"Whoa, partners. Time out here." At the low note of warning in Luke's voice, both boys blinked. Raine glanced Madelyn's way and winked.

"How come you're here today?" Alex demanded, the dispute forgotten.

"I brought someone special to meet you guys." When he glanced Madelyn's way, she felt a warmth spread. "This is Madelyn."

Identical pairs of brown eyes studied her. "You're pretty, like my mommy," Matt chirped, grinning.

And you're going to make some special lady very happy some day, Madelyn thought as she tweaked one bare foot. "Thank you, sir."

"We have cookies!" Alexander exclaimed with rapture in his eyes.

"Yeah, what kind?" Luke asked, his greedy gaze sweeping the sparkling counters with a surprisingly boyish eagerness.

"Peanut butter choc'late chip!"

"Only they're for after," Matthew amplified somberly.

"After what?"

"After pumming, a course." Alexander swiveled his head Madelyn's way, his eyes brimming with curiosity. "Are you and Unca Luke married?"

Her stomach contracted. "No, sweetie. He's my doctor."

He wrinkled his little brow. "Are you sick?"

"No, buddy, she's going to have a baby."

"Like when Auntie Stacy had B.J.?"

"Exactly." Luke started to put Matt down, only to have a vicious pain claw through his back. He froze, then breathed into the spreading agony, willing the spasm to ease.

"Put me down now, Unca Luke," Matt ordered, kicking him in the thigh.

"In a minute, buddy." Luke fought to keep his voice

steady. But it cost him, and he clamped his jaw shut against a groan. Raine shot him an anxious look.

"Luke, are you all right?"

"Yeah. Fine. Just stiff."

Disbelief tightened her lips. "It's your back again, isn't it?"

"Don't start," he warned, narrowing his gaze. From the corner of his eye, he saw Maddy frown and wanted to kick something. Since even that was beyond him at the moment, he settled for a scowl.

Freeing her hands, Raine shot him an exasperated look before plucking an impatient Alex from his arms. She set him on his feet, then took Matt. "You idiot," she said before settling the boy on his already moving feet. "You know you're not supposed to lift—"

"We're in a hurry here, Raine." His voice was a whip, lashing shock over Raine's face.

"Luke, there's no call to be so rude!" Madelyn's soft rebuke had him grinding his teeth against the impulse to spill out an explanation that would only sound like a bid for her sympathy.

"Take care of little mother here," he told Raine, jerking his thumb Maddy's way. He knew he was being a jerk, but anything was better than folding up at her feet. "I have work to do."

Chapter 8

"Harriet moved here after her husband died," Raine said as she plucked a brown frond from an otherwise thriving Boston fern tucked into a corner of Mrs. Finkle's crowded living room. "She couldn't decide what to keep and what to sell, so she decided to keep everything. Eight rooms of furniture crammed into five."

"It does seem a bit overwhelming," Madelyn admitted, looking around for a place to sit. The Victorian fainting couch seemed a safe bet, and she settled gratefully onto the red velvet upholstery.

Because Stacy MacAuley had yet to return, Raine had taken the twins with them when she'd shown the house, corralling them in the fenced backyard with stern admonitions to behave themselves. Ten minutes ago, when Raine had checked on them, the boys had been hunting snails. Madelyn's experience with Emily's brood had taught her not to push for too many details.

As she and Raine had walked through the Victorian's five rooms, Raine had been as efficient as any rental agent, pointing out amenities and answering her questions about shopping and other services in the area. In return, Madelyn had given her a brief rundown on her pregnancy and Doc Morrow's search for a specialist. Raine was immediately supportive, assuring her that Luke was indeed a marvelous doctor. Her sons were proof of that, two little miracles who might never have been born if it hadn't been for Luke's skill and attentive care.

"So what do you think?" Raine asked, turning and spreading her arms.

"In the profound words of my students, I am truly blown away." Madelyn picked up a crazy-quilt pillow and ran a finger over the year 1886 embroidered in a child's hand on one of the silk patches. "Who would believe it? A darling house completely furnished right down to the salt and pepper shakers and a car to drive. It's almost too good to be true."

Harriet's car was a five-year-old Buick that still had a new-car smell. It was Madelyn's for as long as she occupied the house. Though the rent was higher than she'd budgeted, the money she'd save on a rental car more than made up the difference.

"Once you sign the rental agreement, you can arrange to have the phone and utilities transferred to your name."

Madelyn's gaze swept the tastefully cluttered room. "It's been my experience that every silver lining comes with a dark cloud," she said as much to herself as Raine.

"This one is wrapped in gray fur and goes by the

name of Precious, thought heaven knows she's not,''
Raine said with a grimace.

"A cat with eyes as beautiful as hers has to have a
few redeeming qualities.''

Harriet's darling was a Russian blue, a breed known
for its strength—and bad temper. The instant they'd
walked in, Precious had hissed and snarled, then tried
to bite Raine on the leg. A quick spritz from the spray
bottle Raine had prudently brought with her had sent
the cat racing under Harriet's bed, where it continued
to snarl.

"When I talked to her accountant earlier to tell him
I had a hot prospect, he said he'd be in until noon.''
Raine glanced at her watch. "If I call him now, you
can probably get to his place before he leaves.''

After returning to the hotel from the accountant's
office with her copy of the rental agreement tucked in
her purse, Madelyn made arrangements to have her
rental car picked up, then grabbed a quick lunch in the
dining room before checking out. By the time she
shoved her empty suitcase under the guest room bed,
the Victorian cottage was already beginning to feel like
home.

On the way back to Mill Works Ridge, she'd stopped
at a discount store to buy some tops and shorts, as well
as a supply of paperback novels before heading for the
supermarket Raine had recommended. She'd also
picked up a couple of cute cat toys.

Deciding that now was as good a time as any to try
to make friends with her roommate, she walked down
the short hall connecting the two bedrooms. The one
she'd chosen for herself faced the street and had the

most amazing canopied bed. The last time she'd seen the cat, it'd been crouched under the tall frame.

"Precious, are you under there, sweetie?" she crooned as she bent down to lift the crocheted dust ruffle. The thick pecan-colored carpet smelled faintly of shampoo and felt springy against her fingers as she lightly ran the toy mouse back and forth over the pile. "Aunt Maddy has a special treat for you, pretty girl."

Exotic green eyes glared at her through the gloom, reminding her of the Cheshire cat. Except there was no sign of a grin.

"I know what it's like to miss someone so much you just want to curl up in a ball and sleep. It hurts to know you've been left behind, doesn't it? But you're luckier than I was, darling. The person you love will come back. Mine never did."

She froze, her words echoing in her head. Now why on earth did she say that? Hunkered down in the shadows under the bed the cat blinked back at her, a low growl rumbling in its throat for an instant before it pounced. It was only when she felt those sharp claws raking her hand that she remembered the spray bottle.

"All right, I'll give you that one because I wasn't paying attention, but from now on you are going to start behaving yourself." Ignoring the rumbling growl coming from beneath the bed, she went into the bathroom separating the two bedrooms. The first-aid kit she'd bought was still on the counter, along with the rest of the necessities.

Silently congratulating herself on her foresight and efficiency, she tore the protective plastic from the flat metal box and had just opened the lid when the doorbell rang. After grabbing a tissue, she hurried through the crowded living room, feeling surprisingly lighthearted. Expecting to find Prudy or Raine on the porch, she was already smiling when she opened the door.

It was Luke who stood there on the doorstep, looking windblown, achingly tired and endearingly awkward. He grinned, shifted on those long powerful legs, his thumbs hooked in his belt loops. Beyond her control her breath hissed in, and those annoying ribbons of awareness unfurled inside.

"Looks like you're already settled in," he said, his gaze taking in the cotton T-shirt and baggy shorts with the drawstring top. "Looks real comfortable. At least a twelve."

"A twelve?"

"My staff was almighty impressed with your, uh, style. When I got back to the office after seeing to Mrs. Gregory, Dorie made me promise to ask you where you bought your shoes. She was guessin' Neiman's."

Bemused, Madelyn nodded. "They're right. I have wide feet, so I can't buy shoes just anywhere."

His gaze dipped to her bare feet. To the toes she'd painted fire-engine red to give her courage. Those same toes curled into the thick area rug as he slowly lifted his gaze. Suddenly she was having trouble breathing properly. A part of her hated him for that. A part of her hated him for everything that had gone wrong during the past twenty-two years.

"So, uh, you fixin' to become a Blazers fan?"

"Blazers?"

Her senses scrambled as his grin flashed, creasing one hard cheek into a surprisingly boyish dimple. "Portland Trailblazers? A bunch of tall millionaires?" His gaze dipped to the front of her shirt, then jerked back to her face.

"Oh, right, basketball," she blurted, then glanced

down at the unfamiliar logo splashed across her breasts. Lord help her, her nipples were as hard as pebbles—and perfectly outlined beneath the stamped-on letters. She went hot from her hairline to her painted toes. Damn him, she thought. "Actually I didn't notice what it said," she said a little primly. "The shirt I mean. Just that it was on sale."

"It would be, bein's they pretty much tanked their year."

"I'm not much for sports actually, although I do go to all the Cougars games of course."

"I'm mostly into fly-fishing myself."

It surprised her that he would have the patience to match wits with anything smaller than a half-wild dogie. "I guess you no longer compete in rodeos?"

"Not for a long time, no." He shifted his weight again, his gaze going toward the cherry tree in the side yard. "So you took the house to get the tree?"

"Something like that, yes." She fought to stop the rest of her poise from unraveling. "I appreciate your help."

"Not much help to it. You and the house just seemed right for each other somehow."

Luke was already regretting the impulse to check on her. Because his hands felt too big and too rough, he shoved them into his back pockets. "Actually I dropped by to see if you needed any help movin' furniture or maybe grocery shopping, but you look like you have things pretty much under control."

She took a breath. "Uh, would you like to come in? I can make coffee, or I have lemonade."

Luke reminded himself of times he'd had coffee with Raine or Prudy or Stacy. Madelyn was a part of their world now. Unless he wanted to avoid the closest thing to family he had these days, he had to find a way to coexist with her. They might even become friends of a sort. "That coffee, is it fresh ground?"

Her eyes smiled as she stepped back. "Is there any other kind?"

"Not in this lifetime."

Harriet Finkle obviously had a thing for antiques, he noted as he circled an upholstered chair with knobby legs and a matching ottoman. Enough chairs and tables and whatnots to fill a house twice the size of this one, by the looks of things.

Careful to keep his hands tucked close as he side-stepped a round table with delicate porcelain doodads skating on the glossy surface, he followed her through the dining room and into a small sunny kitchen done up in yellow and white. There were more antiques here, a big cabinet with a tin front and a smaller one by the back door. Old kitchen utensils covered the walls. Big as he was, he'd best not make any sudden moves.

"I met Miz Finkle once, at the twins' christening. She was leaving the next day to go bear hunting in Alaska. I was impressed as hell with her grit."

Madelyn tossed him a look over her shoulder. "She included her itinerary with her list of instructions and insurance papers for the car. This week she's in Sri Lanka."

Madelyn had left the bag of Zimbabwe beans on the counter when she'd unpacked the groceries, along with the coffee grinder and coffeemaker she'd bought after discovering that Harriet apparently drank only tea.

When the beans were ground, she opened a new package of filters and set about brewing the first pot in her new state-of-the-art coffeemaker. The first time she'd tasted coffee had been on Luke's lips.

While the coffee dripped, he walked to the back door, dipped his hands into his back pockets and looked through the window at the backyard. "Pretty maple tree yonder. Not as big as the cottonwoods you have down your way, but sturdy enough for a swing."

She felt her face go soft. "My brother Hal and I had a swing—and a cottonwood. I liked the swing, hated the cottonwood. I sneezed for two solid weeks when the cotton was flying."

"On the ranch we had a jacaranda right next to the porch. My mama used to go crazy trying to keep the yard tidy, but she put up with it because she loved the flowers. The first summer after my stepmother moved in, she talked my daddy into cutting it down."

She remembered him talking a little about his family. From what he'd said, and even more what he hadn't said, she suspected his home hadn't been a happy place after his mother had abandoned him and his father. That summer they'd met, his stepmother had just had a baby. To her surprise he'd had a walletful of pictures to pass around. That had been one of the reasons she'd been so sure he would never abandon a child of his own.

"How's your sister? Shari, right?"

"Yeah." He rubbed his hand over his belly. "She's fixing to get married. My dad is havin' a fit. Glen's a nice enough guy, a mechanic for North Star Trucking in Phoenix. Pop thinks he should go to medical school. Wants me to pay for it."

"What does Glen want?"

"To fix diesels. Shari's the one who wants to go to medical school. She has this idea we could be partners someday."

"Would you like that?"

"Guess I must since I agreed to front her for a year to see if she can hack it."

Madelyn crossed her arms and inhaled the tantalizing aroma of brewing coffee. "Your dad must be very proud of you."

He shrugged, glanced down at his scuffed boots. "For a long time we didn't talk much."

"He sent me the sweetest letter. I...still have it."

"I figured he was doin' something like that when he asked for your address." Luke reached up to straighten an antique trivet hanging on the wall. "When he found out about the baby bein' adopted, he broke my jaw."

"Oh, my God." She pressed her fingers against her own jaw. "Did you...did you hit him back? Is that what happened to your knuckle?"

"I didn't hit him. Didn't even want to." His mouth flattened. "I was just glad he didn't use his bullwhip."

She went cold inside. "Surely he never—"

"Once, when the sheriff caught me boosting a six-pack from the minimart."

"How old were you?"

"Old enough to know better," he said with a half smile.

"Is that why you quit school and started rodeoing?"

"No, I quit school because I was stupid enough to think I knew everything important." Suddenly restless, he opened cupboards until he found coffee mugs. "Don't look so sad, Maddy. Pop and I get along fine now."

She took the pot from the burner and poured one cup before replacing the pot. He glanced down at the steaming mug, a quizzical look on his face. "Which one of us is going without?"

"Me," she admitted before indulging in a self-pitying sigh. ''I had my miserly eight ounces for break-fast.'' She inhaled the rising steam lustfully. ''After this baby is born, I'm going to drink an entire pot to celebrate.''

She started to pull out her chair, only to have him beat her to it. ''Guess you're not fixing to nurse,'' he said after accepting her thanks with a polite nod.

''Oh, but I am. Why?''

''Read the literature Esther sent home with you and you'll know why.'' He pulled out his own chair and sat, angling his body sideways to accommodate those long legs. His jeans were frayed at the hem and worn white at the knees, just as they'd been when he'd rid-den. His boots were worn but good quality.

''Where's the hundred-dollar cat?'' he asked as he wrapped one big hand around the mug to draw it closer.

''Under the bed I intend to use. We're negotiating territorial rights.'' She held up her scratched hand.

''Want me to take a look?''

''No, I'll just douse it with antiseptic.''

''Don't let it go too long.'' He took a sip, then sa-luted her with the mug. ''Nice and strong.''

''Thanks for sharing that,'' she muttered, and he burst out laughing. The rich infectious sound cut to the quick, spreading warmth and something akin to pain.

''Sorry.'' He took another, slower sip, his strong throat working as he swallowed. ''How about your folks? Are they well?''

''Daddy injured his back when an engine slipped. He handles the paperwork now. Last I heard he was thinking of selling his interest to Hal.''

''Are they excited about this baby?''

''Not very, no.'' Restless, she got up to pour herself a glass of milk. ''I wish someone would make milk in capsule form,'' she muttered as she carried it back to the table.

Luke smiled, but his gut burned. He wanted to pull her onto his lap and tell her he was excited about her baby. Hell, he was so thrilled he kept smiling at odd times, just thinking about the look she'd have on her face when she held her baby for the first time. But that was personal and private. "You're taking calcium supplements, right?"

"Four horse pills a day." She took a tiny sip, then grimaced and licked her lower lip. She had a beautiful mouth, soft and silky and wonderfully responsive.

"As soon as you can, I'd like for you to arrange to tour the birthing suites at Port Gen, and while you're there, make your delivery reservation. I'll write you an order to have your blood work done so it'll be on file."

"Esther gave me a list of Lamaze classes."

"You'll need a partner," he said, taking his seat again.

"I think I might ask Raine."

He nodded. "I heard enough of your conversation yesterday to figure out Mr. Foster is givin' you some trouble."

"He's worried about what folks will think of him."

"Did he throw it up to you about our baby?" he asked because he had to.

She dropped her gaze. "Yes, at first, but after I made myself into a perfect wife, he forgave me."

Luke's temper kindled, white-hot and threatening. It caught him off guard, and it was all he could do to pull it back before it flashed. "That jerk didn't deserve you," he grated through a tight jaw.

Her smile was edged with some dark emotion. "I think he'd argue the point, but after he rejected this child, I stopped caring about what he thinks or wants or doesn't want.''

It was tempting to dump his anger on a man he'd come to detest. Too tempting. ''None of this would have happened if I hadn't let you down.''

''It's tempting to let you believe that, but the truth is I signed the adoption papers, not you. I...'' She stopped and made a visible effort to swallow.

''Maddy, don't,'' he ordered gruffly, his entire body going taut against the need to pull her into his arms. Only the certain knowledge that he would be lost if he did kept him from moving.

She cleared her throat. ''Sorry. I had a...a pregnant moment,'' she said with a shaky laugh. ''That seems to happen a lot these days.''

He managed a smile that felt stiff. ''I'm used to it.''

Averting his gaze, he studied a splash of sunlight on the kitchen tile. It had been a mistake accepting her as a patient. His feelings had gone deeper than he'd thought. Maybe too deep.

He glanced up to find her watching him. In the sunlight her hair was the color of sun-ripened wheat, and her lashes were tipped with gold. He wanted to tell her she was the most beautiful woman he'd ever seen, but he didn't have the right. ''Maddy, maybe this isn't such a good idea, your being my patient.''

Madelyn felt a jolt of alarm. ''What do you mean?''

''There's a reason doctors don't treat kin. In a crisis a doc needs to be totally detached and rational. Personal feelings can get in the way. *Will* get in the way, in fact.''

''But we're not kin, and besides, you delivered Raine and Prudy. You obviously have feelings for them.''

"Raine and Stacy MacAuley came to me as patients first. Prudy and I became friends after her miscarriage, so yeah, she was a friend when I delivered Chloe, but you're the mother of my only child."

She couldn't think about that now. "I rearranged my life so that I could have the best doctor possible. That's you, Luke. Whatever happened in the past is finished. This baby is what counts."

His jaw tightened. "All right, we'll keep things as they are for now. Just to be on the safe side, though, I'm going to arrange a consultation visit with Karen Winslow so she'll be aware of potential problems in case you go into labor when I'm not available."

"Is she a specialist in high-risk pregnancies, too?"

He nodded. "She was one of my residents before she went into private practice, the best I've ever had. What I know, she knows."

On the surface that sounded perfectly reasonable, even conscientious and certainly prudent. "That makes sense of course."

"I'll have Dorie set it up and give you a call."

"All right."

He downed the last of his coffee and got up to carry the cup to the sink. "Before I go, you'd best give me your number here."

"It's on the phone." She rose to walk past him to the end of the counter where a portable unit was half-hidden behind a crock full of wooden spoons. Dauntingly efficient, Harriet had left both pad and pen nearby.

"Amazingly Harriet doesn't have an answering machine, but I intend to get one the next time I go shopping," she said as she tore the paper from the pad and handed it to him.

He tucked it into his wallet before thanking her for the coffee. Both fell silent as she walked him to the front door and opened it.

"You and your baby are important to me, Madelyn." His voice was suddenly steel hard, his eyes intense. "But you need to know that I'm walking a very fine line here between the personal and the professional. If there comes a time when I'm in danger of crossing it, I'll turn you over to Winslow whether you agree or not."

She wanted to argue. She wanted to resent him, but as she watched him head down the walk toward his Jeep, she realized she was in grave danger of losing some of that objectivity herself. It was a troubling thought.

Chapter 9

Madelyn called her mother at five Oregon time. After making a note of Madelyn's phone number and address and asking about her visit with the doctor, Rebecca Smith had gone straight for the jugular.

"The talk's startin' up again, Maddy Sue. Miz Groves down at the In 'n Out mentioned how some folks are sayin' the baby's not Wiley's, which is why he up and divorced you so quicklike."

"That bastard!" Madelyn cried in helpless fury. "I knew he was up to something."

"Madelyn Sue Smith, you were raised up better than that!"

"I'm sorry, Mama." The apology was automatic, the result of thirty-nine years of parental admonitions. The truth was she wasn't sorry at all.

"Wiley Roy's doin' his best to defend you, but like he told your daddy and me, this is such a small town.

He was thinkin' it might be a good idea if you were to relocate permanentlike after the baby's born.''

Something in her mother's tone had her going cold inside. "Is that what you and Daddy want—for me to leave town for good?"

There was a pause that seemed to go on forever before her mother said stiffly, "It might be for the best, what with your daddy's blood pressure and all."

"I see."

"Honey, it's not really such a bad idea," Rebecca rushed to assure her, sounding enthusiastic for the first time since she'd come on the line. "You've always talked about living in the city, and El Paso's not that far. You could even go to Houston or maybe even Dallas. You can always get yourself a good job, especially if you resign, instead of getting yourself fired."

"Who said anything about my getting fired?" Madelyn said quickly, her stomach suddenly queasy.

"No one yet, but like Wiley said, the board of education frowns on scandal."

"What scandal?" Madelyn's voice rose, but she didn't care. "I'm having my husband's child. He's the one who divorced me. The one who's stirring up all the gossip so that he looks like the wronged party. Saint Wiley the Martyr."

"Madelyn!"

"I'm...no, I am not sorry," Madelyn said firmly, even though her throat went dry. "Wiley Roy Foster is a pig."

There was another pause, during which Madelyn heard the sound of voices outside the kitchen door. An instant later someone knocked on the screen. "I have to go, Mama," she said as she levered herself to her feet. "Someone's at my door."

"Maddy, your daddy and I only want what's best for you." Her mother's tone dripped with hints of accusation that had an apology quivering on Madelyn's tongue. Instead, she set her jaw and walked to the door.

"I'll call next Sunday, Mama. Hi to Daddy." She hung up before she dug herself any deeper into her mother's bad books.

After setting the phone on the counter, she drew open the door to find Prudy and Raine standing on the small porch. Prudy had a large pizza box in her hand and a huge smile on her face.

"We brought dinner. Pepperoni and mushrooms with a side of anchovies for Precious."

"And dessert," Raine added, peeling back the lid of a plastic container to reveal brownies slathered in dark chocolate.

"Forgive me if I drool," Madelyn said with a laugh as she stepped back to let them enter. For the first time in years she felt young and happy—and, she realized with a stutter of surprise, free to do or be exactly what she pleased. Take that, Mr. Wiley Bastard Foster, she wanted to shout as her new neighbors made themselves at home.

"I have lemonade from a jug," she offered, her hand on the fridge door. "Or milk," she added belatedly, glancing at the glass that was still nearly full.

"Lemonade, please," Raine decided, stripping off lids. Prudy asked for the same.

Madelyn debated. Pitchers were for guests. Cartons were for family, she decided, putting a pitcher on the table before searching the cupboards for glasses.

"Who's watching your boys?" she asked Raine over her shoulder.

"Case." She and Prudy shared a devilish look.

"When I left, Chloe and Lily were playing with their Barbies on the floor, and Case was sitting on the couch with a twin clamped under each arm, watching *Winnie the Pooh* for the gazillionth time."

"Case sounds like a wonderful daddy," Madelyn said, finding plates and a spatula to serve the pizza.

Prudy glanced up from the pizza she'd just uncovered and smiled, her eyes going soft. "He wasn't always. But he worked at it, and now I can't imagine him any other way."

Madelyn's heart yearned as she dealt out the plates. Reminding herself that a child didn't need two parents to feel cherished, she pulled out a chair and settled into it.

"Luke called this afternoon," Raine offered as she took the chair opposite Madelyn's. "Said he tried to reach you at the hotel, and when they told him you'd checked out, he called to see if you'd taken this place. He sounded relieved when I told him you had."

"That's our darling L.J.," Prudy said, her amber eyes carefully innocent. "Always looking out for his friends."

Madelyn took a sip of milk. Talking about Luke in anything but the most impersonal terms was more difficult than she'd expected. "He stopped by earlier and offered to move furniture," she forced herself to admit.

"I hope you let him," Prudy said, her eyes taking on an impish twinkle. "There's nothing like furniture moving to show the biggest toughest guy who's really in charge."

Madelyn blinked. "It never occurred to me."

"He apologized for snapping at me," Raine added as she helped herself to a slice of pizza. "Even offered to come over and unstop my toilet as penance."

"Why should L.J. think he needs to pay penance?" Prudy demanded, separating two slices of pizza.

Raine shrugged. "He had a testosterone moment this morning when I asked him if his back was hurting him. I'd already forgotten it of course, but since he opened this particular door, I'm not passing up an opportunity to make him pay just a little."

"I didn't realize Luke had a back problem," Madelyn ventured as she settled her napkin on her lap.

Prudy opened her mouth, then shut it. Raine gave her a curious look before explaining, "Luke was on the rodeo circuit when he was just a kid. I don't know all the details because he won't talk about those years, but from the little tidbits I've picked up here and there, I gather he was thrown and injured his spine."

"Is he in much pain?" Madelyn asked, remembering the hard wince that had crossed his face.

"I have a feeling he is. He limps sometimes, too, though he tries to hide it. I mentioned it once and he nearly took my head off." Raine's grin flashed. "As you no doubt noticed."

Madelyn exhaled slowly. "I feel as though I should apologize."

Raine studied her for a moment, speculation in her eyes. "Are you always this eager to take the blame?"

"No, of course not. I…" Her voice trailed off as she realized she did feel guilty because Luke had turned surly.

"I'm sorry, that was horribly rude," Raine said with a sigh. "Obviously Morgan's passion for asking nosy questions has rubbed off on me." She leaned forward to take another bite. "I'll now fill up my mouth so that I won't be tempted to ask how long you and Luke have known each other." Her eyes took on a teasing sparkle. "Although if you should feel the need to unburden yourself, Prue and I are completely willing to listen."

Caught off guard, Madelyn nearly choked on the milk she'd been sipping. "I...he's my doctor."

"He's my doctor, too, but he never looked at me with those gorgeous blue eyes the way he looks at you."

Madelyn felt a pressure in her chest. "We have a professional relationship, nothing more."

"Maybe now, but once..." Raine lifted her eyebrows. "The man I saw this morning would lie down and die for you—and count himself blessed."

Madelyn didn't believe that for an instant. "Guilt will do that sometimes," she said before she remembered she scarcely knew the women across from her.

"I agree with Raine," Prudy contributed softly. "It wasn't guilt I saw at the Mallory when he was ordering me to take care of you."

Better to get the truth out now, Madelyn decided. Part of it, anyway.

"We met once when we were just kids. Seventeen and eighteen. He came to my hometown to compete in the rodeo at the fairgrounds. He was big and wicked and handsome as the devil himself. Even better, he had a number pinned to his shirt and a reckless look in his eye." She sighed now at the memory of the wild excitement that had shot through her.

"He asked me for my ponytail ribbon to tie around his arm for luck when he rode." Her smile mocked the gullible girl she'd been. "After he took first place, he refused to give me back my ribbon. Said he was going to wear it every time he rode from then on."

Raine's expression said that she understood perfectly. "And of course you fell in love on the spot."

"I thought so at the time. Or maybe I only remember it that way now to ease my conscience." She picked up her milk and sipped, her hand steady even as her stomach performed flip-flops. "We used protection every time, but I still got pregnant. I wrote him, and then I waited for him to come back and marry me." She took another sip, but her throat was still dry. "He showed up two weeks after I'd given our daughter up for adoption."

"Oh, my God," Raine whispered over the sound of Prudy's in-drawn breath.

"I'm so very sorry," Prudy said softly as she reached out to squeeze Madelyn's hand. Madelyn thanked her with a smile.

Raine's expression was thoughtful. "Morgan asked me once if Luke had ever been in combat. When I asked him what he meant, he explained that Luke had 'old eyes,' like someone who'd seen too much suffering or been terribly wounded himself. Or maybe both. Since I'd never seen that in Luke myself, I laughed it off—until now."

"He swore the letter I'd written him had followed him from rodeo to rodeo. Maybe it had. By the time he came back I hated him too much to care."

"And now?"

"Now we have a professional relationship, nothing more." She reached for a slice of pizza and took a bite. Then, like the good hostess she'd trained herself to become, she smiled brightly and changed the subject.

As Luke let himself into his house on the hill, his back was a solid sheet of agony. He had just hit the exit ramp closest to his place when the hospital had beeped him. Because he'd seen too many accidents caused by idiots trying to drive and punch out a number on a cell phone at the same time, he'd pulled into the nearest strip mall to return the call.

Marlene Gregory's vitals had begun to fluctuate. Though he wasn't on call, Marlene's frantic husband had insisted that the attending doctor call him in to check her over. The problem hadn't been serious, simply a fine-tuning of the meds they were pumping into her, but it had taken a good three hours before he'd felt comfortable leaving her.

Now he craved sleep, but he knew he'd never drop off with his back in a tangle. Heat usually helped, especially a long soothing soak in the oversize tub with the built-in Jacuzzi jets.

Moving slowly, like a has-been rider with more scars than sense, he walked through the silent rooms to the bathroom off the master bedroom. The early-afternoon sun cast a lemony glow through the long frosted window, but his mood was anything but sunny.

Holding his breath against the stab of pain he knew to expect whenever he moved, Luke leaned over the oversize tub to stop the drain and turn on the water.

After adding a full carton of Epsom salts, and while the tub filled and steam rose to fill the bathroom, he went into the adjoining bedroom to strip down, returning buck naked to perform the slow stretches the head of physical therapy had prescribed for him. By the time he shut off the water and flipped on the jets, the steam was as thick as hot fog, running like tears down the slick white tile and turning his skin damp.

Jaw locked down against the pain, he slowly inched his aching body into the churning water. Gripping the handrails, he eased himself back until the pulsating water was aimed directly at the bunched muscles.

Little by little the knots unraveled and the worst of the pain eased. He was tired, he realized, and the hot steam was making him sleepy. Because his eyes wanted to close, he let them. Immediately his mind turned to her, as he knew it would. As it had since the moment he'd seen her name on that chart in his office.

His sweet sunny Maddy Sue, with her bubbling personality and eager willingness to offer a scruffy semi-loser unquestioning love. At eighteen he hadn't had a clue how rare that kind of love really was. Hell, he'd hadn't had a clue about much of anything important in this life. Like loyalty and trust and keeping promises.

He'd been raw for a long time after he'd found out exactly how irresponsible he'd been. After he'd left her house, he'd spent months trying to forget. Slamming into bars with a chip already on his shoulder and his eyes peeled for the toughest SOB in the place, riding horses that no one else would take and, on one memorable occasion, shoving his way into a turf brawl between rival biker gangs. Anything to force a fight so that he'd have an excuse to use his fists. He'd lost track of the times his nose had been rearranged, his ribs busted and his knuckles bloodied. Crazy as he'd been then, it had been easier dealing with a faceful of blood than the remorse that had been eating him alive.

It had taken him a good year before he'd gotten disgusted enough with himself to clean up his act. By that time, though, he'd seen the inside of a half dozen local jails and had been well down the long slide into the gutter.

He'd talked his daddy and stepmom into letting him come home and enroll in high school again. He'd been a nineteen-year-old junior with lousy study habits and a bellyful of remorse, trying to cram two years into one. He'd nearly quit a dozen times, but every time he thought he couldn't handle the humiliation or the hard slog of studying one more minute, he thought of Maddy, alone and scared, being kicked out of school and losing her friends one by one. When his fellow students had laughed behind his back when he fumbled an easy question in class, he'd imagined her holding her head high as she walked along the streets with her big belly, pride her only friend.

Worst of all were the times he walked through the halls and heard the lilt of a young girl's laughter or seen the sassy swish of tumbled blond hair. He'd ached then with the kind of pain no drug can touch. The kind that had had him riding Cochise for endless punishing hours until they'd both been dripping sweat and breathing hard. And then he'd walked the exhausted horse home, his leg muscles burning from the long punishing miles and his eyes stinging.

It had taken him years before he could look himself in the eye when he shaved and not be ashamed of the man staring back at him. He'd tried to remake himself into a man Maddy could respect, even if she would never love him again, tried as hard as he'd ever tried anything in his life. His first few years in college had been an exercise in patience and sheer willpower. He'd hated going to classes, hated bending his will to the professors', hated the long tedious hours of studying.

Somehow he'd gotten through it. Every day since, he'd tried to be the best man he could be for that same reason.

More than anything he wanted to start over with her,

but he couldn't, and he felt like a prisoner doing hard
time.

Shifting restlessly, he opened his eyes and stared at
the ceiling. It scared him some to think what might
happen if he relaxed the rigid control over his emotions. It scared him more to realize just how easily he
could fall in love with her again.

One slip, one mistake, one lapse in judgment because he was thinking like a man in love, instead of a
physician, and she could lose that precious baby.
Worse, she could die.

His gut twisted with fear, and he squeezed his eyes
shut. Please, God, he prayed with silent anguish. Please
don't let me fail her again.

Chapter 10

Mondays were always hectic, jammed with patients who'd had problems over the weekend and had to be shoehorned into the office appointment calendar. Consequently Luke was running almost forty minutes behind by the time he slipped into room four, where Maddy was waiting for him to conduct an ultrasound.

Several of his colleagues shared a tech who conducted the tests, but he preferred doing them himself to minimize the chances of missing something important. And yeah, because he never tired of seeing the little ones nestled inside their mamas' tummies. His own private reward. And, he realized now, part of his punishment.

"Looks like you called it, Mama. It's a boy, sure enough."

The baby was curled into a cozy little ball, but as Luke moved the wand over her belly, the little guy gave a protesting jerk, then stretched out, one hand punching out toward the intruder. Belligerent little dickens, he thought with a surge of raw affection.

"He's so perfect," Maddy whispered, her heart in her voice. "And…bigger already." Her eyes shone with tears of happiness, and he felt his throat close. It stunned him to realize he wished with all his heart this was his child he was watching.

"Looks like he's got him a temper," Esther said softly, watching the screen.

Luke stole a few moments to enjoy the baby's antics before attending to business. While Esther and Madelyn discussed names, he took a series of pictures. Finally satisfied, he allowed himself to watch Maddy as she studied her son with something akin to awe on her lovely face. No wonder he'd fallen in love with her on the spot. It hit him, then, what he'd just admitted. What he'd fought against admitting all these years. It had been too scary at eighteen to accept, this need he felt to be with her. At forty it was hands-down terrifying.

"Luke? Is something wrong?"

It took him a moment to realize he was standing frozen, staring at another man's child swimming around in her belly. He shifted his gaze to her face.

"Seen enough?"

"No, but I know you're busy." She took one more quick look at the screen before he lifted the wand from her belly. "How does it look? The fibroid?" she asked as Esther wiped the gel from her skin.

"It doesn't look any bigger, which is the good news. It's still there, which is the not-so-good news." He turned off the machine and collected the Polaroids. "Give me a few minutes to look them over and we'll talk in my office."

* * *

Maddy exhaled slowly. Relief was making her a little dizzy. "I can't believe it. The myoma's actually getting smaller." She forced her gaze away from the two photos she'd been comparing, the one she'd brought with her and the one Luke had just taken. He'd circled the fibroid on each. Even with an uneducated eye she could see the difference. Doc, who thought the fibroid would get bigger, was wrong, she thought. Happily, wonderfully wrong. Or was he?

"Should I be excited?" she asked Luke.

His eyes crinkled behind the scholarly glasses. "Encouraged."

"But this is positive news, right?"

"Very positive."

"So it's safe to celebrate?"

"As long as that celebratin' doesn't include heavy lifting or dancin' on tables." His mouth slanted briefly in a smile as he opened a file drawer to pull out several sheets of paper. He selected one, passed it over. "This is the diet I recommend. You're okay on weight, so just keep doin' what you're doin'."

She scanned it quickly, then sighed. "Only one cup of coffee."

He smiled again. "And no chocolate."

That got her attention. "Sadist," she muttered.

"Yeah, I know. Being the bad guy is part of my job."

"I don't think you're a bad guy, Luke. Just the opposite, in fact."

After giving her a startled look, he handed over another sheet. "Here's a list of warning signs. I expect you to call immediately if any of these show up." His gaze pinned her hard. "And I do mean immediately,

Maddy. Day or night. If I'm not in my office, my service can always reach me.''

''You're my doctor. I'll do anything you say.''

He nodded, all business. The man with soft eyes who'd watched her baby on the screen was gone. ''No heavy lifting, no horseback riding, rest when you're tired, let your body regulate your sleeping, get as much fresh air and sunshine as you can. I prefer that you walk for an hour a day, instead of working out, though yoga's okay.'' He hesitated, then glanced down, his face blank. ''Sedate sex is permitted, with a considerate partner.''

Just like that, she was hot all over. Even though there wasn't even a hint of anything more than professional briskness in his tone, her body was suddenly alive and…lusting.

But it wasn't any man she wanted, she realized with a sharp jolt of dismay. It was Luke's body she wanted to feel thrusting inside her, hot and hard and potent, his big hands she wanted to feel caressing her swollen breasts. His exultant cry she longed to hear mingling with hers when he took her to a place she'd found only with him. Denial shuddered through her, followed by an emotion she realized was desperate longing.

''I'm not interested in sex with any kind of partner, Dr. Jarrod.'' She iced her tone in hopes of icing her mind.

It was anger now simmering in those blue eyes, and she wondered if he had a temper. From the hard set to his jaw and the dangerous line of his mouth, she suspected he did. When he spoke again, the steely edge to his voice confirmed it.

''That wasn't an offer, Mrs. Foster, only information.'' He slapped her folder shut and got to his feet.

"Call me if you have a problem. Otherwise I'll see you in one week."

Without waiting for an answer he tucked her chart under his arm and walked out.

Dr. Morrow's receptionist sounded perky and young, no more than eighteen was Luke's guess.

"Yes, sir, Dr. Morrow's expecting your call," she said after he'd stated his name and his reason for calling. "Please hold."

Expecting to wait, he was surprised when Morrow came on the line almost immediately.

"Dr. Jarrod, I appreciate the call, especially so soon." Though as rough as Texas grit, Morrow's voice was surprisingly soft-spoken. "How's Madelyn doing?"

He shifted his gaze to the two ultrasound photos arrayed side by side atop Maddy's chart. "Better than she thinks."

"Guess I'm not following you, son."

"You went to a lot of trouble to convince Madelyn she needs a high-risk specialist when we both know she doesn't."

"She has a submucous myoma, which could present a very grave risk to both her and the baby."

"It could—if it were in a position to block the cervix, which it isn't. Or if it continued to grow, which it hasn't. In fact, it's gotten noticeably smaller in the three weeks between ultrasounds. Even though she'll need careful monitoring, there's every reason to believe she'll have a normal pregnancy and a normal delivery."

"Now that's something I couldn't know for sure, which is why I set up the consult."

"Consult, my ass. It was a referral. She came to me as a new patient, scared to death because you convinced her she was going to lose that baby."

"No, sir, I told her no such a thing. She was already as jumpy as beans on a skillet, workin' herself into knots. You must have read about her preeclampsia." His sigh was heavy. "I blew that one, son. Just plain missed it. This time I wasn't about to take any chances, so I laid out the risks and my own reservations about my ability to treat her properly, which to my mind is exactly what the Hippocratic Oath requires me to do."

Luke actually squirmed at the mention of the oath he'd made it a point to memorize. So far he hadn't crossed the line, but he'd come within a razor's edge. "If you were worried, why didn't you send her to Baylor for a real consult, then have Marston or Wong monitor her progress long distance?"

"Well, you know what they say about hindsight bein' twenty-twenty."

"Hindsight my ass. During her first pregnancy she had two sub-myomas, both of which had shrunk to half their original size by the end of her second trimester, a fact that I suspect you failed to mention to her."

Morrow chuckled. "Danton always claimed it was well nigh impossible to fool you. Looks like he was right."

Luke sat up so quickly his back screamed. "You want to explain that?"

"Not much to explain. Dan Stone and I were in the same fraternity at Texas Tech. He went on to Stanford Medical, I went to Houston, but we kept in touch. Once, over drinks at a conference in San Francisco about fifteen, sixteen years back, he told me about a student of his who went rodeoin' every summer to pay his tuition. Guess you can imagine how surprised I was when he mentioned your name.''

''I have some idea.'' It wasn't often he got sucker punched, but Morrow had done a damn good job of it.

''Claimed you were the most conscientious student he'd ever had. Driven to be the best, he said. Like a man with something to prove. He also told me about the spill you took the summer of your second year and how you did one semester in a wheelchair and the next on crutches. Said you were strapped for cash and he was worried you'd have to drop out. Wouldn't take his money, he said, so he arranged a loan from a fund we both contribute to.''

Luke felt a jolt of anger, an even stronger jolt of hurt that the man he considered a role model and friend had been spreading around his private business to strangers. ''Is there anything he *didn't* tell you?'' he asked sarcastically.

''Impossible to say since I have no idea of what all he knows about you. What he did say changed around a few things in my mind, which is what's important.''

''What the hell are you talking about?''

''Guess you call it personal redemption. The way you turned yourself into the kind of man I'd be proud to call my friend. It made me wonder if I was wrong to encourage Maddy to give up that little one for adoption.''

The shock that shot through him had his pulse pounding in his throat, making it difficult to breathe. ''I thought it was her parents' doing.''

''It was, in part.'' Morrow's sigh was disturbingly heavy. ''But she would have held out if I'd offered to help her. All through her pregnancy and even after the baby was born, she kept saying you'd come back to marry her. That in spite of all the garbage folks were spilling all over your name, you were a decent man who would take care of her and the baby. Even when she was screaming in pain, she was saying you hadn't abandoned her. To my everlasting regret, I convinced her she was wrong.''

Luke hadn't lost his temper in years. He didn't intend to lose it now. So he eased back and took a couple of deep breaths. ''I should kill you for that,'' he said calmly. It surprised him some that he meant it.

''If I thought it would change the past, I'd hand you the gun.''

''I don't need a gun.''

''I kinda figured that would be the way of it.'' Morrow cleared his throat. ''You asked me why I sent you Maddy when she doesn't need a specialist. Maybe she doesn't medically, but she *does* need you. Very desperately, in fact. And I think you need her.''

The truth made Luke surly. ''Bull,'' he spit out, wishing he had the energy to hit something.

''What are you now? Forty? Forty-one? And never married. Not even close, according to Danton.''

Luke felt something give in his jaw. ''My private life is not up for discussion, Morrow.'' He put a cold warning in his voice that few men had ever dared challenge.

''Now Maddy, she did marry of course,'' Morrow went on as though Luke hadn't spoken. ''Almost had to if she wanted to hold her head up in this town again, though I tried to encourage her to take a job someplace else. She's loyal, though. Claimed her mama would miss her, though God knows Rebecca Smith doesn't have a loving bone in her body.''

Recalling the wintry eyes that never once warmed,

even when they lit on her daughter, Luke had to agree. "Maybe Maddy loved Foster." The words came out hard and tasted lousy.

"Wiley Roy Foster's a cold fish who damn near sapped all the life out of her, though thanks to that vein of sweetness she never lost, he didn't quite manage to turn her into a repressed bigot like himself. Worst of it is, he's also a damned hypocrite, running on about being a role model to his students, even when I was treating him for a venereal disease he picked up in Juarez."

Luke went cold inside. "Madelyn…?"

"No, fortunately not, but I treated her just in case. I told her Wiley had picked up a bug from some bad fruit and that's why I wanted her to take a course of antibiotics." His voice went hard. "That SOB Foster deserves a public whipping."

The rage was a throbbing in Luke's head. "A public castration is more like it," Luke grated through a clenched jaw, earning a bark of laughter from the man on the other end.

"Rumor has it he's hinting that this baby Madelyn is carrying isn't his."

This time the word Luke used was as filthy as Foster's character. "If you don't stop him, I will."

"Don't worry, he's not the only one who can start rumors. Or phone in a tip to an ambitious newspaper reporter about certain prominent local citizens who frequent a well-known whorehouse south of the border, a reality that I intend to explain very carefully to Wiley Roy this weekend during the golf game I set up, just the two of us."

When Luke realized he was flexing his hand, the one with the patched-together knuckle, he pulled himself back. "I'll call you Monday to see what his answer is."

"Do that." Morrow cleared his throat again. "About the referral, call it unprofessional if you want—hell, it *is* unprofessional, no sense denyin' it, but I care about Maddy. My wife and I weren't blessed with children, and she's as close as I'll ever get. It's like she's been walking through life for a long time."

Luke closed his eyes and tried not imagine what Maddy's life had been like. But it had been there in her too-calm eyes and in that pulled-back hairdo. His gut poured out acid. "If you're trying to make me feel lower than a skunk's belly, Morrow, you're doin' a damn good job."

"You mistake me, son. I'm explaining, not blaming. See, it's like this. When I mentioned your name, something flashed on her face before she pulled it back. Something bright and sassy and...purely wonderful. For just that moment she was the firecracker she used to be."

Luke couldn't do more than close his eyes and hurt as Morrow went on. "Maybe she still loves you. Maybe you still love her—only you know that. Fact is, though, I think you've earned yourself another chance to win her back. What you do with it is up to you."

It was almost six-thirty by the time he'd returned all the phone calls Dorie had piled on his desk during an especially busy Monday. His office manager, Gladys Delaney, had just left, locking the front door behind her. The rain had started again, pelting the windows in a monotonous rhythm. An ambulance had just pulled into the bay outside the trauma unit, its siren shutting off abruptly, leaving a sudden void.

Tossing off his glasses, he rubbed his eyes and gave some thought to stretching out on his office couch for a quick nap before he had to head to the hospital for rounds. Deciding he was too tired to move, he leaned back and closed his eyes. Instantly she was there, in his mind, watching the ultrasound screen with a soft smile on her face. In spite of that fine-boned hauntingly lovely face that made him think of a painting he'd seen once, she was solid all the way to her soul. A woman a man could sink into when the loneliness cut too deep.

The things Morrow had said—and yeah, what he hadn't said—were still in his head, waiting to be sorted through. He wasn't sure what he felt about the old man's interference. He wasn't even sure what he intended to tell Maddy. He just knew he had a lot of serious thinking to do.

Luke was just finishing rounds on Friday when his beeper went off. "That's all for today, ladies and gentlemen," he said, handing the chart he'd been consulting to the senior obstetrics resident, Jamie Conover.

Nearly as tall as he was, with spiky black hair and a wicked sense of humor, the woman had more potential than discipline. Because Luke saw too much of himself in her, he'd ridden her hard from the moment she'd been accepted as a first year in his service.

"I'm sorry about the mix-up with the tests for Mrs. Yuan, sir," the long-legged corn-fed Missouri native said as she walked with him to the nearest wall phone. "I should have double-checked the names."

"Damn straight you should have, Conover. You got lucky this time. Next time an alert nurse might not catch your mistake."

Misery seemed to settle over her like a widow's veil. "Yes, sir. I mistook Yuan for Luan."

"Everyone gets one mistake with me. You've just had yours. One more and you're out."

"Yes, sir. I appreciate it."

Luke checked his beeper, then punched out the number. "Karen, it's Jarrod."

"Sorry to get you out of rounds, Doctor, but you said you wanted a second opinion on Mrs. Foster." It had been three or four years since Karen Winslow had worked under him, but her voice still carried a typical resident's eagerness for approval when she spoke with him.

"I appreciate your help, thanks."

"I know how protective you are of your patients, Luke, and I appreciate the vote of confidence—and I mean that most sincerely." She cleared her throat. "Oops, hold on, let me get my glasses."

Reining in his impatience, Luke pressed his aching back against the wall and watched two orderlies pushing a bed toward the elevator. He had another appointment with Maddy one week from today, and he was hoping to reassure her one more time.

"Okay, here we go." As Winslow detailed her findings, which were all but identical to his, Luke felt some of the knots in his belly unraveling. "…so unless something untoward happens, which is always possible of course, it's my opinion Mrs. Foster can look forward to a full-term pregnancy and a normal delivery."

Chapter 11

T ry as he might, Luke couldn't pinpoint the exact moment when he'd actually agreed to play host for the twins' birthday party.

He'd forgotten all about it until Raine had called to tell him how excited her boys were at the idea of riding real horses, And by the way, he had remembered to reserve the picnic area at McMinn's Stables for Saturday afternoon, hadn't he? That had been last Monday. Fortunately Sally McMinn liked him, so he'd been able to arrange things on short notice—after he'd agreed to pay twice the going rate.

Now midway through the festivities he found himself in the saddle with Alex perched in front of him, walking Molly sedately around the exercise ring. Next to him Pax sat astride Sweet Sue with Matthew wriggling like an excited eel and talking a mile a minute. For a guy who'd grown up riding mules in the hills of

Kentucky, the man sat a horse damn well. Better than most, Luke admitted to himself, if not to Pax.

Turning his head, Luke searched the picnic area until he spotted Maddy's bright yellow straw hat, the one with the artificial fruit around the band. While he'd been in the barn saddling the mares, Raine and Pax had strung streamers from the trees and blown up about a million balloons.

Maddy had brought Morgana and the boys along later, dressed in tiny denim cowboy vests she'd made herself. She looked breathtakingly young and pretty in a sleeveless cotton top the color of sunshine and perky white shorts that revealed a satisfying amount of smooth tanned thighs. Now that her center of gravity had shifted, her hips tended to sway a little when she walked, and her fanny filled out those shorts to blood-heating perfection. He'd been uptight and on edge ever since.

While the others were playing on the swings or in the sandbox in the playground, she and Morgana were busy picking daisies along the fence line. They looked so right together—the pretty lady and the happy little girl, one so fair, the other dark.

"She's an exceptional woman, Maddy," Pax said quietly. "Reminds me of a nurse I knew in 'Nam, a blueblood from Boston who went into nursing after her Marine-captain husband was killed. Took care of a bunch of orphan kids in her spare time."

Luke grunted something noncommittal. Pax grinned, but beneath the brim of the Aussie hat, his eyes were sympathetic. "It's hell, isn't it? Knowing you messed up and wanting to make things right so damn bad you wake up with a knot in your gut night after night?"

Luke tightened his grip on the reins. If Alex hadn't

been perched in front of him, he would have spurred Molly into a dead run straight at the open gate.

"Anybody ever tell you to mind your own business, Paxton?" he grated, instead.

Luke might have figured the insensitive jerk would just laugh. "Just about everyone, Jarrod."

Morgana Paxton had exquisite bone structure, the shimmering black eyes of a Bedouin princess and the innocent smile of an angel. It had taken Madelyn about five seconds to fall in love with her.

"How come you talk funny, Aunt Maddy?" she asked, leaning against Madelyn's side. She smelled like bubble gum and happy little girl.

"Because I'm from Texas, sweetie, which is a place far away from Portland." Seated at one of the picnic tables scattered around the grassy area under a towering pin oak, Madelyn finished tying the last stem in the daisy crown she was making before placing it on the four-year-old's glossy black hair.

"Folks down where I live think y'all up here talk funny, too," she added, exaggerating her drawl to make the little girl giggle.

"Uncle Luke talks funny, too. Daddy says that's 'cause he's a cowboy and cowboys are s'posed to talk slow."

"Uncle Luke said girls can be cowboys and own ranches, too," Tory MacAuley proclaimed before plopping down next to Madelyn on the bench.

"Is that what you want to be when you grow up, a rancher?" Maddy asked, surprised that such a dignified little girl would be interested in eating dust and bucking hay.

"Maybe." Tory reached up to flip one of her thick

brown braids over her shoulder. "When I turn seven, Uncle Luke's going to teach me how to ride Molly all by myself. Right, Daddy?" She turned to look at her father who was stretched out in the deepest part of the shade with his son fast asleep on his chest.

At the sound of his daughter's voice Boyd opened one eye and offered her a drowsy smile. "You bet, Peaches," he said before closing his eyes again.

"I'm going to be a ballerina," Morgana declared firmly. "My teacher said I was the best Tinkerbell ever. And next year I get to be a toy soldier in *The Nutcracker*." She glanced up and her face split into a huge grin. "Aunt Maddy made me a daisy crown, Uncle Luke. See?"

A shadow fell across the table as Luke reached out to touch one of the bright-eyed daisies with a blunt forefinger. Preoccupied with the girls, Madelyn hadn't seen him approach. After saying a polite hello when she'd arrived, he'd pointedly avoided her. It was that way at all the gatherings they both attended. If she was in one room, he was in another. If she sat down at a table, he got up. Even the mommies had noticed.

Prudy claimed he had no choice. As her doctor, he couldn't risk getting involved. In the office he was pleasant but all business, answering her questions in full, asking questions of his own about her physical condition but never anything personal. It was exactly what she'd told him she wanted, a strictly professional relationship. There wasn't one good solid rational reason why she should feel hurt because he was avoiding her.

"I reckon that's just about the prettiest crown I ever saw, Miz Morgana," he drawled softly.

Instantly Tory's mouth turned down. Madelyn

started to offer to make her one too, but Luke beat her to it. "I'll bet that if you were to pick some more of those daisies yonder, Aunt Maddy would make one for you, too, Peaches."

Tory's head came up, her brown eyes shining. "Would you?" she asked eagerly.

"I would love to, sweetheart," Madelyn declared. "But I'll need nice big daisies with strong stems."

"I'll show you which ones," Morgana offered, scrambling to her feet.

"Watch out for bees," Madelyn called after them as they took off running toward the pasture fence hand in hand. Giggling little-girl laughter floated back to them on the warm breeze, as bright as hope.

"I think you've just made aunt-of-the-year," he said, angling one hip over the end of the table and crossing his arms.

"They make it easy to love them," she said softly. He smelled of horses, sunshine and virile male.

"Does it still hurt to think about her, our baby?" His quiet question drew her gaze to his. It surprised her that he would ask. In the several weeks she'd been here he'd avoided all but the most clinical questions about their baby.

"Yes, it hurts, but not as much as it did once." She softened the admission with a smile that had him dropping his gaze. "Morgana's very like I imagined Jenny to be at four." She let out a slow careful breath. "Except for the eyes. I always saw her with blue eyes. Her…her daddy's eyes."

Luke glanced up. It cost him, but he kept his gaze steady on hers. "You called her Jenny?"

She nodded, her smile bittersweet. "Even before I felt her move, I would…talk to her, and it didn't seem right somehow to just call her baby. I knew it would be a girl.'' She gave a sad little laugh that had him biting down hard. ''Don't ask me how, but I just knew, just like I know this one is a boy.''

Jenny Jarrod. Luke rolled it over in his mind, letting the pain wash over him. ''I like it,'' he said, his voice husky. ''It has a dainty sound.''

She picked up one of the daisies and touched a neatly rounded nail to the bright center. ''She was only five pounds, two ounces, but she had the loudest cry in the nursery. And a temper, too.'' Madelyn turned to watch Morgana and Tory gathering flowers. ''It's helped, seeing how happy Morgana is with the Paxtons. Even though Doc swore the couple that took her were wonderful loving people, I've always worried.''

Luke swallowed hard. He hadn't cried since his mother had taken off, leaving him with a broken bitter man who'd forbidden him to ever mention her again. He realized now that a man could cry without tears if the hurt was great enough.

''Did you ever contact them?'' he asked.

''No, I gave my word I wouldn't. Everyone told me it was for the best.'' She plucked a petal from the daisy and let it fall. ''A clean break, a fresh start.'' She plucked another petal. ''A few years ago I registered my name and the date and place of her birth in the national database. In case she wanted to find her birth mother.'' Madelyn looked up, her cheeks pink and her mouth vulnerable and soft ''You could do the same thing, you know. The database is for fathers, as well as mothers and children.''

He struggled to draw breath past the grinding pressure in his chest. ''I'm not sure I could face her.''

''She's happy, Luke. We have to believe that.''

He reached out a hand to brush a stray curl from her cheek. "I wish…" He saw the girls approaching then and dropped his hand.

"It wasn't your fault you didn't get the letter in time."

Her words stunned him. "Maddy—"

"We got the daisies, Aunt Maddy," Tory bubbled.

"Nice big ones like you said," Morgana added, dumping what had to be a bushel of daisies onto the table. As Maddy turned her attention to the girls, he knew what it was like to grieve.

Luke rode low in the saddle, bent over the mare's neck as the palomino's long legs ate the trail angling upward away from the corral. Perched on the bench next to Madelyn, Tory shaded her eyes and watched horse and rider disappear over a distant rise.

"How come Uncle Luke rode away so fast?" she asked, glancing up at her father, who was bending over the picnic table, diapering his cooing son.

Boyd flicked her a smile before fastening one of the tapes. "Maybe Molly needs exercise."

Madelyn looked up from the daisies she was knotting together. "Isn't it bad for his back to ride that hard?" she asked, her gaze on the dust still rising from the trail.

"Doubt he's thinking about that right now." Boyd lifted B.J. into his arms, deftly dodging the right hook the baby aimed at his jaw. "Last time I saw him ride like that he'd just heard that his mother had died."

Madelyn shifted uneasily on the hard bench. "You've known him for a long time, haven't you?"

"As much as he lets anyone know him, yeah."

"Is it ready yet, Aunt Maddy?" Tory asked, shifting from one foot to the other, her eyes bright.

"All ready, sweetheart." With a dramatic flourish, Madelyn fitted the daisy tiara over Tory's head, then stood back and cocked her head. "Now we have two beautiful princesses on the ranch."

Tory beamed. "Am I really beautiful?"

"Well, actually, it's more like gorgeous. But if you don't believe me, ask your daddy."

"Beyond gorgeous," Boyd said, his expression besotted as he looked from one little girl to the other. "Both of you."

Morgana's smile bloomed as bright as Tory's. "C'mon, Tory, let's go show Chloe." Beaming, the two girls took off running. Madelyn and Boyd watched them in silence for a long moment.

"You're very lucky," she said quietly. "All of you."

"I'm not a religious man, but I count my blessings every day." His voice was husky, his eyes thoughtful when they shifted her way again. "When I lost my first wife and child, Luke literally kept me from blowing my brains out. He talked to me for hours and some time during the conversation he told me about you and your child—and he wasn't kind to himself in the telling."

B.J. made a little snuffling sound before poking his thumb into his mouth. Madelyn reached out to smooth his wispy curls, and he offered her a drowsy grin around that tiny thumb. "Does it ever go away, the terror that it'll happen again?"

"It fades. Marrying Stacy and having our children has helped." Boyd glanced down at the sturdy little boy snuggled against his shoulder, then at her belly. "Won't be long and you'll know that, too."

Yes, she would have the baby, but who would Luke have?

"I didn't come to Oregon intending to cause him pain, but I realize now that I did."

"If there's any hurting going on, he's doing it to himself." Boyd looked toward the ridge line. "When I was fighting the feelings I had for Stacy, he pushed me up against a wall in his office and told me I'd damn well better stop feeling sorry for myself and grab hold of the lady before someone else beat me to it." His smile was rueful. "That was when I found out he'd gone back for you, with the ink still drying on his bachelor's degree and a ring in his pocket."

"But he didn't," she said, her voice hollow.

"He did, Maddy. Drove up to your house in a new suit, his proposal all rehearsed. Claims he was even wearing a tie." Boyd grinned, shook his head. "It seems there was a party going on," he continued, his grin fading. "Your wedding reception. He arrived one day too late."

Madelyn froze, her eyes locked on the daisy in her hand. Slowly she lifted her gaze. "I didn't know."

"You weren't supposed to." Boyd smiled again, briefly this time. "He didn't give me all the details, but I gather he bought a bottle, drove to the first motel on the highway out of town and spent your wedding night getting blind drunk." He hesitated, then added a little gruffly, "Luke told me about your husband. I suspect it's a good thing Texas is so far away."

She shifted her gaze to the other side of the picnic area where the others were gathered around the picnic table, preparing to cut the cake, she suspected. "All my life I've been trying to be what someone else wanted me to be. Except for those four days with Luke. With him I was…just me.''

"It's tearing him apart, Madelyn. Trying to ignore his feelings so that he can take care of you properly. He thinks he's handling it, but I've been where he is, and sooner or later he's going to blow wide open."

Boyd's jaw was hard and his expression troubled. "When I couldn't save my first wife, I went a little crazy. Understandable, the shrinks said. Part of the grieving process. Except it was worse for me because saving people is what my life is all about. I think, if I'd been the one performing the C-section to try to save her, instead of Luke, I would never have been able to pull myself back after she died."

Madelyn managed a shaky laugh. "I get the point."

"I figured you would."

She plucked one of the daisy's petals and wondered if she dared play the "Loves Me, Loves Me Not" game. "Luke's lucky to have a friend like you," she said when she realized he was watching her with worried eyes.

"I like to think I'm your friend, too, Maddy."

"I'd like to think that, too, Boyd."

"Sign here and here," Gladys ordered Luke, leaning forward to stab her pen at the *X*'s on the bottom of the lease renewal for his office suite.

He picked up his pen, then put it down. "I'm gonna hold off on this for now."

Her eyebrows shot up. "You do realize your lease runs out at the end of next month, don't you?"

He moved the lease to one side. "There's no hurry."

"There's also a waiting list for space in this building."

He gave her a warning look. "Anything else I need to sign?"

"No." She glanced at her notebook. "Dr. Ybarra phoned to express his thanks for the consult last month. Lampson Pharmaceuticals wants to talk to you about the clinical trials for their new fertility drug, and Dr. MacAuley would like a return call at your earliest convenience. The rest of the messages are routine stuff."

While Gladys stacked the reports and letters he'd already signed, he sifted through the stack of pink slips. On the bottom was a check made out to the Open Door Clinic. A quick scan of the amount and signature had him sighing.

Two weeks after he'd taken Maddy on as a patient, the two of them had gone a few rounds about his fee. At first she hadn't believed him when he told her he never accepted more from personal acquaintances than their insurance coverage. After wrangling with him for a good ten minutes, she'd finally given in. What she hadn't done, he'd just come to realize, was accept his conditions. Instead, the little mule had donated her share to the clinic.

"She must have put it on my desk after her appointment this morning," he said as he handed Gladys the check.

A quick look had her grinning. "Guess it makes sense now, all the questions she asked about the clinic last time she was in. And no, I didn't tell her you were the private party who covered fifty percent of the operating costs, but I think she figured it out, anyway." Gladys tucked the check into one of the folders in the stack she'd brought with her before getting to her feet.

"Anything else you need before I call it a day?" she asked at the same time the intercom buzzed.

"Nope. Have a good weekend."

"It'll be productive, anyway." She grimaced. "I'm painting the living room."

Luke watched her go, then, tired to the bone, grabbed up the phone. "Yeah?" His voice came out too harsh and too impatient, and he winced.

"Dr. Fabrizio on four." Dorie's stiff tone had him wanting to punch something. "Perhaps you recall ordering me to put her through the minute she returned your call?"

"Sorry, Dor, I didn't mean to growl."

"So what else is new these days?" she said before disconnecting.

Feeling like a low-crawling worm, Luke picked up his pen and scrawled himself a note to buy Dorie a giant bag of chocolate-coated peanuts before punching line four.

He'd been playing phone tag with psychotherapist Daniela Fabrizio for two solid days. The last time he'd seen her had been at her husband's funeral in May. White-faced and stoic, she'd accepted his condolences with her chin high, but he'd seen the agony in her eyes.

She and Mark Fabrizio had grown up together in southern Oregon where both his family and hers made wine. He and their ten-year-old daughter, Lyssa, had been returning from a visit to his parents when a drunk driver had forced them into a bridge abutment. Mark had been killed instantly. Lyssa had survived, but her face had been severely scarred.

"Hey, Danni, thanks for getting back to me."

"Sorry it's taken so long. My youngest brother and

his wife just had twins, and I took Lyssa down to Jacksonville to meet her new cousins.''

"How's she doing?''

"Better. She still misses her dad, but we're coping.'' Daniela cleared her throat, and when she spoke again, her voice was brisk. "Your message said you wanted an unofficial consult?''

"Yeah, a second-time mom, twenty-eight weeks. Her first was twenty-two years ago.'' He went on to describe Maddy's first pregnancy. "She was pretty torn up when she had to give up her daughter, and now she's terrified she'll lose this baby, too.''

"Understandable, under the circumstances. I'd be happy to talk to her if you think it would help, although I imagine she needs your reassurance more than mine.''

"I'm working on that, which is one of the reasons I asked for the consult. I've been doing some reading about delayed stress among adoptees and birth moms. From what I've picked up so far, opinion seems to be divided about the emotional benefits of the two meeting later in life versus the dangers of invading someone's privacy or stirring up buried angers. I'd like to know your thoughts.''

"Each case is different, Luke. I've known cases where the reunion precipitated great joy and healing, others where it only made the pain worse. So as I said, it depends on how eager each party is to make contact.''

"Very eager, I think. Though she promised never to actively search for her child, she put her name in the national database.''

"And the daughter? She's how old now?''

"Almost twenty-two.''

"Old enough to make her own choices certainly, so that's a plus. Has she ever tried to contact the mom?"

"Not to my knowledge, no." He swiveled his chair to the side and looked out at the rain-swollen clouds hanging over the hospital. "I had this idea that if Madelyn knew her daughter was happy and thriving and…didn't hate her for giving her up, it would ease her mind about the decision she'd made."

"And what if the daughter isn't happy or thriving, or in fact does hate her, then what?"

Then he wouldn't tell her, he thought as they said their goodbyes.

Tucking the phone against his shoulder, he consulted his Rolodex for Case Randolph's private number at the precinct house. He caught Case as he was locking his desk drawer. Two minutes later he had the name of the best private investigator in the city.

Chapter 12

Luke was late for his own party. Not that he realized it *was* a party, Madelyn hastily reminded herself as she glanced once more at her watch. The hands had measured off no more than a minute since the last time she'd checked.

Hovering between the MacAuleys' back and front doors, she wanted to pace, but now that she'd lost sight of her feet, she had a tendency to bump into things, so she vented some of her nerves by checking the party buffet spread out on Stacy's dining-room table.

"Maybe I should call the hospital to see if he's tied up in a delivery," Prudy thought aloud, glancing at her watch. Tonight she was dressed in a lavender mini dress with emerald-and-silver art deco earrings. Next to the tiny nurse, Madelyn, in a yellow silk shirtdress and pearls felt like an overfed canary.

She'd seen Luke only once since the twins' party, at her regular visit. It was then that Esther had mentioned the shirt his office staff had bought him for his birthday, which had come and gone ten days ago without anyone on Maternity Row knowing about it.

The surprise party had been her idea and she'd orchestrated every detail. She wanted it to be perfect. She'd also wanted him to be surprised. It had been sheer luck the monthly poker game had already been scheduled for tonight.

Everyone was there—the Randolphs, the Paxtons, even Detective Sergeant Don Petroff, Case Randolph's longtime partner and surrogate grandfather to Chloe and Lily. Teddy-bear gruff and endearingly homely, he reminded Madelyn of Doc, so of course they'd become instant friends.

It had taken her longer to warm to Prudy's tough-cop husband. Bigger than most with a body worthy of a *Playgirl* centerfold even at forty-nine, Case had brought to mind a barely domesticated jaguar the first time Madelyn had laid eyes on him.

After getting to know him better, however, she'd come to realize that his heart was about as soft as the kiss he now pressed to his younger daughter's auburn hair.

"Daddy, when is Uncle Luke gonna get here so we can s'prise him?" three-year-old Lily asked as she turned her face up to his.

"Soon, scooter," Case promised.

Content, Lily stuck her thumb into her mouth and rubbed her cheek against her daddy's wide chest. Madelyn could almost hear Case melt. There was something especially poignant about a tough man so obviously in love with his own child, she thought, the pain of all that Luke had been denied stabbing through her.

"Don't worry, Maddy, he'll be here," Stacy said

with a quick glance at the front window where four-year-old Chloe was acting as lookout, peering through the curtains for Luke's Jeep.

"Maybe we should have told him this was going to be a party for him," Madelyn worried aloud before glancing at her watch again.

"Only if you wanted to make sure he didn't come anywhere near the place," Case said, smiling reassurance at her over Lily's bright curls. "Jarrod's not much for sentimental stuff."

"That's because he's lived alone for so long," Prudy said, leaning over his shoulder to nibble her husband's ear. "Remember how grumpy you were before you came to your senses and married me again?"

Case scowled, but his hand went up to cover Prudy's, trapping it against his shoulder. "Cops aren't grumpy, honey. We're laconic."

Don grinned. "Damned straight."

"Maybe you should call his beeper number," Stacy told Boyd over the sound of the twins' chattering.

"He said he'd be here, Stace. Give him—"

The portable phone atop an old-fashioned barrister's bookcase shrilled, and Stacy leaped to answer.

"No, wait!" Prudy exclaimed before Stacy could punch the button. "It's poker night. Boyd should answer, or L.J. will wonder why you're still here."

Stacy carried the phone to Boyd, then hovered at his shoulder. As Boyd listened, his grin faded. "Sure you can't shake loose?" Shifting his gaze to Madelyn's, he shook his head. "I understand. If you can't make it, you can't make it."

The air seemed to go out of the room in one big whoosh as Boyd handed the phone back to Stacy.

"Looks like we'll just have to go on with the party without the guest of honor."

"But he has to come!" Tory cried, her eyes dark with dismay. "It's *his* party, with presents and everything."

"Uncle Luke doesn't know that, peaches," Boyd reminded her. "He thinks it's just a regular poker game, remember? Daddy told him that because we wanted to surprise him."

"Call him back and tell him it's really a party. Tell him Aunt Maddy made her special cake and we have ice cream and presents and fried chicken." Before Stacy could stop her, Tory snatched up the phone. "What's Uncle Luke's number, Mommy?"

As Boyd and Stacy exchanged troubled looks, Madelyn felt a jolt of alarm. Next to her Prudy let out a small huff of air before staring down at her sequined sneakers. Madelyn was familiar enough with body language to feel distinctively uneasy.

"Peaches, Uncle Luke had been working really hard and he needs his rest like Daddy does sometimes when I've been operating all night."

"But—"

"I'll tell you what, we'll just put the presents in the den and have the party next week," Stacy said quickly, her smile bright. "That way we'll get to have twice as much ice cream and cake."

Tory grumbled, but Prudy placated her and the others by suggesting a videofest complete with predinner goodies. The walls shook with noise as the assorted offspring bumped and jostled one another on the way to the den while the adults set about refilling drinks and filling plates.

It was ten minutes before Madelyn could corner

Boyd alone in the kitchen where he'd gone to get Raine a glass of wine. "What gives, Boyd? Why did everyone look so uneasy after Luke called?"

Boyd dug in a drawer for a corkscrew. "I don't know, Maddy. Disappointment, maybe?"

"No, it was more than that." She studied his face. It was expressionless. Not a good sign. "Is it me? Is that what you're trying not to tell me? That he never comes around anymore and you're blaming me?"

His head came up. "Absolutely not! You can put that right out of your mind."

"Then what is it you're not telling me?"

"Just that he's been looking kinda tired lately, that's all."

Madelyn heard the truth in his voice, but she also saw the tension in his jaw. She doubted that Boyd would deliberately lie to her, but she suspected he wasn't telling her the entire truth, either.

"It's his back, isn't it? Because of the riding?"

Boyd concentrated on drawing the cork and pouring wine before turning to face her. His gray eyes were sympathetic—and hooded. "Whatever it is, he's handling it."

"It's serious. I can see it in your eyes."

Boyd dropped his gaze, a tiny muscle ticking violently in his jaw. "Even if it is, it's not something I can discuss with you, so please don't ask."

"But I can discuss it," Stacy said as she reached Madelyn's side.

Boyd's gray eyes narrowed ominously. "Stace, don't."

"Don't glare at me, Boyd. Prudy told me what happened, not you, so I'm not breaking your confidence."

Boyd sighed. "Don't expect me to protect you if the

man explodes at you the next time he sees you," he muttered before picking up Raine's glass.

Stacy reached up to rub her finger over the furrows in his brow. "Don't worry, sweetheart. If I can handle you in one of your tempers, I can handle Luke."

One side of his mouth curled up before he leaned down to brush a kiss over her smile. "Don't say I didn't warn you," he told her before disappearing into the dining room. Stacy watched him for a moment, then returned her gaze to Madelyn's face, her fond smile fading.

"What doesn't Luke want me to know?" Madelyn asked, her voice thin.

"About six weeks ago his leg just gave out on him and he folded up in the OR. Boyd's afraid if he doesn't have surgery soon, he might end up damaging himself irreparably."

Madelyn drew in a sharp breath. "What exactly do you mean by irreparably?"

Stacy hesitated, then sighed. "Worst-case scenario, he could end up paralyzed for life."

"Oh, my God." Madelyn felt the blood drain from her face, and she groped for the edge of the counter to steady her wobbly legs. "I had no idea."

"He threatened both Boyd and Prudy with grievous bodily harm if they breathed a word to you or anyone else. Prue had already told me about Luke's canceling the surgery, so—"

"What surgery?"

"Apparently Boyd had him talked into having the disks repaired. After he saw you in his office, he called and canceled."

Madelyn was stunned. That he would do that for her

was almost more than she could handle. "Damn him," she whispered. "I could just...just—"

"Throw your arms around him and kiss him for caring about you and the baby enough to risk so much?" Stacy suggested blandly.

"Something like that," Madelyn muttered, glancing around for her purse. "After I give him a piece of my mind."

Luke lay on his back trying not to breathe any more deeply than he had to. After he'd phoned Boyd, he'd given in to the scalding agony and swallowed two of the powerful painkillers he used only when he wasn't on call. So far they'd done little more than make his head fuzzy and his gut queasy.

Dumb ass that he was, he'd known better than to spur Molly into a gallop, especially over rough ground, but he'd been hurting too much to care. By the time he'd left the stables last Saturday he'd been hard-pressed to stand up straight enough to walk to his Jeep. Spending the rest of the weekend flat on his back had staved off crippling spasms, but the tortured muscles were still giving him fits.

A hectic week hadn't helped, but he'd hung in okay. Just as he'd been congratulating himself on skating through, he'd gotten a call from the ER. A three-car pileup on I-5 had resulted in multiple injuries. One of the worst was an expectant mom with belly trauma. That both mom and baby had survived was a miracle in itself. That the crash hadn't brought on labor was even more miraculous.

Six hours of surgery had saved the mom's life without precipitating premature labor. By the time he'd left

the OR, his leg was hurting so badly it had been all he
could do to drive himself home.

He'd fallen asleep in the Jacuzzi, then jerked awake
when the nightmare had hit again—the sweat-soaked
stomach-knotting one where Maddy was screaming his
name as some man in black tore their baby from her
arms. He hoped to hell the narcotic pumping through
his system would keep the bad dreams away. At least
for a couple of hours anyway.

He was just drifting off when the doorbell rang, jolt-
ing him awake. Adrenaline shot through him as he
ground out a curse. It was MacAuley of course. Come
to hassle his patient, damn his conscientious hide.

Luke gave a few testing breaths, then lifted his head.
The groan exploded before he could bite it back.
Slowly he returned his head to the pillow and closed
his eyes. The sound of his front door opening had them
popping open again. It was then he remembered the
house key he'd given Stace a few years back so that
she could take in his mail while he'd been in New York
for a conference.

"Get the hell out of my house, MacAuley, before I
call the cops and have you hauled off for trespassing,"
he hollered over the sound of approaching footsteps.

He smelled her an instant before he opened his eyes
to see an angel in shimmering yellow framed in the
doorway, her glorious hair drifting around her face.
The drug had dulled his will, so by the time he remembered he was supposed to separate himself from his
personal feelings, he'd already noticed the ripe curves
of her breasts and the pale pink perfection of her
mouth.

"I should brain you over the head with that ugly
monstrosity of a lamp for putting yourself through

this,'' she muttered as she crossed the room toward him.

"You shouldn't be here," he said, then winced at the harsh croak that he'd meant to sound firm.

"*You* should be in the hospital, getting ready for the operation you should have had six weeks ago. And don't blame Boyd for breaking a confidence," she added when he was about to do just that. "He refused to say a word. I found out from another source."

"It seems," he muttered, "I need to have a talk with a certain copper-haired nurse."

"It wasn't Prudy, and stop guessing."

She took a breath, her eyes suddenly huge. He fervently hoped those weren't tears he saw glistening. Because he was damn sure he couldn't handle tears on top of the embarrassed anger fermenting in his mushy brain.

"You canceled it because of me, didn't you?"

"It's discretionary surgery, Maddy. I postponed it a few more months, that's all."

"I heard you fainted in the operating room." Her voice wobbled and he nearly groaned. He hadn't seen this coming.

"I didn't faint." Maybe the lights had gone dim for a couple of seconds, but he hadn't been out. Not even close. Something popped in his jaw, and he forced the muscles to relax. It was then he remembered he was sprawled on top of the bed naked because it hurt too much to draw back the covers.

Being helpless made him want to rage. At himself mostly. "I appreciate your concern," he said tightly, "but I don't want you here."

If she heard him, she gave no sign. "Your back is in spasm, isn't it?"

"No, it's a little sore, that's all." Even as a kid he'd been a lousy liar. Once he'd figured out he was going to get whomped on twice—once for lying and again for whatever he'd done wrong—he pretty much stuck with the truth. The expression on her face now had him wishing he'd worked a little harder on perfecting his lying technique.

"Where's your heating pad?"

"Damn it, Maddy, I'm your doctor, not your patient."

"Not any longer. You're fired."

"The hell I am," he shouted, then sucked in as the pain nearly took him under.

Nostrils flaring, she advanced on him. "Six weeks ago you did your best to get rid of me."

"I didn't—"

"And they say women are fickle."

"That isn't funny."

"I mean it, Luke. As of this moment I am Dr. Winslow's patient." She slipped her purse from her shoulder and dropped it to the floor by the bed before glancing around. "Where do you keep your extra pillows?"

The painkiller was filling his head with gray cotton, but he managed to keep his attention focused on her long enough to demand, "What the hell do you want pillows for?"

"My father had back spasms, and it always helped him to put two pillows under his knees and two under his head."

"Madelyn, go home. This isn't doing either of us any good." His voice came out rough and angry, startling her into looking at him.

"Shut up, Luke. I'm going to take care of you, like it or not." He was already scowling when he saw the emotion turning her eyes liquid. God help him, it looked like love.

Something raw and desperate staggered out of the darkness inside him. It was the need to be loved and to love in return, he realized, the kind that came from the depths of a man's soul.

He didn't deserve a second chance. Maybe she wasn't even offering. Right now, this minute, he only knew he was tired of being alone. Tired of wanting what he couldn't have. Later, when he wasn't hurting, he would sort things out with his conscience.

"Suit yourself," he muttered. "But for God's sake throw a sheet over me before I curl up and die of embarrassment."

She let out a little yelp of laughter. "I've seen you naked before," she said, her voice way too sultry for a man in his condition to handle.

"Yeah, but not half-dead and…puny."

"Not on your worst day," she murmured, or maybe he just hoped that was what she said.

"Linen closet's in the hall."

Frustration ran though him as she disappeared, only to reappear a moment later to spread a sheet over him. Her hands were efficient as they smoothed it over his chest. He felt himself sinking again, his tired sore body desperate to shut down. Not once in all the years since his mother had walked out while he'd slept had he allowed himself to sleep while someone else in the house was awake. Especially a darlin' sexy female who smelled like a whole field of wildflowers.

His eyes drifted shut and he forced them open again. But his lids were so heavy and his damned lashes screened all but a wedge of suntanned throat framed by her lapels. Silk against silk again, he thought, then imagined himself slipping those pearly little buttons free one by one until there was only the silk of her skin and the ripe curves of her breasts.

Knowing he would burn in hell for violating his oath, he let his gaze linger on the swell of her belly—not as a doctor but as a man who wished with all his heart and soul that he'd put that sweet little baby boy in her womb. Because he was too tired to fight anymore, he lifted a hand to that glorious belly, earning himself a good hard kick in the middle of his palm. Atta boy, tiger. Don't take nothin' from nobody.

"You picked out a name yet?" he asked, or tried to.

"No, not yet."

"Tough little guy, needs a…strong name."

"I'll remember that."

He tried to stay awake when he felt her hands in his hair, stroking the sweat-damp strands away from his face, but he didn't seem able to find the strength, so he simply tucked her hand against his chest and stopped fighting.

Luke was still sleeping soundly at midnight when Madelyn wandered into the kitchen in search of something to eat. These days she slept when the baby slept, which wasn't all that often. At the moment her little toughie was wide awake and playing a particularly wild and woolly game of kickball.

Pausing at the door between the kitchen and dining alcove, it took her a minute to find the light switch. The kitchen was small, but streamlined, the appliances built in, the counters nearly bare and gleaming white. Like the rest of the rooms she'd seen, it was as austere as a monk's cell. Wincing at a particularly painful kick in the vicinity of her left kidney, she pulled open the fridge door and rummaged through the pitifully bare shelves, looking for sustenance.

The two packages of Snickers bars tempted her briefly, but she made herself reach for the extra-large jar of peanut butter, instead. The bread was stale, but she was too hungry to care.

She ate in the dining alcove off the kitchen, at a chrome-and-glass table in front of a window overlooking a part of the city she'd never seen before. Lights twinkled like fireflies in the purple darkness, and in the distance, traffic moved in a serpentine pattern on the valley floor.

Living here in a house hanging over the side of a hill was akin to living in an eagle's nest, she thought, sipping juice. A solitary lair for a solitary man. There was no yard for children to play, no neighbors to drop in with pizza and chocolate, no sense of family and belonging. The perfect place for a loner who filled his days with work, instead of the wife and children he needed so desperately. Just as she'd filled hers with her own work and charity functions and gardening. Anything to keep from feeling too deeply.

She suspected it hadn't really worked for either of them.

Feeling sad and little disoriented, she poured herself another glass of juice, carrying it with her into the master bathroom. Damp towels lay in a heap next to the oversize tub still filled with water that had grown cold long ago.

His clothes were there, too, scattered on the tile floor where he'd dropped them. Since the rest of the house was almost surgically neat, she suspected he'd been hurting too much to tidy up after himself.

After setting her glass on the marble sink, she set

about draining the tub and hanging up the towels. His shirt and jeans and dark blue briefs went into the wicker basket that served as a hamper. When the room was tidy, she picked up her glass and went to check on him again.

He was still lying on his back, one arm flung out toward the empty side of the queen-size bed, the other fisted on his bare chest. A funny little shimmer of purely female appreciation ran through her at the sight of those magnificent shoulders.

At seventeen she'd never seen a more perfect example of manliness. One look and she'd wanted him to be the first to make love to her. According to one theory, sexual attraction was purely chemical, an inexplicable mix of pheromones and neural receptors. Nature's way of bonding a fertile female with a potent male. According to another, it was mystical, one soul calling to its mate. Whatever it was, it was still there, that overpowering need to be in his arms.

Instinct told her he didn't like himself very much. She suspected he hadn't liked himself for a very long time. Perhaps forever. She knew the feeling of course, but the therapy she'd undergone as part of her training had helped her cope with the guilt.

She wanted to help him, but she wasn't sure how to go about it. She wasn't sure about anything when it came to Luke. She just knew he was important to her—and not just as her doctor.

He was going to be angry when he woke up, she decided, trailing her gaze over the character lines that hadn't been part of his face at eighteen. Angry and embarrassed that she'd seen him at his most helpless.

Well, she'd been embarrassed, too, darn it. That morning in the Mallory. He'd simply bowled over her protests and went about caring for her. Two can play that game, Lucas Oliver Jarrod, she thought with a private little smile as she set the juice on the nightstand next to his beeper.

Five minutes later, wearing one of his shirts over her bra and panties, she eased herself down next to him on the bed. His lashes fluttered, and he frowned.

"Maddy?" His voice was rusty and threaded with disbelief.

"Go to sleep, Luke," she soothed, turning on her side and taking his hand in hers.

"Baby?" he muttered.

"He's fine."

His mouth moved. "Sorry...not mine."

"So am I," she murmured on a suddenly shaky breath. And then, just as he'd once done, she lifted his hand to her lips and brushed a kiss over his scarred knuckle.

He smiled then, a soft dreamy smile that should have looked odd on such a masculine face, but seemed poignantly touching, instead. "Keep you safe, sweetheart," he murmured. "Even from me."

It was then, at that moment, she realized she still loved him.

Chapter 13

Madelyn awoke to a gray morning and the steady drumming of heavy rain on the roof. Still drowsy, she experienced a moment of blank confusion before she recalled the night before.

Life in Oregon was anything but boring, she decided as she rolled to her back. Surprise shot through her when she saw that Luke was awake and watching her.

"How are you feeling?" she asked softly.

"Better."

She studied him a moment, then decided he was telling the truth. Beneath the inky stubble, his skin was still too pale, but the jagged pain splintering his eyes was gone. Exhaling in relief, she eased awkwardly to the side.

"How long have you been awake?" she asked when he continued to watch her without speaking.

"A while." The lines bracketing his mouth deepened. "You were dreaming. I was afraid to wake you."

She frowned. "How did you know?"

Silently he brought one hand to her cheek. His blunt fingertips came away wet. His jaw turned hard as he curled those strong skilled fingers into a fist against his belly.

She had been so wrong about him, she thought. Years and years wrong. A part of her grieved for all they'd missed. "It's a dream I have a lot," she admitted, stretching her legs nervously. "You were teaching Jenny to ride and she was laughing." Madelyn offered a quick smile. "Like the twins."

"I have this dream, too. She comes to me as a patient and I...turn her away. And then she..." He broke off, his jaw white, but the nightmare image was already in her head. Failing the ones he loved most was his worst fear, she realized with sudden insight.

"Don't hate yourself anymore, Luke," she pleaded. "You don't deserve it."

"You don't know how much I want to believe that." His gaze shifted to the ceiling, his face stony, his breathing quickening. His sadness was a living thing. "I don't know how to make things right, Maddy. Not for her. Not for you."

"But you did try to make things right," she said, rushing her words in an effort to reach him. "Boyd told me you came back for me."

"Man talks too much," he muttered.

She couldn't prevent a small smile. "I think he was trying to plead your case with me."

He considered that, then sighed. "It was my damn ego. I wanted to look good for my girl, so I stopped in El Paso to buy a suit. It was too tight in the chest and the tailor had to alter it. I should have just showed up in my jeans."

He sounded so disgusted she had to fight to keep from laughing. "I thought of you on my wedding night," she said, turning to her side. "My friend Emily gave me this French silk negligee with yards of lace. It was wonderfully slippery against my skin, and when I put it on, I imagined your hands slipping under all that lace—"

His head turned fast, his eyes hot. "What's really going on here, Madelyn?" he demanded, his voice barely controlled.

"I'm trying to tell you I want to make love with you again, you obstinate mule!"

Those hot needy eyes went blank, and then a hard flush took over his face. "It has to be the meds." He reached out to brush her hair away from her face with a hand that visibly trembled.

"Don't look so scared, Luke." Because she was terrified she lifted her chin and smiled. "I'm not asking you for any kind of commitment. In fact, that's exactly what I *don't* want. For the first time ever I'm free to make my own choices and live my own life. Right now, I want to find out if what I think I feel for you is real or…some leftover fantasy."

Giving in to her own repressed longings, she burrowed her fingers through the hair on his chest. The muscles beneath the sun-burnished skin rippled, beyond the control of his will. Air whooshed from her lungs as his hand whipped down to grab her wrist.

"Maddy, stop. I'm just hanging on by a thread here."

She inhaled the clean scent of his skin and her senses scrambled. "Is it your back? If it hurts, I—"

"It's not my back, damn it." His chest rose and fell

in a ragged sigh. "I desperately want to kiss you, but I can't kiss you without wanting to make love to you."

"But that's what I want, too! And I have it on the best authority that it's safe, as long as my partner is gentle." She touched his face, saw emotion flash in his eyes. "You're the gentlest man I know."

"Physically it's safe, yes, but—"

"Please, Luke. I've been so empty for so long." She pressed against him, her belly rubbing his as she arched upward. "Make love to me, Luke. Please."

He looked a little stunned. "You need to know the way it has to be, Maddy. If I kiss you, I can't deliver your baby. Even if you change your mind, I won't change mine, so if you're not sure, tell me now."

"Do you trust Dr. Winslow?"

"I do, yes." His answer came without hesitation and with his gaze steady on hers. Like a sigh the last of her reservations fell away.

"Then I won't change my mind."

Luke thought he groaned. He was pretty sure he shuddered. He framed her face with his hands and angled his head. Her gaze was intense on his, her lashes half-closed, her lips parted slightly in an invitation that would tempt a stone statue. These past weeks had taught him just how far from stone he was inside.

He drew back, breathing hard. Fumbling a little, he piled pillows behind him before drawing her into his arms. The part of him that had been missing slipped into place, and he breathed a silent heartfelt prayer as he cuddled her closer, while one hand stroked her hair.

"I never forgot, Maddy, not for one minute. Even when I told myself I had, I remembered how sweet you tasted."

He kissed her then, because nothing could stop him.

It was the kind of kiss without passion, one that he'd never given any woman but her. One that came from deep inside where he hid dreams too fragile to expose to the light. It wasn't only sex he wanted, though God knows he did. No, it was healing he sought, for them both.

She made a little sound, her hands curving over his shoulders. Her lips were moist and eager as she sought to deepen the kiss. Gladly, eagerly, he complied, shaken now by the depth of the feeling she aroused in him.

"You were always with me," he told her between kisses. "In my dreams, during the day when I thought I couldn't read one more word, digest one more fact." He stroked her cheekbone, using the back of his hand because his fingertips were too calloused to use on that soft skin.

"I dreamed about you, too," she whispered, nuzzling his hand. "A thousand times I regretted sending you away."

It hurt to realize he could have come back sooner and been welcomed. "No more regrets, Maddy. Promise me."

In answer she brought her lips to his. Like a torrent held back too long, need came rushing up from deep inside him. He felt her unfolding, little by little, letting down barriers, while his own were crashing. This was the woman who completed him, the light in his dark, the laughter in a world that had been gray and stark for such a very long time.

"Maddy," he breathed against those soft lips. "My Maddy girl." He put everything into those three words. His hopes, his remorse, a desperate longing to put laughter into those beautiful eyes again.

"Sit up, honey, and let's get you out of this shirt."

She went hot inside and out. Her body was so much older now, no longer slender and athletic the way he'd liked her. And her hips were huge. Wiley had hated her in slacks.

"You first," she said, her fingers shaking a little as she tugged nervously on the sheet. And then she remembered—he was already naked.

"Honey, you've already seen it all, what there's left of this old boy, anyway." Looking a little nervous, he rubbed his hand over his belly. "Couldn't do more than a dozen sit-ups if my life depended on it."

Madelyn ran her hand over her tummy, her lips curving. "At the moment I can't even do one."

"I love your body just the way it is, sweetheart." He undid one button, then nudged the cloth aside to kiss her shoulder. "Every adorable sexy thirty-nine-year-old inch of it." He freed another button and kissed the spot just above her nursing bra. "I love to feel your skin against my hands and I love the way your body shivers when I touch you." Another button slipped free, and he dropped a kiss on her tummy before glancing up, his gaze intense on hers. "And I love the way you're looking at me right now. Like you wish I'd hurry."

Madelyn moaned, as his hands smoothed over her belly. "Lean forward, honey," he ordered gruffly. Between kisses he rid her of her bra, then cupped her breasts in hands that brought life into the world. When she moaned, his gaze lifted to hers. "Tender?"

"A little," she whispered on a rush of pleasure.

"I'll be careful," he murmured before bending to run his tongue around each distended nipple. She dissolved then, her mind fogging until there was only his hands, his mouth. The husky words that seemed to come from deep inside.

He suckled, then stroked until she was moaning helplessly. He moved lower, stroking her belly with slow reverent movements that told her without words how much he cared. His breathing grew harsh. Sweat glistened on his skin and hers where their bodies touched.

Adrift, she felt his hands on her thighs, drawing her panties from her. And then hands were gently parting her legs. The bed dipped as he changed position. He touched her gently, then slipped a finger inside her, drawing a moan from her as she writhed, and then his mouth was there, kissing her intimately, deeply. Sensation after sensation rolled over her, each one more delicious than the one before.

She felt the tremors start, then bunch. Her hands turned frantic, clutching and twisting the sheet beneath her. Just when she knew she would go mad with wanting, she exploded, ripple after ripple of the sweetest heat moving through her body. It was then he replaced his mouth with his hand, taking her up and over again until she was all but sobbing with the sheer joy of it.

"Open your eyes, honey," he ordered, his voice harsh with strain. Her lids fluttered, then opened. He was on his knees positioning himself between her spread legs. His body was fully aroused—and only a short fast thrust from penetrating hers.

"Oh, my," she whispered. "Did I do that?"

His laugh was surprisingly boyish as he slipped his hands under her buttocks to gently lift her. "Nobody else, honey." Anticipation was a fever in her blood, and she writhed impatiently.

His gaze on hers, he leaned forward, probing gently.

"Feel how much I want you," he whispered fiercely. He was so large that for a moment she was frightened. Determined to give him pleasure for pleasure, however, she braced herself for the intrusion. But instead of thrusting inside her, he merely rubbed himself against the sensitive nub—hard friction against soft moist heat—until she felt herself climbing again.

This time she cried out as she splintered, then sobbed his name. Breathing hard, he lowered her gently and bent to kiss her. Her eyes closed and she felt herself floating.

"Sleep, sweetheart," he whispered before brushing a kiss across her parted lips. She made an incoherent sound, then smiled as she felt him draw the sheet over her. She thought he whispered something more, something her subconscious struggled to hold. And then she slept.

Water bubbled and swirled around his naked body, and soap-scented steam soaked little by little into his pores, slowly loosening the tension trapped in just about every muscle of his body.

When he'd left the bedroom, he'd been so aroused it had been all he could do to get himself into the tub without groaning. It still amazed him that he'd been able to stop himself from burying his ache deep inside her. But he'd wanted her too much to risk surrendering control.

Until this moment he thought he knew all there was to know about living with mistakes, the kind that make a man's gut burn at odd moments and turn his nights into a minefield of guilty regrets and painful longings.

He'd been wrong. In the hour since he'd left her curled up like a sated kitten, he'd come to realize just how much this mistake was going to cost him if she left him. For starters, a large chunk of what little peace of mind he'd managed to carve out for himself.

One kiss and he'd been hers again. Mind, body and soul. He wanted it all now, a home she would fill with her own personal brand of sunshine, instead of a house on the hill where he kept his clothes and slept when he wasn't working. A little boy they would raise together. A real family of his own, instead of borrowed moments with someone else's sons and daughters.

A life, instead of an existence.

It was part of his nature to ride full out in any contest, using every ounce of determination in his psyche to get what he wanted. This time, though, the choice had to be hers. Still, he figured it was only fair to show her all the reasons she should choose him.

Problem was, wooing a lady gently wasn't one of the skills he'd acquired over the years. During the years he'd been slogging through one school after another, what free time he'd had was usually spent sleeping.

Occasionally, when loneliness had driven him to seek out a few hours of feminine companionship, he'd simply walked into a student hangout and sat on a bar stool. Sometimes he found a lady who had more to offer than bright chatter and a sexy body, sometimes he didn't. Either way, he'd always been scrupulous about his intentions. No promises, no expectations. It was the same with the few relationships he'd had during the past few years. Whenever the lady in his life had gotten that nesting look, he'd extricated himself as gently as possible. With Maddy, however, he wanted strings and commitment and a lifetime of being tied to her.

Damn funny how life worked, he thought as he eased

forward to stretch muscles one twitch away from knotting tight again. When she'd wanted him, he'd run. Now, when he wanted her more than he wanted to take that next breath, she wanted freedom.

It would cost him, but he'd let her call the shots. For now.

Madelyn awoke to the delicious smell of coffee and a sweet lethargy that made her want to purr. Rolling onto her back, she yawned, then yelped as the baby gave her a vicious one-two punch.

"Gave you a kick, did he?"

She glanced up to find Luke standing in the doorway. Her heart tumbled. "Six points at least."

His gaze roamed her face, his eyes guarded. Clean shaven now and his hair brushed into rough order, he was fully dressed in jeans and a blue-and-white plaid shirt, tucked neatly into the low slung waistband.

"Would coffee help?" he asked, holding up the mug in his hand. She felt a little giddy, knowing that this honorable man wanted her.

"Would whimpering get it into my hand any sooner?"

"No, but a good morning kiss would help."

"Then rustle those studly buns, cowboy."

His grin was an endearing mix of cocky and shy. "Yes, ma'am."

It took two tries but she managed to push and wriggle herself into a sitting position by the time he reached her. His free hand cupped the back of her head as she lifted her face up to his, her heart already racing.

"Good morning again, gorgeous lady," he murmured before his mouth covered his. His lips were warm and hungry. She tasted need and impatience and a steely strength. Sensation spiraled in a slow unfolding tendril all the way to her womb. She dug her fingers into the thick unyielding muscle of his forearm. When he drew back, she wanted to beg for more.

"Tastes good," she said, instead.

"I'll say." This time his hand closed into a fist in her hair. This time his mouth was avid and demanding. She felt herself opening, her hunger matching his. He drew back finally, his eyes dark between even darker lashes. His eyes glittered as he handed her the mug, then wrapped her other hand around it securely.

"I'd planned to take you to lunch, but I just got a call. Sally Pritchard's contractions are five minutes apart." He glanced at his watch. "How about dinner, instead?"

Knowing her expression mirrored the disappointment she felt, she shook her head. "Case is planning to surprise Prudy with dinner at the new seafood place in Lake Oswego, and I promised to baby-sit Chloe and Lily." She blew away steam, then took a desperate sip. Feeling slightly more human, she watched him fill his pockets before strapping on his watch. It was then she had a sudden thought. "I'm free Saturday night, if you are."

He sent her one of those bone-melting grins before coming over to give her another long mind-scrambling kiss. "You got yourself a date, sweetheart." He got to his feet again and headed for the door.

"Drive carefully," he ordered gruffly. Though he moved stiffly, she was relieved to see that he wasn't limping.

At the door, he paused and turned to look at her. "One more thing, darlin', I surely do love the way you look sittin' there naked in the middle of my bed."

She uttered a little squeak when she realized the sheet had slipped down to her waist. Her blush started at her toes and ran like a fever all the way to her hairline. He was laughing when he left.

Precious was waiting by the back door when Madelyn let herself in a few minutes past nine. The reproachful look in the exotic green eyes had her giggling out loud.

"Mama's sorry, darling. She didn't mean to abandon you."

In reply Precious trotted to the spot at the end of the counter where the two dishes bearing her name in raised letters stood side by side. After staring disdainfully at the one that was supposed to be full of food by now, she looked up to meow piteously.

"No, you are not starving and you know it," Madelyn informed her firmly. Precious blinked, then twitched her tail and tried a growl.

Madelyn grinned, enjoying the game they'd played for weeks now. "You know what, Precious? You're just like a certain cowboy I know. Scared to death someone will find out what a softie you really are."

After putting her purse on the counter, she slipped out of the slicker that had come nearly to her toes and folded it carefully over one of the chairs. Then she fetched a can of the designer cat food Harriet had specified in the list of instructions she'd left.

A rumbling purr filled the kitchen as Precious dug in, attacking the feline version of chicken liver pâté as though she'd been stuck in a tree for a week.

Though Madelyn had made herself a peanut-butter-and-jelly sandwich before leaving Luke's place, he'd been out of juice. After pouring herself a glass, she opened the curtains and stood watching the rain as she sipped. Above the lush crown of maple leaves the sky was a solid gunmetal gray without even a hint of blue.

Monday was her day to help out at the preschool where Morgana, Lily and Shelby were enrolled, and the children tended to act up when they were stuck inside. On Tuesdays and Thursdays she volunteered at the hospital as a pink lady. Wednesdays she baby-sat for the twins while Raine took a mental-health day. Reminding herself to visit the video store this afternoon while she was out shopping for groceries, she went to check her messages.

The first message was from Raine wanting to know about Luke's condition. The second was from Case asking if she could come an hour earlier than they agreed with a P.S. asking her to let them know about Luke. The third and fourth calls were hang-ups, something that had happened several times in the past few days. The last message had her heart racing.

"Hi, little Buddha, just wonderin' if you got home okay." Surprisingly husky, Luke's drawl curled down inside her and warmed her heart. "It's eight-forty-seven and I'm still at the hospital, waitin' for the newest little Pritchard to make his appearance. Appreciate a call when you get home, okay? Extension here is 462." There was a pause before he added in a surprisingly shy tone, "I sure do miss kissin' you, honey."

Her good mood restored, she flipped through the book for the number of the hospital switchboard, then dialed. Jarred a little by the operator's Southern accent, Madelyn realized she'd gotten used to the hard Yankee consonants and clipped way of speaking.

"Maternity, Mrs. Klein."

"Dr. Jarrod, please."

"I'm sorry. Doctor's unavailable." There was a brief pause. "Is this Mrs. Foster?"

"Why, yes, ma'am, it is."

The voice warmed. "Doctor asked me to remind you to call Dr. Winslow's office for an appointment first thing tomorrow morning. Said you'd understand why that was so important."

It was still raining at four on Saturday as Madelyn sat at the kitchen table reading over the settlement papers that had arrived late Friday afternoon by express mail. According to her attorney, Jorge Cruz, dealing with Judge Berdette had been akin to walking through a roomful of rattlers blindfolded. Clearly worried, he'd advised her to sign the papers immediately, then overnight them back to him so that he could get them filed as soon as possible.

She'd just reached for her pen when the phone rang.

Luke had called twice this week, but he'd been rushed and their conversations had been short. Heart speeding, she reached for the portable and punched the button.

It was her mother. "Seems to me a woman who's trying to have her a healthy baby wouldn't be out gallivanting at all hours," Rebecca said without preamble.

Closing her eyes, Madelyn sent up a little prayer for patience before saying pleasantly, "I'm sorry I missed your call but I was baby-sitting for a friend. If you'd left a message, I would have called back as soon as I got home."

"You know I hate talking to those machines, girl." Her mama's sigh was long-suffering. Madelyn realized she no longer felt the familiar pinch of conscience that usually accompanied one of her mother's complaints, and she smiled to herself. Could it be she was finally developing a backbone? "How's daddy's arthritis?" she asked politely.

"Worse than ever. Doc Morrow's getting senile, if you ask me. Telling your daddy he needs to move around more, instead of taking it easy the way anyone with sense knows you have to do when your joints are swollen up."

"Doc does have a point, Mama."

"There you go again, defendin' that old quack."

"You didn't think he was a quack when he agreed with you about my giving up my baby," she said a little too sharply.

Her mother's indrawn breath was like a slap. It was on the tip of Madelyn's tongue to apologize, but she caught herself before the words spilled out. Why should she apologize for defending a friend? "In case you're interested, Mama, I'm feeling fine, and so is the baby. It's a boy, by the way."

The silence that followed seemed hours long, but suddenly Madelyn didn't care whether her parents accepted her child or not.

"Does Wiley Roy know?" her mama said finally, an unnatural edge to her voice.

"No. I haven't spoken to him since the night after I arrived in Oregon."

There was another silence, shorter this time and followed by a heavy sigh. "I thought he mighta called with the news, but I guess it's up to me to tell you."

"Tell me what, Mama?"

"Wiley Roy's gone and asked Arletta Tremaine to marry him."

This time Madelyn was struck dumb. The youngest daughter of one of Wiley's golfing buddies, Arletta was scarcely twenty-five, if that. According to Wiley himself, she was the biggest airhead that ever stepped onto the first tee at the country club. The fact that she had implants the size of grapefruits and a tendency to giggle adoringly at his corny jokes no doubt prompted Wiley's change of heart.

"Seems to me I heard Arletta talking once about how she wanted six children."

"Guess it don't matter none, since Wiley went and got himself a vasectomy a few weeks back."

"I hope he told Arletta."

"Well, of course he did, Maddy Sue. Wiley's a gentleman."

"If you say so, Mama," she said.

"Oh, I almost forgot," her mama said just as Madelyn opened her mouth to make an excuse to hang up. "I got me a call yesterday from some girl by the name of Tricia Wilson. She said she was a friend of yours from college and stopped by on her way to Dallas to talk to you about some alumni thing or other. Miz Barlow saw her on your porch and told her about you being gone to Portland for two more months. Seems this Tricia was real anxious to get in touch with you, so Miz Barlow gave her my number here at the house."

Madelyn searched her mind and came up blank. "There was a Patricia Alden who lived down the hall from me my senior year. We called her Trish sometimes. Maybe Wilson is her married name." Madelyn tried in vain to remember the girl's face. "Did you get her number?"

"No, she said she was traveling, so I gave her yours."

Madelyn remembered the hang-ups on her machine and wondered. "No sense worrying about it, I guess."

She glanced down at the papers bearing Wiley's signature and wondered if Arletta would be able to make him happy.

"If you talk to Wiley, give him my best wishes," she said, meaning it.

After calling her a double-dyed fool for letting such a good man get away, her mama hung up.

Slumped wearily in front of the nurses' station, Luke scrawled his initials next to a change in meds for Carrie Denney before handing the chart back to charge nurse Margot Stanley.

"Is that a four or a seven?" she asked, stabbing her pen at one of his scribbles.

"Seven." After thirty-eight hours without sleep during which he'd seen three mommies through to delivery, he was damn lucky he could hold a pen.

"Full moon this weekend," Stanley said as she filed the chart. "Thank goodness I'm off."

"Me, too."

"Uh-huh."

"Honest. Winslow's covering."

"Winslow should have her head examined." At the sound of a sultry female voice Luke turned to find Karen Winslow approaching, looking as chic as a model in her surgical scrubs. "Can I buy you a cup of coffee, Doctor?" she asked after exchanging greetings with Stanley.

"Guess you can, yeah."

Straightening took effort. Walking without a limp took more. Luke managed both, but he knew he was running out of time.

"I tried to return your call earlier, but you were delivering a baby, and then I was,'' she explained as they walked toward the elevators at the end of the corridor.

"Mama of twins decided to deliver early." Passing the nursery, Luke smiled at a proud grandpa making faces through the window at a little redheaded darlin' in a bassinet.

"I heard it was fairly dicey for a while."

Luke didn't want to think about how close they'd come to losing a very special lady—and the babies she'd risked her life to carry. "Mama has a history of heart problems."

"How's mommy doing?" Winslow asked as he punched the elevator button.

"Sleeping. Babies are in the neonatal intensive care unit. Paul Melendez thinks they'll make it." The elevator doors opened and a tech pushing a patient in a wheelchair exited.

"I assume you called about Mrs. Foster?" Winslow asked as they stepped together into the car.

"Yeah." Luke punched the button for the basement, then braced his back against the wall. "I think it's only fair I tell you this case is…a little complicated."

Winslow's tired gray eyes gleamed with sudden speculation. "You're involved?"

"Guess we are, but only after she made it clear I was no longer her doctor." He met her curious gaze steadily. "You have my word."

"I never doubted that for a moment, Luke." She smiled. "I'll take good care of her for you. You have *my* word on that."

"I appreciate it." The car jolted to a stop and they stepped out.

Five minutes later they were settled at one of the tables in the cafeteria. "Just to be sure, I did another

ultrasound, but nothing's changed since the last one,''
Winslow said before digging into her cherry pie.

Luke toyed with the heavy mug and wondered how
to phrase his next question. Finally he gave a mental
shrug and went with his gut. "Don't take this wrong,
okay, but I want your word on something else, too."

She glanced up, her fork poised halfway to her
mouth. "What's that?"

"That if you detect the slightest hint of a problem,
you'll call me so we can talk about it."

"Certainly, Doctor." Her gaze cooled, and he cursed
the lack of tact that had gotten him in trouble more
than once.

"Karen, it's not that I doubt your professional judgment. Just the opposite, but I've had eight or nine more
years of experience. And the signs of potential trouble
are tough to spot, even for me."

Her gaze turned thoughtful. "Would it ease your
mind if I faxed you my examination notes after each
visit?"

"Guess it would, yeah. Thanks."

She took a bite, swallowed, then gave him a com-
miserating look. "It's hell being on the other side, isn't
it, Doctor?"

He laughed. "Pure misery, darlin', and that's a
fact."

Chapter 14

"If L.J. misses *this* party, I'm going to brain him with that huge historical novel we bought him, wrapping and all," Prudy declared as she glanced at the clock. It was nearly four. Luke was due at seven.

"I haven't heard from him since Wednesday morning," Madelyn admitted before licking icing from her finger.

Raine glanced up from the canapés she was arranging on her mother's silver tray. "Maybe he's scared."

"Of what?" Madelyn scoffed. "Certainly not of rejection. I practically threw myself at him."

"Boyd ran away from me for a while," Stacy said as she placed a tray of cold cuts in Madelyn's fridge. "He was afraid he hadn't laid his demons to rest and didn't want to hurt me. Maybe Luke feels the same way."

Raine nodded. "It makes sense. After we lost Mike,

Morgan felt so guilty he withdrew into his work so he wouldn't have to feel.''

Surprised, Madelyn glanced up. "Mike?" she asked.

"I was pregnant when Morgan and I married. Our son died in a skiing accident when he was eight. Morgan blamed himself because he'd canceled out on the trip at the last minute."

"I'm so sorry," Madelyn said softly.

Raine smiled. "He told me later the hurt was so bad he couldn't deal with it, so he exhausted himself with work."

"You have to admit Luke is a workaholic," Prudy contributed helpfully.

"And he does feel guilty," Raine added. "It's in his eyes every time he sees you with one of the kids."

"When Boyd told me Luke had gone back for me, I thought…well, you know what I thought," Madelyn muttered, slathering icing on the cake.

Stacy smiled. "That he loved you."

"A logical conclusion," Prudy added, waving celery.

"I'd put money on it," Raine declared before carrying plates into the dining room.

"Maybe then, but I'm not so sure now."

"Could be he wants more than sex this time," Prudy offered before taking a bite.

"That's just it! I'm not sure what I want, but if we never spend time together, how will I ever find out?"

"Now that you've officially become Dr. Winslow's patient, he's free to court you." Raine glanced pointedly at the bouquet of white carnations on the kitchen table.

"The card just said thanks for taking care of him," Madelyn complained, but her face softened.

"He invited you to dinner," Stacy reminded her.

Madelyn stared at the swirls of chocolate decorating the cake. "Why do I think I'm making a terrible mistake?"

"Because you're scared, too," Prudy declared firmly. "Love's like that. One minute you're floating on this pink cloud, the next you're terrifed and looking for reasons to run away."

"I see the Jeep," Chloe said, turning away from Madelyn's front window, her eyes shining. This time it looked as though they'd actually get to have a party.

"Okay, everyone out of sight," Madelyn ordered, her stomach fluttering.

The four little girls giggled as they raced into the spare bedroom. Prudy and Raine joined Stacy and Boyd in Madelyn's bedroom where they'd gone to change B.J. Grinning, Don gave her a quick hug for luck before shambling after the girls.

By the time the doorbell rang, Madelyn was alone in the living room, wishing fervently she'd never come up with the surprise-party idea. All week long she'd looked forward to seeing Luke again. Now she was going to have to share him with a houseful of people.

Second time's a charm, she told herself as she straightened her long-sleeved silk tunic and walked to the door. Harriet's grandmother clock began chiming seven.

Luke stood on the doorstep, his face half-hidden by the brim of a dove-gray dress Stetson hat. Instead of the faded cotton shirt and jeans worn paper thin at the stress points, he wore a navy blazer skillfully tailored to accommodate his wider-than-average shoulders, and tan sharply creased slacks that broke perfectly over highly polished dress boots. Beneath the blazer, he wore a crisp pale-blue shirt, which was open at the throat to reveal the dark chest hair that had tickled her nose.

"Your date's here, ma'am," he drawled as he removed his hat and ran one big impatient hand through his glossy hair. It was a familiar gesture, one she'd stored away, then made herself forget.

"And right on time," she said when her senses stopped jangling. "I'm impressed."

His gaze swept over her briefly before it returned to her face. It wasn't a brazen look, and yet Madelyn was painfully aware of her nipples hardening and tingling inside her bra.

His mouth slanted. "I'm thinking I'd better stop off and buy me a tie before dinner."

"Are you saying I'm overdressed?" she asked, glancing down at the lavender shirt and conservative navy skirt that was a decent inch below her knees.

"Guess I have to admit to bein' partial to the way you looked sitting in my bed, but I like you all polished up, too. Although I gotta admit it intimidates the heck out of me." He was teasing of course, she realized, considering the obviously expensive clothes and glossy black boots that must have cost more than her entire outfit.

Wiley had been a fanatic about always buying the best. It gave her a small jolt of satisfaction to realize that Wiley's shoulders never filled out a classic blue blazer the way Luke's did.

"Come on in while I get my purse." She stepped back and he followed. She heard a muffled giggle, and his head came up.

"Was that the cat?"

"No, uh, actually—"

"Surprise!"

"Happy birthday, Uncle Luke."

The room was suddenly filled with children, shouting and laughing. Luke froze, then went pale. "Was this your idea?" he asked as the twins tried to climb his legs.

She nodded. "Are you angry?"

Instead of answering, he hooked one hand around her neck, leaned down and kissed her until her toes were curling and her blood sizzled. She swayed a little when he let her go.

The room broke into wild applause, and she blushed.

"Not bad, hoss," Boyd said, grinning. "For an old guy."

Don Petrov left at ten. He was the last. Before the others had left, the ladies had made her promise to leave everything until tomorrow, and she'd meant to do just that. But as soon as she and Luke were alone, she was so nervous she couldn't sit still. "I think I'll just tidy up—"

He caught her before she took more than two steps, swinging her into his arms. "Not a chance, darlin'. I've been waitin' all night to have you to myself again."

One hand dove into her hair at the same time his mouth came down on hers. Her senses scrambled and her bones melted. She tasted chocolate and a lonely man's need before he drew back. Unsteady on her feet, she clung to him, her belly tucked hard against his. His grin was a little crooked as he smoothed back the hair his hands had made into a tousled mane.

"Don't get me wrong, honey—the party was damn near perfect, but I thought it would never end."

"Is that why you tore into your presents like one of the twins on a rampage?"

The look he gave her held a touch of that same boyish devilment. "Nah, that was pure greed."

A laugh bubbled up in her throat. "I was so afraid you'd get a call and have to leave."

"Not a chance. I had Winslow cover me tonight."

She blinked. "But you thought it was just dinner."

"Dinner with you, Maddy. Nothing is more important than that." He linked his arms around her and bumped his belly against hers. He'd taken off his jacket and rolled his sleeves. "How's baby tonight?"

"Worn-out from all the partying," she said with a laugh.

"How about Mama? Is she worn-out, too?" Though teasing, his voice held a note of concern.

"More like sleepy. I tend to fade with the sun these days."

Frowning, he ran a measuring gaze over her face. "Then I'd better get out of here so you and baby can get some sleep."

She drew a shaky breath. "Not before you unwrap my present."

"I thought the party was your present."

She shook her head. She felt a little giddy as she took his hand and moved it to the top button of her silk tunic. "Start here." She'd tried so hard to make her voice into a sexy purr. Instead, it wobbled. Feeling like a perfect idiot, she gave a little cry and buried her hot cheek against his shoulder.

"I'm terrible at this," she muttered against the unyielding muscle.

He choked a laugh. "Sweetheart, if you were any more terrible, I'd be dead."

She groaned. "I'm sorry."

"I'm not." As though to prove his point, he took her hand in his and pressed it to the hard ridge of his arousal. "That's how much I like your present, sweetheart."

Emotions flashed through her mind until she was a little dizzy. It was pure bliss, having this strong man turning to putty because of her.

"I can't seem to stop wanting you," she whispered helplessly. "Is that wrong?"

His eyes went dark. "Not where I'm standing." His mouth aligned with hers, came down softly. Her lips were ready, aching. His kiss was gentle, yet edged with fire ready to kindle.

"Definitely sweet." He nibbled at her lips, pushing the tip of his tongue into the corner of her mouth, then withdrawing it, teasing her, tantalizing her, finally deepening the kiss until her senses reeled.

She liked the feel of his big hard body rubbing slowly against hers, caressing her, provoking her, and she loved the feel of his hands stroking her arms, her breasts, her belly. Heat rocketed through her, and she rubbed against him, letting his chest abrade her nipples until the tiny peaks turned hard and aching.

She let out a gasp of pleasure, delighting in the shower of sensations. Heat and chill, throbbing pulse and bone-melting sighs. Her body began to hum and then to vibrate with a primitive force, and she ran her hands over his shoulders and down his arms.

Between kisses, he stripped her of the silk tunic. His muscles bunched as he stripped off his own shirt and unbuckled his belt. Caught up in her urgency, she unfastened her bra and tossed it aside. Impatient now, they finished undressing quickly.

His eyes glittered as he watched her. "You take my breath away," he whispered, his hands reverent as they caressed her belly. Arching upward, she pressed against him, her mouth seeking his. He moaned, then kissed her passionately and deeply before breaking off to scoop her up into his arms.

"Luke, your back!" she protested as he swung her around.

He bent his head and kissed the curve of one breast before asking, "Which way to your bedroom?"

"Through the hall to the right."

She buried her face in his throat and felt the rapid throbbing of his pulse against her cheek.

"Boy, howdy, look at that!" he said when he caught sight of Harriet's canopy bed. "Can't imagine any man with blood in his veins sleeping in a bed with ruffles on the pillows and shiny beads hanging over his head."

"They're seed pearls," she said with a nervous smile. "When you look up, they...they shimmer in the moonlight like little stars."

"I still say it'd be plum embarrassin' for a man to have him a heart attack and have to lay there until the paramedics came, knowing what they'd see when they got there," he teased as he reached down with one hand to jerk back the embroidered coverlet.

He kissed her again, slowly this time before lowering her to the soft feather tick. The bed dipped as he joined her. And then he was kissing her some more. Her lips, her eyelids, her earlobes. His hands smoothed over her, finding every curve, every pulse point, every singing nerve ending until she was nearly crazy with wanting him. She moved restlessly, her hands reaching for him, urging him to fill her.

"Easy, honey," Luke whispered, his own needs

tearing at him like a wild thing. Gently, tenderly, he cupped his hand over the mound between her legs, kneading and stroking until she arched upward, crying out, her eyes flying open, then glazing over with a stunned pleasure.

Even as she shuddered, he braced his weight on his hands and eased the tip of his shaft into her slowly, allowing himself only a few inches of pleasure, watching her face, her eyes, the trembling of her soft lips as she murmured his name.

"Is it good?" he asked, desperate to please her.

"Yes," she whispered, her voice thick.

Slowly he began to move, fighting a clawing need to take his own pleasure in one hard pounding thrust. Instead, teeth gritted, he rocked back and forth against the velvet walls sheathing him. She writhed, then sobbed, her hands clutching at his straining arms.

He felt the little tremor start deep inside her. Her eyes flew open, shining and stunned. "Come inside me. I want to feel you inside me."

Carefully he pushed deeper, watching her face for signs of pain. But it was only pleasure he saw as her head arched back. His desire rose in a hot punishing wave, but still he held back, his harsh breaths rasping through the quiet room. She was moaning and tossing her head from side to side. She was slicker now, and he risked another slow thrust.

She arched against him, her belly gloriously exposed. He moved his hand to the place where her body and his joined, rubbing rhythmically while his own need clawed deep. With one final controlled movement, he tipped her over and then, while her body still pulsed against his, gave himself to her.

Chapter 15

The rodeo was noisy and dusty and hot. Flags flew from the top of the grandstand and at intervals around the dirt ring. The air smelled of horses and humanity and, now and then, when the wind gusted, well-oiled leather.

Luke had been tied up at the hospital until noon, so they arrived after the events had started. Their seats were dead center in the covered section of the grandstand and close enough to the action to see the contestants grimace when something went wrong or grin when it went right.

After explaining that he'd missed breakfast, he'd eaten his way through three hot dogs to her one. Between bites, he'd kept up a running commentary on the calf roping and barrel racing, even predicting the scores within a point or two.

The stands were packed with moms and dads and kids enjoying the fresh air and sunshine—and each other. Almost everyone wore a cowboy hat, many purchased from one of the stands set up outside the grandstand.

Luke's, too, was regulation rodeo, a white straw Stetson with a narrow black ribbon band, well seasoned and shaped perfectly. She thought it was just about the sexiest hat she'd ever seen.

Pretty much like always, he was dressed in a plaid shirt with the sleeves rolled tight against his biceps and his usual Wrangler that hugged his butt and tested the heavy zipper. Instead of a number pinned to the shirt, however, he wore a butter-soft buckskin vest. Her heart had tumbled when she'd seen him, then tumbled harder when he'd lifted her off her feet for a long slow sensual kiss.

Every time she was with him he went out of his way to touch her hand or stroke her hair or catch her up for a hug. It was as though the two of them were starting over fresh, without guilt or shame or even any expectations today. By tacit agreement, neither spoke of the past. Or the future. What they had now was the moment.

When he'd asked her to go with him to the rodeo, she'd been afraid it would stir up bad memories. It had been precisely because she'd been afraid that she'd accepted. For too many years she'd let fear rule her life. Fear of disappointing her parents again. Fear that she wouldn't measure up to Wiley's image of the perfect wife. Being afraid had made her prissy and boring and…just plain dull.

Her lips curved as he nudged his hard thigh closer to hers. "View's different from up here," he said.

She shifted her gaze from the ring where the last of

the barrel racers had just finished. "Better different or worse different?"

"Close up, a whole lot better." His grin flashed. "Smells nicer, too." He leaned closer to inhale her scent. "Makes a man want to beg." He nuzzled her ear until she shivered, then drew back, looking a little cocky. "Can't look up the ladies' skirts from here, though."

She gave him a punch on his biceps. It was like hitting rock, and her knuckles sang. "Watch it, buster. I'm the jealous sort, you know."

His eyes crinkled. "Seems to me I remember your head turnin' a time or two when a good lookin' cowboy walked by."

"What can I say? I can't resist a tight pair of buns in a tight pair of jeans." She leaned closer, rubbing her arm against his. "Do you know what I want to do then?"

The look he gave her was pure heat. "Careful, darlin', this is a public place."

"I want to take a great big bite out of one of those buns."

He made a strangled noise in his throat. "Tonight, in that sissy bed of yours, you can bite me all you want, sweetheart. Wouldn't mind a lick or two, either, were you to be so inclined again."

Now it was her turn to choke. The last time he'd stayed over, she'd given in to the fantasy she'd had at the Mallory and explored him with her hands and her tongue. His reaction then had been both vascular and personal.

Heat suffused her as the public address system crackled to life again. "All right, folks," the announcer boomed, "this next event is a battle of horse and rider to see who's boss. For those of you new to rodeo, we have us two judges up here in the booth, and they're going to be rating both the animal and the contestant on a scale of one to twenty-five. Perfect score is one hundred, which, folks, is not real easy to come by.'' He went on to explain that points were given for the cowboy's use of the blunted rowels of his spurs and the amount of fight he can generate in his mount.

"So the harder the horse fights to buck you off, the better it is," she guessed aloud.

Luke nodded. "That's about the way of it, yeah. Since he's bigger and stronger and a whole lot faster, the trick is figuring which way he's goin' to twist a split second before he does it."

"Have you ever gotten a perfect score?" she asked as he took another bite of his hot dog.

"Twice," he admitted after swallowing. "First time was Christmas and a half-dozen birthdays rolled into one. Second time was just Christmas."

She reached up to wipe a speck of mustard from his lower lip, and he nipped her finger with his strong white teeth before sucking on the pad. "Behave yourself," she ordered as his eyes turned dark.

"Now that's not gonna be easy, darlin', considering the way you and baby fill out that shirt." The naked desire in his eyes sent little shivers running over her skin. Every time they were together she fell more in love. For his part, he never mentioned the word, but several times, when she'd turned quickly enough to catch him off guard, he'd been looking at her in a way that made her think he wanted more than a temporary affair.

"Number forty-two's gonna start this out for us today, folks,"

Though leaner than Luke had been at eighteen, the man climbing the rails of the chute had the same swaggering moves and cocky grin as he slung his legs over the top rail, then glanced up at the announcer's booth.

"Cody Gresham comes to us from Stockton, California, the third Gresham brother to compete in this event. This is his first year on the circuit, by the way, so give him an encouraging hand, won't you?"

The crowd responded, whooping and whistling when the young man waved his hat and grinned.

"Kid's not gonna make it much past a second or two," Luke predicted.

Eyes shaded by the straw hat with the pink ostrich plume he'd bought her on the way in, Madelyn studied the lanky young man with the number forty-two pinned to his shirt while the handlers struggled to calm a reddish-brown horse with a black mane and tail.

"He looks pretty confident to me," she reflected aloud.

"See the way he's jokin' with the guys hanging around the chute?" Luke said.

She nodded. "Whatever he's saying it must be funny."

"Point is, he should be pullin' inside, instead of playin' to the crowd."

She turned to look at him. Beneath the brim of his hat, his face was surprisingly relaxed, even boyish. "Is that what you did—pull inside?"

"After I got tired of spitting out arena dirt and nursing bruises, yeah."

She remembered that moment vividly, she realized now. Right up until the minute he'd slipped his arm from around her shoulders in order to ready himself for his ride, he'd been incredibly loving, his grin a lazy slash against his deep tan and his eyes filled with devilment. The instant he strapped on his chaps, however, he'd been as cool as ice, his jaw hard and his eyes narrowed.

There'd been a wildness in his eyes then that had fascinated her even more than it frightened her. It was the same wildness she'd seen in the eye of the horse in that frozen instant when Luke had lowered himself into the rigging. Both would resist taming. Both would fight to the death before surrendering. And yet, only one would win. It was that same fierce drive to win she suspected he brought to the practice of medicine.

The chute opened then, and the horse shot out as though jet-propelled, all four legs a good two feet off the ground. Screaming in fury, he twisted and spun, desperate to rid himself of the unfamiliar weight.

Arm reaching for sky, head down, the rider struggled to hang on. The crowd roared encouragement as he raked the bronc with his spurs. On the edge of her seat, Madelyn clutched Luke's arm and used her own body language to help the young rider.

"Kid just lost his seat," Luke predicted an instant before the cowboy went sailing over the bay's head. A collective groan went up as the contestant hit the dirt hard, then rolled, trying to escape the flashing hooves. He almost made it and then, at the last minute, one hoof clipped his shoulder. He collapsed in a heap like a rag doll.

Digging her nails into Luke's forearm, Madelyn bit her lip as a silence spread out in a ragged wave. Paramedics raced toward the downed cowboy. It was only when Luke's hand covered hers that she realized she was biting her lip.

"My guess would be a broken clavicle. Coupla

weeks and he'll be ridin' again—and most likely makin' the same mistake.''

She exhaled slowly as the cowboy waved the white-clad medics away before struggling to his feet on his own. Holding his arm tight against his belly, he limped toward the side of the ring.

"Macho idiot," she muttered as a cheer went up.

"Man doesn't have a choice if he doesn't want to be tagged a wimp for the rest of his career."

"Oh, for heaven's sake," she began, only to have Luke duck under the brim of her hat to give her a imperious kiss. She lost her ability to breathe, then couldn't seem to breathe enough. She loved the way he was always touching her or kissing her.

"You have a soft heart, sweetheart," he said with a grin as the announcer assured the crowd that Gresham was suffering nothing more serious than a "busted collarbone."

She burst out laughing at the smug look he slanted her. "Is that what you did—sit up and swagger off when you were hurt so badly that last time?"

His jaw went hard and a shadow crossed his face before his grin flashed, the one that said it was no big deal. "Nah, I just lay there and bawled."

She didn't believe that for a minute. She also knew he'd never admit how terrified he must have been at the thought of never walking again. She shivered a little.

"You okay?" he asked, his hand on hers.

She smiled. "I'm very okay," she said. "In fact, I'm having a wonderful time."

"Folks," the announcer said, "this pretty bay mare up next comes all the way from Mehan Brothers Ranch in Durango, Colorado. Goes by the name of Misty, which is a right pretty name, but I have it on good authority from Buck Mehan himself she's just about the meanest little lady he's ever seen—and you folks who are personally acquainted with Buck know he's a real expert on females of all persuasions.''

Laughter rippled. Luke tugged his hat a little lower, hiding a grin, she realized.

"Ridin' Misty today is last year's grand champion, Derek Rainwater.''

A cheer went up, followed by a buzz of anticipation. Madelyn gave Luke a curious look. "Is he talking about your friend Buck?''

Luke nodded. "About a year after I left the circuit, he lost a leg when his mount fell on him.''

"Is he the one who got you the tickets?''

"Yep. Had to promise to have a drink with him later to get 'em, though—unless you have a problem with that.''

She considered, then shook her head. "I liked Buck—even if he did try to seduce me on the dance floor.''

Buck met them at the main gate about a half hour after the las'. event ended, ambling toward them with a slightly unsteady gate that aroused Madelyn's protective instincts. His weathered face creased into wide grin as he approached, his gaze taking in the possessive arm Luke had slung over her shoulders.

"Now that's a right satisfyin' sight, you two together again.'' His voice reflected thirty years of a pack-a-day habit, but his brown eyes twinkled with genuine delight as he held out his hand.

Luke slid his arm from her shoulders and stepped forward, putting his body between her and his old friend. Instead of shaking Buck's hand, however, he dropped the man with a quick left jab to the jaw. It happened so fast she didn't even have time to gasp. One minute the grizzled cowhand was standing with his feet planted wide, the next he was sprawled on his backside, a dazed look on his face.

"That's for puttin' the make on my lady, you horny SOB," Luke drawled as Buck tested his jaw for cracks.

"Heckfire, son, that was more'n twenty years ago and I was half-drunk."

"Maybe, but I'll drop you again if you so much as twitch in her direction," Luke warned as he extended a hand to help the older man to his feet.

Buck staggered a little before finding his balance. Luke's expression didn't change, but Madelyn saw him shift to the balls of his feet, just in case Buck started to topple.

"No offense, ma'am," Buck said, sweeping off the straw hat that had stayed glued to his head, even as it had snapped back hard.

"None taken." She smiled ruefully. "I never would have mentioned it if I'd known he'd take it personally."

Buck's grin was slow coming and a little off kilter. "Tell you the truth, ma'am, it was worth a sore jaw to see hoss here all fired up again. Last time him and me were together, he was flat on his back and half-dead from all the cutting they'd done on him to put that stiff backbone together again."

Seeing Luke's expression darken, Madelyn offered Buck a bright smile. "Thanks so much for the tickets, Buck."

"Why, you're more than welcome, ma'am." Mischief kindled in his eyes as he flicked a glance Luke's way. "Soon as hoss here mentioned you two were spending time together, it just seemed fittin' somehow, bein's how you met and all."

At her side again Luke slipped a protective arm around her waist. "You got some idea where you want to have that drink I owe you?"

Smitty's could have been located on any corner in any small town in Texas. The air smelled of stale cigarette smoke, spilled beer and enough sexual heat to kindle a decent-size brushfire. The young flame-haired waitress had a wiggle in her walk and a tiny pearl stud in one nostril. She also knew exactly how far to bend over to ensure a good tip.

"Two more of them long necks for me and hoss here, and another club soda for little Mama here," Buck ordered before stuffing a five into the rolled-up hem of her skin-tight cutoffs.

"Coming right up, handsome," she purred before flicking Luke a look that offered more than a cold one. Gut tight, he refused with a look of his own that had her tossing her head before she sauntered off.

Buck watched her weave her way through the tables toward the bar, a wistful look on his face.

"Time was, I'd be all over that sweet gal by now," he said, then drew himself up short. "Beg pardon, ma'am."

Madelyn's smile forgave him. "How come you're not married, Buck?"

"Nearly was once, but I got cold feet at the last minute and took off on her. Found out later she married a schoolteacher and raised up four young'uns." He rubbed his jaw, a telling look on his face. "Never had the heart to try again."

"It's never too late," Madelyn said.

The band started up again, and couples leaped up to crowd the small dance floor. Buck hitched his chair closer to the table. "When's your baby due?"

Her eyes softened. Luke loved the way her eyes tipped up at the corners when she was happy. If he had his way, those eyes would always smile. "In four weeks and three days—if he's on time."

"So it's a little cowboy not a cowgirl?"

"Yes." Her smile widened.

As Buck talked about his two nieces and nephews back home in Durango, Luke twirled the bottom of the empty bottle on the shiny table, fighting the jolt of apprehension he invariably felt whenever she mentioned the baby. Even though Karen had given her a glowing report just yesterday, he couldn't seem to shake the niggling fear that something wasn't right.

Conscience was part of it, the guilty kind that had him jerking awake in a sweat, wondering if he'd wanted her so much his judgment was skewed. Once he'd been so scared he'd actually driven to his office to stare for a good hour at the latest ultrasound photo Karen had sent over, along with a copy of her examination notes.

"Ain't that right, hoss?"

Luke blinked, then looked up to find both Buck and Madelyn staring at him. "Uh, you want to run that by me again?"

Buck's eyes had a teasing glint, and Luke's gut tightened. "I was just telling Miss Maddy about the time in Albuquerque when Cody Gresham got choked on a piece of gristle and you opened up his gullet with a pen knife so's he could breathe." Buck rubbed two fingers over the bruise riding his jaw, his eyes dark with memory. "How old was Cody then? Ten?"

"Nine." Luke started to tip back the bottle, then remembered it was empty and put it down again. "I was a first-year medical student and still hated the sight of blood," he added for Madelyn's benefit. Just so she'd know he wasn't the hero Buck was trying to make him out to be. "Keeled over in a dead faint when the EMTs finally got there."

"That's a fact," Buck confirmed as he leaned back in his chair and hooked his thumbs in his pockets. "But first he turned a real pretty shade of green."

Maddy giggled, and Luke's heart did a slow roll. She was wearing her hair down, and he was sure he could smell the roses-and-rainwater scent that invariably clung to the thick silk. "My hero," she said, her eyes shining.

Luke smiled back because she expected it, but he knew better. The waitress arrived then, and at the same time his beeper went off. "Do you have a pay phone?" he asked as she shot him a startled look.

"By the rest rooms. To the left of the bar and toward the rear."

He nodded his thanks before scraping back his chair. "Remember what I said, Mehan," he warned before bending to brand Maddy with a kiss that sizzled clear to the toes of his boots.

When he drew away, she blinked up at him, her face the prettiest shade of pink and her eyes glazed. "Save my place," he told her before diving into the crowd.

Madelyn watched him disappear into the crowd, her heart fluttering. She felt young and eager—and special. "Honey, you sure are one lucky gal," the waitress said.

The exaggerated sigh she gave was just enough to have Buck's gaze glued to her breasts.

Madelyn fought a grin as the grizzled old cowboy fumbled in his pocket for another five. Content, the waitress collected the empties and left. "Whooee, that lady sure can...walk."

Madelyn burst out laughing. Buck grinned before taking a long swallow. When he set down the bottle again, his expression had sobered. "I was sure sorry about what happened with your first little one," he said, his voice gruff. "Must have been pretty rough on you."

"Yes, it was." She took a sip of her own drink, her gaze on the dancers.

"Guess you know Luke grieved hard for a long time. Worried his friends he might actually do something stupid, he was that tied up with hating himself."

She frowned, her attention on Buck's seamed face now. "He didn't...do anything, did he?"

"No, but he came close one night in Laredo. It was closing night of the Stampede and we'd been tossing back a few in a biker bar Luke knew about. Neither of us was tracking real good, which is why I figure we didn't notice the four locals following us out. Normally we would have given as good as we got, but they was on us before we had a chance. Took damn near everything but our clothes. Me, I was just glad to have all my parts in place, but Luke, he wasn't about to let 'em have his wallet. Fought like a wildcat, he did, but he was outnumbered."

Buck paused to cast a nervous glance over his shoulder before continuing. "Both his eyes was all but swole shut and he had a busted hand. Me, I was content to lay there and moan, but he was set on going back inside after those ba—dudes. Maybe I'm not real bright, but I figured he'd end up dead, so I stopped him.''

Madelyn blinked. "Stopped him how?"

"Gave him one of them karate kicks right in the jewels, if you take my meaning. Was months before he'd speak to me." Buck shot another glance behind him. "See, the thing is, it wasn't his wallet he was trying to hang on to, but what he had in it. Not that he explained, you understand, but him and me bunked together a coupla times, and sometimes late at night when he thought I was sleeping, he'd take out that red ribbon of yours and run it through his fingers real slow-like."

Madelyn's breath caught. "Oh, Buck," she whispered.

He reached across the table to squeeze her hand. "Luke was real good to me when I lost my leg. Lent me money with no interest until I could get my bearings." His mouth compressed. "Tonight's the first time I've seen him look happy since you two busted up."

Madelyn glanced down at the ice melting in her club soda. "If I ask you something, will you be honest with me, Buck? Even if you think the answer will hurt me?"

"I will." His formal tone surprised her, but perhaps it shouldn't. Even the roughest cowboy had a vein of old-fashioned courtliness in him.

She took a breath. "In all those drunken nights you two spent together, did Luke ever once tell you that he loved me?"

Buck looked down, his body language a perfect example of reluctance. "No, ma'am, can't rightly say he did." He looked up again, his eyes pleading with her over the flickering candle. "But that's only because he's a real private person, you know? On account of

Daddy by Choice

him growing up pretty much on his own after his mama took off.''

She nodded at what he said.

Clearly relieved that he'd smoothed over a rough patch, Buck offered her another earnest smile. ''If anyone deserves a second chance, Madelyn, it's him.''

The big antique clock in the dining room was six minutes fast, Luke noted as he walked past, his stomach rumbling at the smell of frying bacon. While he'd been shaving, she'd started breakfast.

Last night was the first time since they'd become lovers again that they'd slept together in the same bed without making love. She'd wanted to, but it had been a long busy day and her eyelids kept drooping. So he'd simply tucked her against his chest and turned out the light.

It was getting to be a habit, falling asleep with her soft round body draped over him. Twice during the night, he'd jerked awake, his heart racing and his mind alert, only to realize the baby was awake and restless.

Today marked the beginning of her last final month, and he was taking her shopping for baby clothes. And maybe, if he could manage it, a cradle.

She was standing at the sink talking on the phone when he entered the kitchen. Precious looked up from her dish to give him a polite meow. Grinning at the spoiled kitty, he reached into the cupboard for a mug.

As she took a step backward to give him access to the coffeepot he noticed that her face was flushed and her eyes seethed with anger.

''Can't we sue for breach of contract or something?''

Her frown deepened as she listened to the reply. After filling his cup, Luke leaned back against the counter and sipped. She'd changed since coming to Oregon, he realized. Not just physically, but emotionally.

"Well, do what you can, and in the meantime, I'll think about the options you outlined," she said before ending the conversation.

After returning the portable phone to the charger, she shifted her gaze his way and tried to smile. "That was my attorney. It seems Wiley has decided he wants the house."

Luke kept his anger tucked in tight. According to Dr. Morrow, Foster had stopped his campaign of innuendo and sly hints. "I thought he signed the settlement agreement."

"He did, but now he's claiming he signed under emotional duress." Her eyes flashed. "He has the *nerve* to claim he was so upset about losing his son he wasn't thinking straight."

She walked to the fridge and jerked it open, then slammed it shut so hard the trivets on the wall rattled. "How *dare* he?" she shouted before whirling around to glare at him.

"Say the word, honey, and I'm on the next plane to Texas. Five minutes alone with that son of a bitch and I guarantee he'll swear to bein' the hind end of a polecat, if that's what you want."

She stuttered a laugh. "Careful, cowboy, I might just take you up on that."

He put down his mug and drew her into his arms. Maybe in a thousand years of holding her he might take the wonder of her for granted. "What's your attorney say?"

"He's not optimistic. Wiley's attorney is a former circuit judge, and even though he's retired, he wields a lot of influence over his fellow jurists. Jorge thinks

Wiley has a good chance of winning his case and wants to see if he'll agree to let me buy him out for half the appraised value.'' Sighing, she rested her cheek against Luke's shoulder. ''I must have been out of my mind to marry that man.''

He stroked her hair and watched the sunshine ripple. ''Why did you?''

''Mostly because Mama and Daddy approved of him. Daddy kept saying Wiley would make me respectable again.''

It was tempting to dump his anger on a man he'd come to detest. Too tempting. ''Let him have the damn house, Maddy. Stay here and marry me. Now, today, or as soon as we can get a license. Let me take care of you and the baby.''

Her jaw dropped and for an instant her eyes were blank with shock. Then they turned wary. ''That's very generous of you.'' Her voice was unnaturally calm and he started to sweat.

''It's not generous at all, Maddy. In fact, it's damned selfish, but I can't seem to help it.'' He took a breath and felt pressure grind in his chest. ''I love you, Maddy. I'm so in love with you I came close to violating an oath that I revere because I couldn't keep away from you.''

She bit her lip, then shook her head. ''No, you're just telling yourself you love me because you feel sorry for me.''

''The hell I do!'' His voice came out too harsh and too loud. Disgusted with himself, he took her hand and balanced it on his. It was her left, he realized. The one he desperately wanted to see wearing his ring as soon as possible.

''I feel a lot of things for you, Maddy. Some I can

tell you, some that have no words. But one thing I don't feel is pity or sympathy or whatever it is that's got your back up.''

''If you love me, why haven't you said so before now?'' It was a fair question, one he didn't want to answer.

''I pushed you too hard too fast the last time. So this time I was giving you time to get to know me. But that doesn't mean I don't want a lifetime with you.'' A hole opened in his gut. It was the same feeling he'd had an instant before he'd lost his seat and crashed into the dirt.

''Even Buck said you were eaten up with guilt.''

He frowned. ''What's Buck got to do with this?''

''He told me about my ribbon. How you nearly died trying to get it back.''

He ground his teeth. ''Doesn't that prove how much I love you?''

''No, it only proves you're superstitious.''

He smiled because she expected it. ''When I finally read your letter telling me you were pregnant, it nearly sent me to the floor. It was like I'd been kicked so hard I just disappeared.'' He hated remembering, which was why he wouldn't let himself forget. ''I don't have any memory of leaving the house or saddling Cochise. I must have, though, because next thing I knew I was racing the wind out on the mesa. It was panic I was feeling then. Panic that I'd messed up and couldn't make things right.''

Smiling, she played with the button on his shirt. ''I was terrified at the very thought of being a mother. It felt like I'd just stopped playing with dolls, and all of a sudden I was about to have a real live baby to take care of.''

He tightened his arm and inhaled the scent of her hair. It made him think of butterflies and lazy days by the river. "Driving back to Texas, I kept thinking how ignorant I was and how much I wanted to make you and your little one proud of me." His mouth twisted. "Selfish bastard that I am, all I could think about was how you and the baby would be in the stands cheerin' me on when I won Grand Champion."

A bittersweet smile played over Madelyn's lips as she imagined herself standing in the middle of a cheering crowd, her little girl dressed in a frilly dress with a pink ribbon in her hair, laughing out of Luke's eyes at her as her daddy took a bow. Something lovely and warm wrapped around her heart, as healing as a hug. "Don't forget the stomping and whistling," she said.

"You sure could split the air, that's a fact."

"My brother taught me, then got mad as the devil because mine was louder."

"Oh, yeah, I sure remember that whistle of yours." He lifted a hand to smooth her hair away from her face, letting his fingers linger on her cheek. "I do love you, Maddy. And I love your baby. I'd prove it to you if I could, but so far I haven't come up with a surefire plan."

She huffed a little laugh. "I know you think you love me. I think I love you. If it were just me, I'd be dragging you to the altar as we speak. But I have the baby to consider. What if we're only fooling ourselves? What if it doesn't work out?" Her eyes turned bleak. "I grew up with parents who never should have gotten married. I'm not sure why they stayed together, but their constant battles made my brother's and my life miserable."

His gut tightened. He knew what it was like to grow

up listening to his parents spill venom on each other. He knew how it hurt when he found out he was the reason they'd gotten married. A damned accident was the way his old man had put it. "It won't be that way with us, Maddy."

"How do you know?"

"Because in twenty-two years I never stopped thinking about you."

"But maybe that's because we're like survivors of some kind of disaster. What we shared, knowing we'd created a child we would never be allowed to raise or even see again has bonded us in ways we might not even suspect." She took a breath. "Maybe it is love. Or maybe we tell ourselves it is because then what we did doesn't seem quite so selfish."

"Bull! You don't have a selfish bone in your body."

"I'm not so sure about that," she said with a shaky laugh before turning away to pour herself a cup of coffee.

She sipped, then turned back. "Most of the studies I've read say that a woman never forgets the first man she loves, especially if it ends badly. In many ways it—well, let's call it a broken heart—can keep her from bonding with another man. In my case I think Wiley had a lot to do with that, but...maybe not."

"Sounds like a lot of psychobabble to me." Frustration made his voice sharp, earning him a startled look. Because he wanted to shake her, he refilled his cup and held it with both hands.

"No, it's true," she said. "I've never forgotten you, though God knows I tried. Seeing you now, the man you've become, has opened a lot of doors I thought I'd sealed shut. I need to know for my own peace of mind how I really feel."

"So you can move on to another guy someday?"

She took a breath, then nodded, her gaze steady on his. "It's possible, yes. Right now I just want time to make sure what we feel is real and not some mix of guilt and sex and...fantasy."

Fantasy, hell, Luke thought as anger surged. He'd just told her he loved her. Not once had he ever come close to saying those words to a woman. Maybe that didn't rate a brass band to her, but it was pretty damned important to him, and he sure as hell didn't like being told he was suffering from delusions or posttraumatic stress. But maybe she was, he realized suddenly.

"I promised myself I'd let you set the pace this time. So I will. Only there's just this one little thing we need to get straight right off."

She frowned. "What's that?"

"That offer of marriage—it's a one-time deal. If you turn me down, I won't ask again."

Surprise was still settling in her eyes when he set his cup down on the counter with a hard crack and walked out.

Chapter 16

Alone in the small cubbyhole off the ICU nurses' station, Luke dry-swallowed two heavy-duty Tylenol tablets, then chased them down with a swallow of stale coffee. It was a few minutes before nine on a hot sunny Saturday morning, and his head was thick with exhaustion.

He hated emergency C-sections about as much as he hated thinking about his past sins. Too many times the choice came down to saving the mom or the baby, sometimes with only minutes or even seconds to make that choice. This time, though, it looked like both Marla Hanson and her tiny red-haired daughter would make it. Still shaken, Paul Hanson was sneaking rye shooters from the flask he'd tucked into his wife's suitcase.

Damn good idea, Luke thought, giving in to a yawn before flexing his aching shoulders.

As soon as he mustered up the energy, he intended

to take himself home for a hot bath and a day's sleep. Five minutes later he was still working up the energy when Boyd ambled in, his scrubs equally sweat-stained from his long hours in the OR. "Any coffee left?"

"Enough for a mild buzz."

Boyd plucked a foam cup from the stack by the coffee machine and emptied the pot. Then he leaned back against the counter, crossed his ankles and sipped.

"Can't say as I've ever seen quite that particular shade of gray on someone's face before," he said, eyeing Luke over the rim of his cup.

Though it cost him, Luke stood a little straighter. "Then you haven't taken a good look at yourself after one of those marathon sessions you put in."

Boyd snorted. "At least wear your brace."

It was an old argument. "You ever try performing a section wearing a straitjacket?"

"Ever try performing a section flat on your back in traction, 'cause that's where you're heading, hotshot."

"Get stuffed, MacAuley."

"Don't say I didn't warn you." Boyd took another sip of his coffee, his shoulders drooping with the same exhaustion Luke felt throbbing in his own.

"Just talked to Stace. Apparently there's been a change of plan. You're supposed to have Maddy at our place at one next Sunday, instead of two."

"Tell her to call Dorie so she can make the change on my calendar."

Boyd shook his head. "How the hell did you get through med school without a good memory?"

"Wrote my class schedule on my arm every morning." He shifted his weight onto his right leg, hoping the tingling in the left didn't escalate into numbness.

"This baby-shower thing, am I supposed to bring a present or what?"

"The women bring presents, the guys watch the kids. Case figures we can plop 'em down in front of the new big-screen TV Prue got him for his birthday with a bunch of videos and still get in a few hands of poker."

"Is Pax back from New York?"

Boyd laughed. "Yeah, the designated pigeon will be there."

"Have to admit that brightens my spirits some. The man just can't help throwing away his money."

Boyd flexed his shoulders, winced as the stiff muscles protested. "You might as well know the ladies are hoping for a wedding."

"Maddy's not looking for marriage. She's looking for closure."

"What the hell's that mean?"

"Best as I can make out, she wants to spend time with me to prove she was right when she kicked me out of her life."

"You gonna let her do that?"

"I don't see I have any right to stop her."

"Even if you're in love with her?"

His jaw went hard. "Maybe you didn't hear me, MacAuley. The lady isn't looking for a husband. She's into her freedom."

"Raine didn't want Pax, either. He changed her mind."

"Yeah, well, he already had a foot in the door. I'm not even on the property."

Boyd lifted a brow. "Guess you just stopped by for breakfast the other morning when I happened to see your Cherokee parked out front of her place."

"What can I say? She likes my body." Luke flexed his tired shoulders. "Hell, I'm nothin' but a damned sex object."

Boyd had the gall to grin. "Seems to me a man could do worse than have a woman like Madelyn lusting over him."

Luke allowed himself a moment to grieve for what might have been before pouring the last of his coffee down his throat. "I'm outta here," he said, dropping his cup into the trash.

"Don't forget the shower."

"Tell Stace I'll have her there on time. Two o'clock a week from Sunday."

Boyd groaned. "I'll tell her to call Dorie," he said as they left the cubicle together.

Feeling lethargic even though she'd been out of bed for a few hours, Madelyn was tucked up in a corner of the fainting bench reading when the doorbell rang. She wasn't expecting Luke until tonight, but he was the only one who used her front door. Her pulse quickened as she struggled to her feet, then fluffed her hair before going to the door and opening it.

Disappointment ran through her when she saw that her unexpected visitor was a stranger, a thin pale young woman in ragged jeans and a faded Cowboys T-shirt. Taller than Madelyn by several inches, she had masses of dark curly hair so thick it overpowered her features and bony shoulders, which seemed bent by a burden too heavy to bear. For a frozen instant Madelyn saw herself in this sad waif and wanted to weep.

"May I help you?" she asked, deliberately warming her smile.

"I hope so, ma'am. I'm looking for Mrs. Madelyn

Foster.'' The drawl was pure Texan, and Madelyn's curiosity sharpened. A friend of a friend perhaps? The rust-bucket Chevy pickup parked at the curb led her to believe the girl needed help.

''I'm Madelyn Foster.''

She noticed the girl's eyes then, vivid bluebonnet eyes framed by inky black lashes. Madelyn's breath jammed in her throat, then came out in a rush. *Oh God, oh God, oh God...*

''Jenny?'' Her voice was little more than a wisp of sound.

That too-thin face closed up, and those beautiful hauntingly familiar eyes rejected love even before it was offered. ''My name's Tricia. Tricia Wilson.'' Her gaze flickered, then turned distant. ''I found your name in the register of parents willing to make contact. I think you're my biological mother.''

Because her knees seemed to be dissolving, Madelyn groped for the doorknob and held on tight. ''Oh, honey, I'm so glad you found me! I promised not to look for you, but I thought, if you wanted to find me some-day...and you did!'' Flustered, she forced strength into her wobbly legs. ''Please, come in.''

She stepped back, terrified the girl would change her mind and leave. Entering warily, Tricia glanced around. For an instant she looked exactly like Luke the first time he'd laid eyes on Harriet's treasures.

Madelyn felt her insides trembling as she tried to memorize every expression, every curve and line. *Dearest Jenny, you were only four days old and I kissed every inch of your dear funny little face. And I held you until my arms were numb...*

Madelyn's stomach clenched as she saw hints of her own face in the spatter of freckles across the delicate cheekbones and the shape of her chin. But the sooty brows and determined mouth were feminine versions of Luke's. Her daddy's little girl, she thought as her heart wept.

"I…my mother told me that a woman named Tricia had stopped by my house." She laughed nervously. "But you already know that." She realized her hands had grown slippery and she wiped them on her shorts. "Can I get you some juice or a soda? Or something to eat? I have some leftover meat loaf or I can fry some chicken. It's my grandmother's recipe. Your great-grandma, honey."

At the mention of their family tie, those thin shoulders stiffened. "No thank you, ma'am. I ate at a truck stop on the interstate a few miles back." There was pride in the angle of her jaw. So much pride. The kind she'd seen in too many neglected teenagers over the years. Her heart contracted.

"You drove?" she asked, careful to keep her tone even. "All the way from Texas alone?"

"Yes, ma'am."

Madelyn bit her lip, so eager to hug her child it hurt. But first they needed to get past the resentment and anger she sensed beneath the pride. She understood of course. But still, she hoped. "Would you like to sit down?"

"Can't stay but a minute." Both hands clasped tightly around the cheap denim purse, Tricia looked around warily. "Is all this yours?"

"No, it belongs to the woman who owns this house. I'm only renting it until the baby is born."

"Are you going to throw this baby away like you did me?"

Madelyn gasped softly, her hands instinctively cupping her belly. "I didn't throw you away, Tricia," she rushed to assure her child. "I wanted you desperately. Every night when I rubbed lotion on my tummy, I told you all the things we would do together and how much I loved you."

Tricia stared at her in stony silence. This was the child she'd carried in her body for eight long months. There should be a connection, shouldn't there? A subliminal memory of their hearts beating with one rhythm. But those bluer-than-blue eyes never wavered, never warmed. Protecting herself from more hurt, Madelyn thought. Like her daddy at eighteen.

Still, Luke's hard shell had vulnerable places. Maybe his daughter's did, as well. She took a step closer, then froze when Tricia's gaze darted toward the door as if she was getting ready to bolt.

"I know it sounds trite, but I was only seventeen. Not even out of high school. My parents are good people, Tricia, but Daddy's business was in trouble and Mama was sick a lot. I would have found a place of my own, but I had no money, no job. I couldn't even buy diapers for you." She took a breath and worked to steady her voice. "I had no choice."

"What about the guy who provided stud service? Or didn't he want me, either?" The hurt was sharper now, riding just behind that hard cynical shell.

"Your...father didn't know about you until after I'd...given you up."

"Yeah? What was he—a one-night stand or something?"

"We knew each other for four days actually, but yes, I can't lie to you, you weren't planned. But that doesn't mean I didn't love you from the first moment I felt you move."

Tricia's shrug was so terribly casual, like a little girl facing her worst fear alone because she had no one to hold her hand or hug her tight. Is this what her life has been like? Madelyn thought on a wave of renewed anguish.

"He...lives right here in Portland, your father," she said, choosing her words with care. "His name is Lucas Oliver Jarrod. He grew up on a ranch in Arizona, and for a while he competed on the rodeo circuit, until he had a bad accident. Now he's a doctor, an obstetrician. And a wonderful loving man. You...you look just like him."

Her daughter's eyes narrowed, then took on a calculating glint. "Is he rich?"

Madelyn was nonplussed. "To tell you the truth, I don't know. I suppose he's comfortable, although his house is modest and he drives a Jeep and he...he wears old work shirts and jeans most of the time."

Tricia gave her a considering look before wandering over to the ornate player piano tucked against one wall. She reached out to run her fingers over the yellowed keys. It wasn't quite a caress, but there were memories crossing her face now. Pleasant ones, Madelyn realized on a flare of hope.

"Do you play?"

"I used to play a lot—until Felicity sold my piano."

"Felicity?"

"The wicked stepmother." She turned to give Madelyn a mocking look. "My *real* mother died when I was nine. Breast cancer." Her voice thinned, but held steady. The girl had courage, Madelyn thought with a jolt of pride. "Daddy kept saying how his heart was in the grave, and then he up and married his secretary six months later."

"Perhaps he was lonely," Madelyn suggested cautiously.

"Horny as a randy old goat is more like it. And Felicity, she knew just how to play him, too. Gushed all over me, like she couldn't wait to be my mama. Until after the wedding—then I was just a nuisance she shipped off to boarding school."

"Oh, honey, I'm so sorry. That must have hurt."

Again that shrug. That sad stiff vulnerable movement. This time Madelyn saw the helpless pain it was meant to conceal. "I got over it."

"Your daddy lost his mother when he was nine, too."

"Like I care."

Madelyn winced at a sudden kick just below the third button of her sleeveless shirt. "Whoa, that was a good one."

Alarm flared in Tricia's eyes. "Are you all right?"

Smiling ruefully, she smoothed both hands over her belly. "I think your baby brother is getting bored with his little nest."

Tricia's mouth tightened. "Don't call it that! I don't have a brother and you're not my mother."

"Yes, Tricia, I am. You're angry at me for giving you up for adoption, and I can understand that. Maybe you even think your life would have been better if I hadn't, but I promise you, it would have been miserable at best. All I had to give you was my love, but a baby needs warm blankets and good food and…and so many other things I couldn't give you." Shaky now, she braced one hand on the arm of the couch and lowered her bulky body to the plush seat. "I didn't have a choice. Jen—Tricia. I swear."

"Oh, yeah, right; it was for my own good." Her

voice dripped sarcasm and her eyes seethed. Witnessing her daughter's pain had Madelyn's eyes filling with helpless anguish.

"It was! I wish you'd believe me."

Tricia jerked around to stare at the fireplace. "Well, guess what, *Mama*. I have a son, too. He's almost three. I was nineteen when I had him. The state said I was an unfit mother because I danced in a bar, but I scratched and lied and cheated to keep him."

Her child had a child of her own? A little boy? For an instant Madelyn couldn't breathe. "What's his name?"

"Mason Philip Wilson. I call him Mace."

"Mace. I like it." Madelyn smiled. "Do you have a picture?"

Tricia reached into her purse and pulled out a thin wallet. From one of the pockets she took out a snapshot and then crossed to the couch. "This was taken a few months ago."

Madelyn's hand shook as she stared at the laughing little boy who was the image of his mother. "He's adorable," she said when she could speak. "He looks happy."

"He is now. He was sick right after he was born because Chuck beat me while I was pregnant. The doctors thought Mace might be brain-damaged, but he's smart as a whip." A look like guilt crossed her face. "He's also deaf."

"Oh, my God," Madelyn breathed. "Did they put the man who did that in jail?"

"I didn't tell anyone. Chuck told me he'd kill my son if I said anything."

"But the police would have protected you."

Tricia gave her a look that questioned her sanity.

"As soon as they released Mace from the hospital, I took him and left town." Her mouth flattened. It was the same expression she saw on Luke when he was struggling not to feel too deeply.

"Looks like you and me both picked losers," Tricia drawled, her tone flippant.

Madelyn swallowed. There was so much hurt in the girl, so much bitterness. It was like looking at herself for so many lost years. "Your daddy isn't a loser, Tricia. He would have married me if he'd known about you."

"Lucky you."

Swallowing the sharp words that rose to her throat, Madelyn studied the face of her grandson. Here was love and hope. And perhaps healing. "May I keep this?"

"Sorry, it's the only one I have."

After taking one last look, Madelyn handed her the photo. "I hope you'll bring him with you the next time."

Ignoring the tacit plea, Tricia tucked the photo carefully into her wallet again. "I came here because I want to go to college to become a teacher, but I need money. I've got it all figured out how much I'll need." She named a figure, her gaze defiant.

Madelyn took a breath. "I don't have anywhere near that amount, Tricia. I'm a high-school guidance counselor in a small district. I have some savings, yes, but my...my ex-husband is being difficult about the divorce settlement."

Her daughter's chin came up and she looked Madelyn squarely in the eye. "I'm not proud, Mrs. Foster. I'll take what you can spare. Even enough for one semester would help."

"What school?" Madelyn said as she pushed herself to her feet.

"I don't know yet. I haven't even applied."

"I went to El Paso State. Your daddy went to Arizona State, then Stanford."

Tricia's gaze flickered. Madelyn sensed that she was impressed, though trying hard not to show it. A small step perhaps.

Her checkbook was in the kitchen. Excusing herself, she went to fetch it. While she was there, she thought about calling Luke so he'd have this precious chance to see his daughter, maybe for the only time. Because she sensed Tricia would consider it some kind of emotional ambush, she decided to ask her permission first.

When she returned to the living room, her daughter was standing in front of the bookcase built into the wall to one side of the fireplace, studying the titles. "Do you like to read?" Madelyn asked as she sat down to write out the check.

"Yes. Sometimes I think it saved my life." Tricia didn't turn until she heard Madelyn tear the check from the pad.

"I wish it were more," Madelyn told her as she handed her the check.

Tricia's expression was wooden as she glanced at the amount. Though she tried to hid it, Madelyn could see she was surprised. "I'll pay you back someday," she said in a taut voice before folding the check and tucking it into her purse.

"I know your father would—"

"No!" Tricia's voice was as loud as a lash. A jagged fear flashed in her eyes as she hurried to the door.

"Tricia, wait!" Madelyn cried, struggling awkwardly to her feet . "Please don't go! Stay here tonight. I'd like to hear about Mason and you."

But Tricia had already fumbled the door open. "Thank you for the money."

"At least give me an address!" Madelyn cried, terrified that she was losing her child all over again.

"I can't! If Chuck should find us..."

"I won't tell anyone," Madelyn promised, reaching out to touch her.

Tricia flinched away, her momentum carrying her to the porch. "Goodbye, Mrs. Foster."

Madelyn's eyes filled with tears. "Tricia, please, don't go. I've waited so long to see you. Please stay."

"I can't. I'm sorry. Maybe someday." She spun around, taking the steps quickly, then running down the walk to the beatup old truck.

"The license plate," Madelyn thought aloud before turning quickly to retrieve her pen and checkbook. It was only an instant, but even as she grabbed up her pen from the coffee table she heard the truck roar to life.

By the time she reached the door, her daughter was gone.

Chapter 17

Luke was on the freeway when his beeper went off. It took his tired brain an extra few seconds to recognize the number.

Raw fear shot adrenaline into his bloodstream before reason took over. If Maddy was in labor, she'd call Winslow, not him. No doubt she was calling about tonight. To remind him to wear a tie, most likely, to the ballet.

By his way of thinking a man who willingly agreed to encase his gullet in a starched collar and necktie for three hours just so's he could stare at a bunch of skinny ladies and musclebound boys in tights had to be touched in the head—or hopelessly in love.

A grin split his tired face as he flipped on the radio, Vintage Hank Williams boomed from the speakers, his kind of music. Not that damn slow stuff with too many violins that made him restless. As soon as he got home, he'd call her. Maybe rag her a little, but even as he let the anticipation build, he found himself reaching for his cell phone.

She answered on the first ring. As soon as he heard her voice, he knew he'd been right not to wait. "Maddy, what's wrong? Is it the baby?"

"I couldn't make her stay." Her voice wobbled. "I tried, but she was scared, and…and…oh, Luke, he *beat* her."

He went dead calm. His mind narrowed focus. "Take a deep breath, okay? Now tell me who 'she' is."

He heard her gulp. "Jenny."

This time emotion pumped along with the adrenaline. "Our Jenny?"

"Yes, our baby, only her name is Tricia Wilson. She got my name from the database and…just showed up."

The next exit was two miles ahead. He checked his mirrors, then moved right. "You said someone beat her?" Because fury wanted to flash, he iced his mind.

"Yes, her, well, I guess it was her boyfriend." She gulped air again. "We…we have a grandson." She broke down then and sobbed.

Oh, God. "I'm on my way, sweetheart. Just hang in, okay?"

"Okay. Yes."

In his mind's eye he saw her straightening her spine and lifting her chin. "Maddy?"

"I'm fine now, Luke. Really. I just needed to vent. Thank you for listening. But now I'm fine, really. I'll see you tonight." His jaw tightened at the formal courtesy. His instinct told him something was very very wrong. One of his hunches, he thought grimly. He couldn't remember the last time he'd been mistaken.

"Not tonight, now. I'm on my way," he repeated before breaking the connection.

It wasn't record time, but close.

He rang the bell, then tried the door. It was open, and he let himself in. She was curled into one corner of that sissy red couch, a box of tissues on the table next to her and that monster cat curled up beside her. Her face was tearstained and pale, her eyes drenched with unhappiness. His gut twisted into a mean hard knot.

"Sweetheart, are you all right?"

She bit her lip, then shook her head. "Doc was wrong. They weren't good people who adopted her. They were cold and selfish and she...her stepmother shipped her off to boarding school when she only nine. Just a baby."

Sensing her need to talk, he sat down and took her hand, kissing it before flattening it against his thigh.

"Now, start from the beginning and tell me what happened."

Her mouth trembled. "I thought maybe she wanted to connect with her...her birth mother. But she...she just wanted money. That's why she came."

He breathed a curse that had her shooting him a reproachful look.

"I don't blame her, Luke, Not in the least. She wants to go to college and she needs help. Who better to ask than her...parents?"

He thought about his own struggle to finance eight long years. Too many times it had been a choice between eating and paying the electricity bill. His old man might have helped if he'd asked. He'd been too proud to humble himself.

"I told her about you, Luke." She wiped her cheek with the wad of tissues in her hand. "She wanted to know if you're rich. I told her I didn't know." She gave him a curious look. "Are you?"

"Guess that depends on your definition. If you're talking money, yeah. If you're talking things that matter, like a wife and a child or two to love and a home where the rooms don't echo when I come home at night, then no, I'm about as poor as poor can be."

She smiled through her tears. He saw the pity, too, and bit down hard on his lip.

"His name is Mason, our grandson. He looks like...like Tricia. And like you." She tucked her other hand around his. "I tried to get her to leave the picture, but—"

She broke off, her startled gaze dropping to her belly. "Ouch! That kick really hurt."

Something in her face had him going still. "Hurt how, honey?"

"Just...hurt. It still does."

Schooling his expression, Luke ran his hand over her belly. It was slab hard. The placenta could be tearing. An abruption. And if that happened, both she and the baby could die. Helpless terror blanked his mind for an instant before discipline kicked in.

"Maddy, we're going to the hospital now." He stood, then reached down to put an arm around her back.

"But what...why?"

"Trust me, Maddy. Trust the man who loves you." With no time to waste, he scooped her up into his arms and headed for the door. He fumbled a little getting it open and then walked as fast as he could down the walk. Her hands wound tightly around his neck as he carried her to the passenger side. He felt her fear now, and the pain she was trying to hide. His mind filled with images of other desperate women, times he'd lost the battle.

"Open the door, honey," he ordered.

She fumbled but managed to get the door open. "Luke, it really hurts," she cried as he settled her in the bucket seat. "I mean really." Her eyes were dark now with the pain he knew would only get worse.

Without wasting time, he snapped her belt in place, slammed the door, and trotted around to the other side, his keys in his hand. He fired the engine, engaged the gears and made a squealing U-turn. He took the corner fast, fishtailing a little before pumping the gas.

Silently cursing the whimsy that had prompted him to get a Jeep with a manual transmission, he struggled to drive and punch in the number of the maternity wing at the same time.

"Maternity, Stanley."

"Margot, it's Luke. I'm about six, seven minutes out with an abruption. It's Winslow's patient so have her paged. Name of the patient is Madelyn Foster. She's at thirty-two weeks plus. Tell OR to set up for a crash section stat. Alert the best team you have and warn them it's going to be fast and messy. Call trauma and tell them to meet me at the ambulance dock."

"Will do, Luke. Drive carefully."

Madelyn strained forward against the belt, her face paper white and her eyes huge and terrified. "What's happening? Am I in labor?"

"You have a little problem, nothing we can't handle together."

"You won't leave me? Promise you won't."

"Not a chance in hell, sweetheart."

Luke drove with deadly intensity, his gaze welded to the street ahead, reading the flow of traffic the way he'd once read the horses he'd ridden. Tires squealed and horns blew as he ran lights, changed lanes.

"Save the baby," she pleaded. "Please. The baby."

"You're both going to make it, damn it. I'm not losing you. I won't lose you."

She was crying now, great gulps of anguish that tore at that tiny part of him that wasn't intensely focused. "S-something awful's happening. I feel tearing…" Her voice splintered into a sharp cry.

"I swear to God, Madelyn, you are not going to die and neither is your baby."

She was moaning steadily by the time the hospital's south tower came into view. Rocketing up the access road, he nearly sobbed with relief when he saw the trauma team gathered around a gurney at the dock. He recognized Prudy's bright curls and sent up a prayer of thanks.

After screeching to a halt, he climbed out. By the time his boots hit the tarmac, the team had Madelyn's door open, hanging IVs, getting her on the gurney. He intended to go with her but first he had to make sure she was in good hands.

"Is Winslow scrubbed?" he shouted at Prudy over the roof of the Jeep.

"She's in her car, ETA, thirty minutes," Prudy told him without looking up. Madelyn's pain, he knew, must be excruciating. He maneuvered in next to her and grabbed her hand, trotting beside the gurney as they hurried her inside.

"There's only a first year available," Prudy told him, her gaze full of anguish. "You'll have to do it."

"God, no! I can't risk it. What if I make a mistake?"

"You'll do it because there's no other option."

In their haste the gurney swerved and Madelyn screamed.

"Take her right to maternity," Prudy ordered, slapping the button to open the double doors at the end of the trauma unit proper.

Crammed against the wall of the elevator, Luke stroked Maddy's hair, talking nonsense. Her gaze was riveted on him, her eyes glazed with pain. "If I die, promise you'll take my son. Please, Luke. There's no one else."

"You're not going to die." He had to make his voice sharp. Otherwise he would dissolve.

"Promise me," she whispered brokenly.

"I promise."

She tried to smile. "Don't look so...fierce. Scare the baby."

He choked a laugh. "Hang in there, sweetheart. Remember that I love you."

"Love you. Should have told you." She closed her eyes, and Luke bled inside. Straightening, he forced himself to concentrate on essentials, the way he did right before he rode.

"I want you with me," Luke told Prudy as the elevator sped upward.

Alarm and sympathy warred in her brown eyes. "I haven't assisted in years. I'd be too slow."

"Not to assist. To talk to me if I panic."

She nodded, her gaze telling him she understood all that he said and couldn't say. "That I can do." Her grin was a little forced, but it helped.

By the time the elevator doors whooshed open and the team spilled out, Madelyn was unconscious and the baby was in terrible trouble. As he and Prudy raced to scrub up, he went over the procedure he was about to perform. Fast and dirty and clean up later, he reminded himself. Get the baby out first, then see to the mom.

Minutes later, scrubbed and gowned, he hurried into the OR to find Madelyn lying still as death under anesthesia and the belly he loved to caress bared for the incision that would deliver the baby.

The blood drained from his face and the bright lights seemed to waver. "You can do this," Prudy said, her eyes steady above her mask.

He took a breath, muttered a prayer and stepped to the table, his hand already reaching for the scalpel. The tech slapped it into his hand. He made one quick sure slice, then dropped the knife and reached for the baby.

She drifted in a soft white world. There was peace here and sometimes pain, a pinched band across her tummy. Now and then sounds came to her from a distance. Muted beeps, the rattle of metal on metal. The insistent murmur of a man's voice, calling her name.

"Wake up, Maddy. Open your eyes, sweetheart. I need to see your eyes."

The order burrowed through the haze and lingered. He'd come back for her. Her cocky cowboy with the laughing eyes. Or was it a dream? She tried to open her eyes, but her lids felt so heavy.

"That's it, sweetheart. Open your eyes."

She did it then, finding a blurry world that gradually sharpened. Luke was leaning over her, her hand securely clasped in his. His eyes were red rimmed and bloodshot, his skin gray beneath the black whiskers. It hurt her to see him so exhausted. Ravaged.

"You...need to be in bed."

He swallowed hard, then leaned down to brush a kiss

across her forehead. "Welcome back, sweetheart," he murmured as he drew back. "You have a healthy son. Four pounds, six ounces."

She blinked, "I...had the baby?"

"You did indeed, darlin'."

Joy came in a starburst, followed by a wave of profound gratitude. She was a mother again. This time no one would take her child. *No one.*

"Is he beautiful?"

He nodded, his eyes filled with something that looked very much like pride.

"When can I see him?"

He cleared his throat. When he spoke, his voice was husky. "Soon. He had a little trouble breathing at first, so they're keeping him in the neonatal nursery a little while longer just to make sure he's okay."

Her heart lurched. "Trouble?"

"Nothing serious. It's just that he hadn't decided to leave his nice warm bubble yet. I kinda jerked him out before he was ready and he's playing a little catch-up."

She felt disoriented, as though she was a beat behind the rest of the world. "You delivered the baby?"

He nodded. "Karen was stuck in traffic." He kissed her hand, then released her to press a button that elevated the head of the bed. She winced as a scalding pain arced across her abdomen. She touched the spot and found a bandage.

"I had a C-section?"

"I know you wanted to be awake, but there was no choice." He turned to pour her some water, then held the glass while she sipped through one of those silly crinkled straws. It tasted blissful.

"I remember now. You grabbed me up like a sack of potatoes and ran."

"Guess I did. At the time it seemed necessary." He returned the glass to the tray table and she noticed he was wearing rumpled blue scrubs. Her cowboy doctor. "How are you feeling? Any pain?"

"A little." She glanced down. "My belly is still lumpy."

The dismay in her voice brought a smile to his lips. "It'll shrink. Nursing helps."

Nursing? Emotion balled in her throat. Already her breasts were hot and aching. "When can I see him?"

"In a little while. Now that you're awake, we can see about getting you out of intensive care and into a suite."

She looked around to find that she was in a cubicle with glass walls. "Just like a display in a department-store window," she muttered, feeling terribly vulnerable.

"More like Sleeping Beauty," he murmured, brushing back her hair. There were calluses on his fingers, wonderfully rough against her skin.

"How long was I asleep?"

"Long enough to make an old man of me."

She touched his tired face. "Was it the fibroid?"

His jaw tightened suddenly. Something like guilt appeared in his eyes. "No. It was something called a placental abruption. The placenta tore away from the uterus. There were no visible signs it would do that. Nothing Karen could have seen."

But *he* should have seen it, Luke thought as her eyes drifted closed again. He wasn't sure he would ever forgive himself for not doing so.

The birthing suite was a bower of flowers. All her neighbors had sent bouquets and balloons. The gardener who took care of her lawn had stopped by with a miniature rosebush, which he promised to plant for her as soon as she got home.

Stacy had brought an adorable little-boy outfit, and Raine had promised to have the communal bassinet ready to receive the latest Maternity Row baby. Even Don Petroff had stopped by, looking endearingly awkward with a stuffed panda bear under one arm.

Now that the baby was out of danger, he stayed with her in one of those clear plastic bassinets. He was proving to be a noisy demanding roommate. Every two hours like clockwork, he woke up screaming for his dinner.

"Give me a minute to examine your mom's incision, little guy," Dr. Winslow said with a grin as she lifted Madelyn's gown.

Tall and graceful with expressive gray eyes and sunwashed auburn hair, her obstetrician reminded Madelyn of a prima ballerina. "Are you feeling any discomfort in your belly?"

Madelyn glanced down at the neat line of staples. "A few twinges when I move, but nothing serious."

Dr. Winslow flicked her a pleased glance before covering her with the sheet. "Dr. Jarrod was afraid of infection because he had to act so precipitously, but so far so good."

"He saved my life, didn't he?"

Winslow offered her a solemn nod. "No doubt about it. If he hadn't gotten you into surgery when he did, you would have bled out."

Madelyn unbuttoned her gown, then leaned over to lift the baby to her breast. She winced as the eager little mouth found the nipple. She took a moment to enjoy the sensation before glancing up. "It's like a dream, actually. One minute I was fine and the next I was in terrible trouble.''

"Abruptions are like that. The worst part is they usually happen without notice.'' The doctor drew a breath. "I went back over my last examination notes and all the signs were positive.''

"Right before it happened, I was very upset about something that had just happened. Do you think—''

"Absolutely not! These things just happen.'' She smiled. "When I was a resident here, we used to laugh about Dr. Jarrod's hunches. He seemed to just know when something was wrong, even when there were no signs. In this case, looks like he was right.'' After exchanging a few more words, the doctor excused herself and left, nearly colliding with Prudy at the door.

"Good heavens, woman, don't you ever do anything but feed that little rascal?'' Prudy demanded as she sailed in on a burst of energy and color, bright green and orange today.

"Not much,'' Madelyn admitted as Prue pulled up one of the plastic chairs and sat down.

"So, how much has he gained today?'' she asked with a grin.

"Only an ounce, but it's still early.''

Leaning back, Prudy propped her sneakers against the lowered rail and let out a weary sigh. "I really should transfer to maternity. It's so serene up here. Most of the time, anyway.''

Madelyn smiled. "You should be here when all the babies are crying.''

"No thanks.''

Madelyn glanced down. "Have you seen Luke today?''

''Nope. Last time I saw him was yesterday afternoon. He was sacked out in one of the empty suites.''

Madelyn rubbed the baby's padded rump through the soft blue blanket. ''I'm worried about him, Prue. He looked so drained.''

''It was like films I've seen of surgery combat. He had to get the baby out fast, and he did. His hand was rock steady as he was sewing you up. And then, when it was over, he took one step backward and passed out cold.'' Prudy's chocolate eyes darkened as memory passed over her face. ''No one expected it, so we just stood there in shock, staring down at this huge, strong, utterly controlled man crumpled up like a rag doll at our feet.''

Madelyn drew a sharp breath. ''Did…did his leg give out on him again?''

''No, sweetie, it was a delayed reaction to nearly losing you. After we revived him, he couldn't stop shaking.'' She smiled. ''He loves you desperately, Maddy. I've never seen a man more worried. Or more devoted.''

Madelyn drew a shaky breath. She desperately wanted to believe that. ''Then why hasn't he come to see me again?''

Prudy averted her gaze. ''I don't know, Maddy. I wish I did.''

''Guess what, darling boy? We're going home today.''

Her son looked up at her, his tiny mouth pursed in a frown. The hair that had been dark brown when he'd been born was already turning light. She swirled a silky lock around her finger, fascinated by the tiny perfect head.

He was a wonder, this male child with the solemn face. Because she'd yet to name him, the nurses had taken to calling him Peanut. They all adored him.

"Mrs. Stanley says I have to give you a real name today, Peanut. Something strong for my strong little critter."

She sensed his presence an instant before she glanced up to see Luke in the doorway, a huge bunch of white carnations in his hand. Her heart did a slow somersault.

"Looks right, the two of you," he said as he walked toward her. She tipped up her face, eager to feel his mouth on hers. But his lips brushed her forehead, instead.

"How are you feeling?"

"Wonderful." She cast a pointed glance at the carnations. "Are those for me?"

He looked startled, then sheepish. "Guess they must be."

"They're beautiful. Thank you." Her insides quivered. She'd missed him so much.

"I hear Winslow is planning to discharge you today," he said as he stuffed the flowers in the water pitcher.

She nodded. "Boyd and Stacy volunteered to drive me home." But she'd wanted it to be him.

"Good." His gaze dropped to the baby nestled in her arms. "Looks like he's gained some weight."

"Eight ounces so far. He's a real chow hound."

She saw his face soften and held her breath. But when he glanced up, his jaw was hard again.

"You're just in time to help me decide on a name for Peanut," she said, her heart tumbling erratically now.

He shoved his hands into the back pockets of his jeans. "I'm not much good with stuff like that."

"I've picked out two actually. Oliver Lucas. Or Lucas Oliver."

His head came up fast. For an instant his eyes were full of naked longing before the shutters came down. "I appreciate the gesture, but it's not necessary."

"It's no gesture, Luke. I think a son should have his daddy's name."

He swallowed hard before walking past her to the window. His back was ramrod straight as he looked out at the sunshine. "You could have died, Maddy. Both of you. I can't get past that." His voice sounded shredded.

"You saved us, Luke. If you hadn't come when you did, we would have died."

"I convinced myself that Karen would look after you as well as I could. But maybe I was wrong. Maybe I was just fooling myself because I wanted you so much."

"You're not wrong, Luke. Karen did look after me. But as she explained, an abruption can come without warning and in otherwise uneventful pregnancies." She took a breath. "She also said she didn't know of any other doctor who could have done what you did."

His chest heaved. "I thought I'd changed, Maddy. That I was a better man. But I was wrong. I—"

"You stop that right this minute, Luke Jarrod," she ordered, her voice sharp. "I won't have you beating up on yourself like this. No sir, I just will not."

He stiffened, then swung around to stare at her. "You won't?" he asked cautiously.

She shook her head. "Peanut and I have discussed it and we've decided we like Oregon a whole lot better than Texas, so I'm going to take your advice and let Wiley have the house.'' She smiled. ''I consider it a fair trade. I have Peanut, he has a pile of bricks.''

His gaze narrowed. He looked tense enough to shatter. ''I keep seeing you on the table. I keep thinking I let you down. For all my promisin' to take care of you, in the end I failed.''

''It was your voice I kept hearing. Telling me to trust the man who loves me. And I do. With all my heart. As much as I love you.''

He drew a deep shuddering breath. ''Guess Oliver Lucas would be my preference,'' he said, his eyes steady on hers as he came toward her. They were still amazingly blue and full of love. Her own stung with happy tears.

''That's it, then, Oliver Lucas Jarrod,'' she said as he eased down on the bed to take her hand, balancing it on that flat wide palm with its ridge of permanent calluses.

''Before this happened I, uh, called Harriet in Bangladesh. It took some serious negotiating, but she agreed to sell me the house.'' His finger rubbed over the spot on her finger where a wedding band would go. ''I thought I'd give it to you for a wedding present.''

Her breath caught. ''I accept.''

''Just like that? No more figurin' and testin'?''

She choked out a laugh, shook her head. ''Because I was terrified to make another mistake, I almost made the worst mistake of all.''

His grin was a little wobbly when he bent his head to kiss her. It was a sweet healing kiss, with enough licks of hunger in it to have her heart racing. ''I'm crazy in love with you, Maddy Sue. And with our son.''

His hand was infinitely gentle as he cupped the downy crown. "He's mine, Maddy. As much mine as Jenny. I want my name on his birth certificate so he'll know he was always wanted."

At the reminder of their daughter her joy slipped. "She needs us so much." She felt tears well, then spill.

"Don't, sweetheart. Maybe she said she came for the money, but I have a hunch it was more than that. Might be she just has to take her time comin' to trust us."

"Oh, Luke, do you think so?"

"Now that she's found out how special her mama is, there's no way she's gonna be able to stay away." He kissed her again, softly. Smiling, he lifted a hand to brush back her hair. "I guess you'll want to do this wedding thing in Texas, huh?"

She considered, then shook her head. "I want to do it in our own backyard. Under the maple tree where you're going to hang a swing for our son."

His chest rose and felt in a jerky movement, and his eyes were shiny as he looked into hers. "I'd hang the stars for you if I could."

"We have stars, remember? Right over our heads, and after we make love, we can watch them shimmer together." She smiled. "Do you think Harriet will sell us the bed, too?"

His horrified expression had her grinning.

"I'll ask her," he said, "on one condition."

"What's that?"

"If I have me a heart attack while you're wearing me out, you'll drag me into the living room before the medics arrive."

She laughed. "It's a deal."

He kissed her again, a long lingering kiss. Nestled

between them the baby made a little mewling sound, then opened his mouth and let out a lusty wail. Drawing back, Luke took his son in his arms and kissed the angry little face while she opened her gown.

He took a ragged breath, then brought his gaze to hers. There was sorrow there and pain. And so much love. "Every time I held a newborn in my hands I thought about you and our baby, Maddy. Every time I witnessed that…that special moment when the mom sees her child for the first time, I wished with all my heart I could put our child into your arms."

Her lips trembled as he settled Oliver against her breast. "I love you, cowboy," she said as the baby began to suckle. "My hero."

Epilogue

It was a perfect day for a wedding.

The sun was shining. Emily and her husband, Lomax, had been in town for two days, touring Portland and spoiling Oliver shamelessly. Two of a kind, Luke and Lomax had grumbled and groused about dressing up for the special dinner Emily had planned, then behaved like courtly gentlemen, charming the awestruck waitress and darn near every other woman in the Mallory Hotel dining room. Doc Morrow and his wife, Mary Lynette, had arrived right on time last night and were happily playing grandparents. Because her parents had refused to attend, Doc was going to give her away. Luke's family was there, too, his daddy talking bloodlines with Morgan, who was thinking of buying a quarter horse.

The minister had arrived. The caterer had produced a glorious spread. Madelyn had been fussed over and praised by the moms and now stood before the mirror in the bedroom that had become officially theirs yesterday.

Harriet had grumbled a little about giving up the bed, but Luke had managed to talk her into it. She'd refused to budge on the cat, though, and they'd shipped Precious to Spain last week. Madelyn had grieved a little, but Luke had promised to get her a kitten after they returned from their honeymoon in Hawaii.

Oliver, who'd just celebrated his two-month birthday, was going with them. It had been Luke's idea. Part of the bonding thing, he'd told her with a crooked grin. Every chance he got, he held her while she nursed.

Now, as the clock edged toward two on the first Saturday in September, both branches of her extended family were gathered in her backyard. Waiting for the ceremony to begin.

Madelyn was waiting for Luke. He was late for his own wedding.

Fighting nerves and a sinking feeling in her stomach, she glanced toward the street. Cars lined the curb. There was no sign of the Jeep.

"Maybe he parked in the back."

Stacy and Raine exchanged looks. "I'll check," Raine said before hurrying out.

"You look lovely," Prudy said, her eyes glowing. "Like Grace Kelly when she married her prince."

"It's going to be terribly embarrassing if I have to go out there and tell everyone it was all a mistake." She gave a laugh. "I should have married him while he was flat on his back after surgery."

"He'll be here," Stacy assured her.

"But..." Her voice stuttered to a stop when he appeared suddenly, standing in the doorway, looking breathtakingly handsome in a charcoal suit.

"You're not supposed to see me before the ceremony," she protested, her voice shaky with nerves and relief.

His grin was crooked. "I, uh, have this present I want to give you before we do the happily-ever-after stuff."

Prudy and Stacy exchanged grins, then headed for the door. "We'll be outside when you're ready," Stacy said.

"Don't you dare mess up her hair, cowboy," Prudy ordered before disappearing.

"What kind of present?" Madelyn asked suspiciously when they were alone.

His face tightened. "Stay put. I'll be right back."

"But..." She stopped when she realized she was talking to an empty doorway.

Heart racing, she picked up her bouquet and buried her face in the spicy carnations. She was trying to settle her nerves when he was back. Her jaw dropped at the sight of their daughter standing next to him. In his arms he held a little boy with tumbled black curls who stared at her with bright blue eyes. She dissolved for an instant before pulling herself back.

"Tricia?" Her eyes filled with tears.

Her daughter's smile was tentative, her blue eyes guarded. "You said you wanted to know your... grandson." She turned to sign something to the toddler, who cast a shy glance at Madelyn. "That means grandma," Tricia explained, repeating the signs.

Madelyn felt tears welling. "Will you teach me to sign 'I love you very much'?"

Tricia repeated the words aloud as she formed them

slowly with her hands. Maddy did her best to copy the movements, then laughed when the little boy frowned. "What did I do wrong?" she asked anxiously.

"You left out the 'love' part." Tricia demonstrated the difference. "It just takes practice."

Madelyn took a breath. "You could teach us," she said softly. "If you stayed."

Tricia took a nervous little breath. Deep in her blue eyes a glimmer of light appeared, like the first faint flicker of a candle in a night that's been bleak and cold. "I'd like that," she said, her voice tremulous.

Madelyn smiled at her daughter before shifting her gaze to the little boy held so securely in his grandfather's strong arms. "Hi, Mason, I'm your grandma." She smiled and won a shy smile in return. And then she looked into the face of the man who had given her all this. And more.

So much more.

"How did you find her?"

His mouth slanted. "I already had this investigator looking. He'd traced her to Dripping Spring, but she was up here while he was down there." He glanced at their daughter. "She's stubborn like her mama, so it took me a while to convince her to give us a shot at this parent thing."

Tricia's smile was tentative, but Madelyn had seen that same smile before, right before Luke had told her he loved her the first time. Her heart welled. "You are so very special," she said, her gaze fast on his.

His mouth turned vulnerable, but only for a moment. "Darlin', I think we'd best get ourselves married before this old boy breaks down and bawls like a baby."

She heard the gruff humor and she heard the love. Her own control was shaky as she shifted her gaze to her daughter. "It's a man thing," she said on a little laugh. "The tougher the outside, the softer the inside."

Tricia's smile broke free, changing her face. And her life, Madelyn thought. It would take time, but together they would make a family. "He swore you'd kill him if we were late, so I didn't get a chance to buy a dress." Embarrassed, she glanced down at her denim skirt and plain cotton shirt.

"You look beautiful," Madelyn told her. Because she had to touch them all, she crossed the room. "I'd be honored if you'd stand up with me."

Tricia bit her lip and nodded.

Luke watched his wife and daughter fall in love. In his arms was a little boy he already adored. Heart thudding like thunder, he cleared his throat. "If you two will excuse me, my best man and I are supposed to wait at the altar."

Madelyn laughed. "Give us a few minutes and we'll meet you there."

Luke took a breath, hitched Mace a little higher and tucked the emotions that threatened to take him to his knees behind a bad-boy grin.

"Darlin', I'll give you anything you want."

Her eyes sparkled and her smile was a gift from heaven. "I'll remember that, cowboy."

His vision blurred, and for one shining moment he saw an adorable sexy baton twirler in a short skirt looking at him with stars in her eyes. He blinked, clearing his vision. She was still there, his Maddy girl.

His wife and his love. His life.

*   *   *   *   *

Acclaimed author

MARILYN PAPPANO

continues her compelling miniseries

*The men of Heartbreak live by their own rules—
protect the land, honor the family…
and never let a good woman go!*

Look for

ROGUE'S REFORM, IM #1003
On sale May 2000

Only from Silhouette Books
Available at your favorite retail outlet.

And if you missed the first two tales about the
passionate men of Heartbreak…

CATTLEMAN'S PROMISE, IM #925
THE HORSEMAN'S BRIDE, IM #957

you can order them now!

To order, send the completed form, along with a check or money order for the total
above, payable to Silhouette Books, to: **In the U.S.:** 3010 Walden Avenue, P.O. Box 9077,
Buffalo, NY 14269-9077; **In Canada:** P.O. Box 636, Fort Erie, Ontario, L2A 5X3.

Name: _____

Address: _____ City: _____

State/Prov.: _____ Zip/Postal Code: _____

Account # (if applicable): _____ 075 CSAS

*New York residents remit applicable sales taxes.
Canadian residents remit applicable
GST and provincial taxes.

Visit Silhouette at www.eHarlequin.com
SIMHC

Silhouette®
Where love comes alive™

ATTENTION ALL ROMANCE READERS—

There's an
incredible offer
waiting for you!

For a limited time only, Harlequin will mail you
your **Free Guide** to the World of Romance

inside
romance

Get to know your **Favorite Authors,** such as
Diana Palmer and **Nora Roberts**
through in-depth biographies

Be the first to know about **New Titles**

Read Highlights from your
Favorite Romance Series

And take advantage of
Special Offers and **Contests**

Act now by visiting us online at
www.eHarlequin.com/rtlnewsletter

**Where all your romance news
is waiting for you!**

PNEWS

Attention Silhouette Readers:

Romance is just one click away!

online book **serials**

➤ *Exclusive* to our web site, get caught up in both the daily and weekly online installments of new romance stories.

➤ Try the Writing Round Robin. Contribute a chapter to a story created by our members. Plus, winners will get prizes.

romantic **travel**

➤ Want to know where the best place to kiss in New York City is, or which restaurant in Los Angeles is the most romantic? Check out our Romantic Hot Spots for the scoop.

➤ Share your travel tips and stories with us on the romantic travel message boards.

romantic reading **library**

➤ Relax as you read our collection of Romantic Poetry.

➤ Take a peek at the Top 10 Most Romantic Lines!

Visit us online at

www.eHarlequin.com

on Women.com Networks

SEUT1

SILHOUETTE'S 20TH ANNIVERSARY CONTEST
OFFICIAL RULES
NO PURCHASE NECESSARY TO ENTER

1. To enter, follow directions published in the offer to which you are responding. Contest begins 1/1/00 and ends on 8/24/00 (the "Promotion Period"). Method of entry may vary. Mailed entries must be postmarked by 8/24/00, and received by 8/31/00.

2. During the Promotion Period, the Contest may be presented via the Internet. Entry via the Internet may be restricted to residents of certain geographic areas that are disclosed on the Web site. To enter via the Internet, if you are a resident of a geographic area in which Internet entry is permissible, follow the directions displayed on-line, including typing your essay of 100 words or fewer telling us "Where In The World Your Love Will Come Alive." On-line entries must be received by 11:59 p.m. Eastern Standard time on 8/24/00. Limit one e-mail entry per person, household and e-mail address per day, per presentation. If you are a resident of a geographic area in which entry via the Internet is permissible, you may, in lieu of submitting an entry on-line, enter by mail, by hand-printing your name, address, telephone number and contest number/name on an 8"x 11" plain piece of paper and telling us in 100 words or fewer "Where In The World Your Love Will Come Alive," and mailing via first-class mail to: Silhouette 20th Anniversary Contest, (in the U.S.) P.O. Box 9069, Buffalo, NY 14269-9069; (In Canada) P.O. Box 637, Fort Erie, Ontario, Canada L2A 5X3. Limit one 8"x 11" mailed entry per person, household and e-mail address per day. On-line entries and/or 8"x 11" mailed entries received from persons residing in geographic areas in which Internet entry is not permissible will be disqualified. No liability is assumed for lost, late, incomplete, inaccurate, nondelivered or misdirected mail, or misdirected e-mail, for technical, hardware or software failures of any kind, lost or unavailable network connection, or failed, incomplete, garbled or delayed computer transmission or any human error which may occur in the receipt or processing of the entries in the contest.

3. Essays will be judged by a panel of members of the Silhouette editorial and marketing staff based on the following criteria:

   > Sincerity (believability, credibility)—50%
   > Originality (freshness, creativity)—30%
   > Aptness (appropriateness to contest ideas)—20%

   Purchase or acceptance of a product offer does not improve your chances of winning. In the event of a tie, duplicate prizes will be awarded.

4. All entries become the property of Harlequin Enterprises Ltd., and will not be returned. Winner will be determined no later than 10/31/00 and will be notified by mail. Grand Prize winner will be required to sign and return Affidavit of Eligibility within 15 days of receipt of notification. Noncompliance within the time period may result in disqualification and an alternative winner may be selected. All municipal, provincial, federal, state and local laws and regulations apply. Contest open only to residents of the U.S. and Canada who are 18 years of age or older, and is void wherever prohibited by law. Internet entry is restricted solely to residents of those geographical areas in which Internet entry is permissible. Employees of Torstar Corp., their affiliates, agents and members of their immediate families are not eligible. Taxes on the prizes are the sole responsibility of winners. Entry and acceptance of any prize offered constitutes permission to use winner's name, photograph or other likeness for the purposes of advertising, trade and promotion on behalf of Torstar Corp. without further compensation to the winner, unless prohibited by law. Torstar Corp and D.L. Blair, Inc., their parents, affiliates and subsidiaries, are not responsible for errors in printing or electronic presentation of contest or entries. In the event of printing or other errors which may result in unintended prize values or duplication of prizes, all affected contest materials or entries shall be null and void. If for any reason the Internet portion of the contest is not capable of running as planned, including infection by computer virus, bugs, tampering, unauthorized intervention, fraud, technical failures, or any other causes beyond the control of Torstar Corp. which corrupt or affect the administration, secrecy, fairness, integrity or proper conduct of the contest, Torstar Corp. reserves the right, at its sole discretion, to disqualify any individual who tampers with the entry process and to cancel, terminate, modify or suspend the contest or the Internet portion thereof. In the event of a dispute regarding an on-line entry, the entry will be deemed submitted by the authorized holder of the e-mail account submitted at the time of entry. Authorized account holder is defined as the natural person who is assigned to an e-mail address by an Internet access provider, on-line service provider or other organization that is responsible for arranging e-mail address for the domain associated with the submitted e-mail address.

5. Prizes: Grand Prize—a $10,000 vacation to anywhere in the world. Travelers (at least one must be 18 years of age or older) or parent or guardian if one traveler is a minor, must sign and return a Release of Liability prior to departure. Travel must be completed by December 31, 2001, and is subject to space and accommodations availability. Two hundred (200) Second Prizes—a two-book limited edition autographed collector set from one of the Silhouette Anniversary authors: Nora Roberts, Diana Palmer, Linda Howard or Annette Broadrick (value $10.00 each set). All prizes are valued in U.S. dollars.

6. For a list of winners (available after 10/31/00), send a self-addressed, stamped envelope to: Harlequin Silhouette 20th Anniversary Winners, P.O. Box 4200, Blair, NE 68009-4200.

Contest sponsored by Torstar Corp., P.O. Box 9042, Buffalo, NY 14269-9042.

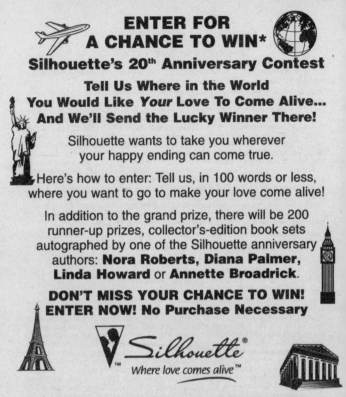

ENTER FOR
A CHANCE TO WIN*

Silhouette's 20th Anniversary Contest

Tell Us Where in the World
You Would Like *Your* Love To Come Alive...
And We'll Send the Lucky Winner There!

Silhouette wants to take you wherever
your happy ending can come true.

Here's how to enter: Tell us, in 100 words or less,
where you want to go to make your love come alive!

In addition to the grand prize, there will be 200
runner-up prizes, collector's-edition book sets
autographed by one of the Silhouette anniversary
authors: **Nora Roberts, Diana Palmer,
Linda Howard** or **Annette Broadrick**.

DON'T MISS YOUR CHANCE TO WIN!
ENTER NOW! No Purchase Necessary

Silhouette®
Where love comes alive™

Visit Silhouette at www.eHarlequin.com to enter, starting this summer.

Name:

Address:

City: State/Province:

Zip/Postal Code:

Mail to Harlequin Books: **In the U.S.**: P.O. Box 9069, Buffalo, NY
14269-9069; **In Canada**: P.O. Box 637, Fort Erie, Ontario, L4A 5X3

*No purchase necessary—for contest details send a self-addressed stamped envelope to:
Silhouette's 20th Anniversary Contest, P.O. Box 9069, Buffalo, NY, 14269-9069 (include
contest name on self-addressed envelope). Residents of Washington and Vermont may
omit postage. Open to Cdn. (excluding Quebec) and U.S. residents who are 18 or over.
Void where prohibited. Contest ends August 31, 2000.   PS20CON_R2